Truth and Forgiveness

BUTLER FAMILY LEGACY

PAT NICHOLS

Truth and Forgiveness by Pat Nichols
Published by Armchair Press
ISBN: 979-8-9860519-3-2
Copyright © 2023 by Pat Nichols
Cover Design by Elaina Lee
Edited by Sherri Stewart

Available in print from your local bookstore or online.
For more information on this book or the author visit:
https://patnicholsauthor.blog
Printed in the United States of America
Truth and Forgiveness is a work of fiction. Names, characters, and incidents are all products of the author's imagination or are used for fictional purposes. Any mentioned brand names, places, and trademarks remain the property of their respective owners, bear no association with the author or publisher, and are used for fictional purposes only.
Library of Congress Cataloging-in Publication Data
Nichols, Pat.
Truth and Forgiveness/ Pat Nichols

Books by

Pat Nichols

Women's Fiction

Willow Falls series

The Secret of Willow Inn
Trouble in Willow Falls
Star Struck in Willow Falls
Bridges, Books, and Bones

Butler Family Legacy series

Big Secrets, Little Lies
Truth and Forgiveness
New Beginnings

Contemporary Romance

Jenny's Grace

Dedicated to our amazing grandchildren, Joy, Jace, and Kinsley, who add so much joy to our family, and to Bri who graced our lives for eleven months before she left this earth for her eternal home.

Chapter One

Six weeks after walking out of the Manhattan office building one last time, Daisy Butler remained suspended in a time warp—unable to move forward until her dad made a decision. She plucked a dried leaf off the concrete walkway running through her family's commercial greenhouse and peered up at the glass ceiling. Dark clouds cast a gray pall across the massive space. Another dreary January afternoon in Georgia soured her mood. She crushed the leaf, let the pieces slip between her fingers, and wandered to the exit.

Outside, she sidestepped a puddle from last night's torrential rain and paused beside the miniature house on wheels parked beside her dad's delivery truck. David Lambert was probably sitting at the camper's dinette with his laptop open. Had her attraction to the investigative journalist unduly influenced her decision to move back home? Had she abandoned a promising career for a man she'd just met two months ago? After he gathered enough evidence to solve the case and finish writing a book about her grandmother Rose's disappearance thirty-five years earlier, would he abandon her to chase down another cold case?

A wind gust nipped Daisy's cheeks and tousled her shoulder-length hair. She pulled her jacket tight across her chest and dashed across the backyard to her mom's private retreat. Inside the tiny clapboard building, the warped floorboards creaked with each footstep. Sheer white curtains fluttered in the breeze from the open window. A bud vase adorned the sill, the white rose symbolic of the ongoing struggle to accept the truth about Rose Fowler.

Daisy's muscles tensed as she dropped onto the hand-hewn wooden bench beside her mom. She scrunched her nose at the scent of damp wood and eyed the open newspaper on her lap. "At least that article didn't appear on the front page."

Poppy Butler tapped the headline. "*Georgia Mega Lottery Winner Remains Anonymous. Winning Ticket Sold at Willy's Convenience Store.*" She pressed her palm against the dark wine-colored birthmark staining her left cheek. "One slip of the tongue, and the whole world will find out that your dad claimed the winning number."

Daisy released a long sigh. "There's a huge difference between him accepting the check and actually cashing it."

Her mother lowered her hand from her cheek and touched Daisy's arm. "Are you having second thoughts about resigning?"

"I underestimated the challenge of transitioning from twelve-plus-hour workdays to zero."

"Like a race car stuck at an endless red light."

"If I'd had the slightest inclination Dad would take this long to decide whether or not to cash that check...what's done is done. Now I need to find some kind of project to keep me busy."

"You could start your own law practice."

Images of Curtis Butler streamed through Daisy's mind. The grandfather she had never met before the Warner law firm assigned her to recruit his business empire. If David hadn't arrived on the scene, her family would never have discovered that Curtis fathered her Aunt Pansy and had a hand in her grandmother's disappearance.

"What do you think, honey?"

"About what?"

"Opening your own office."

"I'm a corporate attorney, Mom. I doubt anyone within a fifty-mile range would need my services."

"Seems these days everyone is specialized." A smattering of raindrops pinged the metal roof. Her mom tilted her face upward. "Years ago when Mama entertained men during rainstorms, Pansy and I pretended this little hideaway was a boat adrift at sea. My sweet sister would peer out the window and describe the whales and dolphins she imagined floating by. One time she wrote a story about landing on an island populated by cats."

Images of dozens of sketchpads featuring her middle-aged, childlike aunt's detailed drawings skated across Daisy's mind. "Her imagination and artistic ability are off the charts."

"Lucky for us one of her imaginary stories about Mama's disappearance brought David into our lives."

"Indeed." Daisy leaned her head back against the wall. "Does Aunt Pansy understand why we need to keep the winning lottery ticket a secret, even if Dad never cashes it?"

"The challenge isn't whether or not she understands; it's her unpredictable comments."

"One more reason to continue stalling her plan to open a bakery."

"We can't deny her dream indefinitely." Daisy's mom set the newspaper on the bench. She scooted to the edge, removed a new scrapbook from an ancient trunk, and opened to the first page.

Daisy ran her finger over the title bearing her dad's name. "Danny Butler's Family Legacy. The sequel to your first scrapbook?"

"At least I won't have to keep this one secret or fill it with newspaper clippings of relatives who don't know us or care if we exist." She turned the page to reveal the family's Christmas photo and tapped her finger on her middle child's image. "Next year's picture will include Lilly's baby—your first nephew and my first grandbaby."

Daisy smiled at the image of her sister standing between her husband Andy and their brother Basil. A lump rose in her throat as her focus shifted to her mother posing beside her dad. The way she turned sideways to hide the birthmark on her left cheek—the blemish she believed obscured her beauty and brought her shame. Other than the birthmark, there was no mistaking she and her mom were mother and daughter. Daisy swallowed as her focus drifted to her own image—her hair tucked behind her ear revealing her faux-emerald earring a shade darker than her eyes. David stood beside her, their shoulders touching. The only non-family member ever invited to pose for the annual Christmas photo. "What goes on the rest of the pages?"

"Pictures. Mementos. One in particular—" She flipped to the next page. "Pansy's last birthday card to your dad."

Daisy touched the card, one of dozens created for family members over the years by her aunt who brought so much joy to their family. "The card that held the winning ticket. Do you suppose her cards will continue to include lottery tickets, all with the same number?"

"I suspect they will. We'll find out when your birthday rolls around."

The rain intensified, drumming the roof with a rhythm akin to brush sticks striking dozens of snare drums. Daisy pointed to the ceiling patch over the window. "Good thing Dad fixed that leak." She paused. "Do you have any idea when or what he'll decide to do about the check?"

Her mom shook her head. "All I know is he's struggling with his conscience."

"About taking the money or what to do with it?"

"Both."

"What do you want him to do, Mom?"

She remained silent for a long moment, as if considering how to answer. "Whatever he believes is best for our family." Daisy's mom closed the scrapbook and placed it back in the trunk. She moved to the window and pushed the sheer curtains aside.

Daisy closed her eyes, pinched the bridge of her nose, and scoured her memory for clues her dad might have revealed. An offhand comment or question during breakfast or supper. Nothing surfaced. Not surprising, considering Danny Butler was a man of few words. She lowered her hand and opened her eyes.

Her mom stared at her, her lower lip clenched between her teeth. "You gave up a lot when you walked away from a promising career. Especially after all those years you spent studying and working hard."

Daisy eased beside her mom. A spider posed in a web stretching between the upper window frame and a rafter. "Family comes in a distant second for Warner law-firm partners. I wasn't willing to make that choice."

"Love of family is a powerful emotion." Her mom swiped her hand across the window. "So is the appeal of huge sums of money."

A sensation akin to a dozen fluttering butterflies accosted Daisy's chest as she stared at the arc her mom created in the condensation. There was no denying one all-consuming fact. Her dad's indecision continued to strain her family's patience and test their loyalty to one another.

Chapter Two

Grateful for the blue sky and a fifteen-degree jump in temperature, Poppy ambled from the greenhouse and climbed onto the back porch of the only home she had ever known—her private world insulated from strangers' cruel stares. She hung her wide-brimmed straw hat on a hook, walked into the kitchen, and breathed in the rich scent of freshly baked chocolate chip cookies—a testimony to Pansy's extraordinary baking skills.

She poured a glass of lemonade and settled on one of six vintage ladder-back chairs—her mama's prized possessions. Gifts from a satisfied client. She traced her finger over the hand-hewn table marred by nicks and spills from years of family meals and school projects. So many memories lived in the room that had served as Pansy and her classroom after that incident when she was eleven. She pressed her hand to her cheek and squeezed her eyes shut as the painful memory escaped. The older boy pulling up her skirt during recess. His smirk when he said she'd need to fix her ugly face if she planned to be a prostitute like her mom. That was the first time she had any inkling about how her mama earned a living.

Desperate to shove the painful memory back into its hiding place, Poppy opened her eyes and focused on her sister and her children's drawings adorning the wall separating the kitchen from the front room. Danny had always found comfort in their simple life, unencumbered by possessions. She understood that his hatred for his father had compelled him to accept the winning lottery check. At the same time, his disdain for wealth kept him from cashing it. Not knowing what lay ahead sent a cold chill creeping up her spine. One little ticket had hurled a gigantic monkey wrench into her predictable, comfortable life.

Poppy pushed off her chair and pulled a cookie from an apple-shaped jar, Pansy's latest thrift-store find. The chewy rich taste of chocolate and brown sugar delighted her tongue and helped ease her anxiety.

Footsteps struck the floor behind her. "I need to buy lots more cookie jars for my bakery." Pansy set her sketchpad and a box of colored pencils on the table.

"Nice hat. How many in your collection now?"

"Thirty-seven." Pansy's brown eyes twinkled above pink cheeks as she fingered her Atlanta Braves World Series logo. "Basil gave me this one. He promised to give me a police hat soon as he graduates and gets his badge. "

The stark reminder of her son's career choice released a bitter taste and forced Poppy to set the half-eaten cookie on the counter. She brushed crumbs into the sink. Obviously the family's potential wealth hadn't altered Basil's plans.

"Maybe tomorrow Danny will give me some money to open my store." Pansy plopped her plump body onto her chair at her end of the table and opened her sketchpad. "It'll look like this."

Poppy pulled a chair beside her sister. Boots, Pansy's black sixty-pound, rescue dog with white front paws, padded in and laid his head on her lap. She stroked his ears while studying the drawing of mismatched cookie jars lined up on a counter. Behind the display an elaborate flower arrangement sat on a cabinet beneath a sign reading *Pansy's Bakery and Flower Shop*. Somehow she had to stall her sister without crushing her dream. "This looks real fancy."

"I'm gonna paint the walls yellow like sunshine and the ceiling blue like the sky."

Boots lifted his head off Poppy's lap, yawned, and sprawled on the floor under the table.

"You know we'll need to do a lot of planning before we're ready to open a store, sweetie."

"We have to buy baking ovens and get some kind of license, like if I was gonna drive a car. Daisy's a lawyer, so she'll help me. We need to go to town tomorrow so I can put this picture in the window of my new store, the one across from Willy's house."

So much for stalling. Poppy reached for her sister's hand. "Do you remember what we told you about keeping Danny's lottery ticket a secret?"

Pansy nodded. "That if people find out he won, they'd want us to give them lots of money." She set her ball cap on the table beside her sketchpad and brushed bangs away from her eyes. "But isn't it okay to give people money if they don't have any?"

Poppy swallowed against the tightness in her throat. How many times had she explained reality to the woman who had the mind of a child and the heart of an angel—the family member whose wisdom sometimes belied her mental capacity? "You know Danny hasn't decided what to do with the check."

"He can put it in the bank." Pansy stood, then poured a glass of milk and pulled a cookie from the jar. "Boots wants a cookie, but chocolate makes dogs sick." Her canine's tail thumped in anticipation as she plucked a dog biscuit from a box and tossed it under the table. "I can bake good-tasting doggie treats and sell 'em in my store." She settled back in her chair and bit into a cookie. "If Papa Curtis loved Mama Rose, how come he didn't marry her like Danny married you?"

Poppy stared at her sister. Where did that question come from? She hadn't mentioned Curtis Butler since her family confronted him and introduced Pansy as his biological daughter. How should she answer? With the truth, that's how. "Because he already had a wife."

"Danny's mama?"

"Yes."

Pansy washed down her cookie with a sip of milk and took another bite. "Is Papa still real sick?"

The image surfaced of Curtis Butler sitting in the straight-backed chair, gripping his cane—the way his suit jacket hung loose on his thin frame. "He is."

"When he dies, will he go to heaven so he can be with Mama?"

Poppy wrapped her fingers around her lemonade glass. Was her question prompted by Sunday's message or simple curiosity? "That depends on who's in his heart, honey."

"Oh." Pansy removed a colored pencil from her box, flipped to a blank page, and began sketching a picture of a man sitting in a chair.

"Who are you drawing?"

"Papa Curtis." She drew a face surrounded by a heart shape on the figure's chest. "I'm giving him the right kind of heart."

Poppy's eyes moistened. If the man who managed a gigantic business empire had one smidgen of Pansy's compassion, he would never have denied her existence or had a hand in their mother's death.

"Is Daisy still David's special friend?"

Poppy suppressed the anxiety-riddled giggle threatening to escape. Her sister's random thoughts unconstrained by a mental filter made family conversations unpredictable as well as entertaining. "You'd best ask David."

"Okay." Pansy pushed away from the table. "Come on, Boots, we've gotta go talk to him."

Poppy grabbed her sister's arm. "Not now, sweetie."

"'Cause he's busy writing his book about Mama?"

"Exactly."

Pansy pulled her chair back to the table and continued drawing. "How come God didn't make me smart like you?"

Poppy brushed a lock of hair away from her sister's cheek. "There are lots of different kinds of smart."

"What's my kind?"

"The way you know how to write good stories and draw and make people happy."

"Tomorrow when I hang my picture in the window, I'll make lots of people happy." Pansy closed her sketchpad. "It's time to go help Danny in the greenhouse." She finished her milk and scooted out the back door with Boots scrambling behind her.

Poppy slumped in her chair. Maybe she should come up with a good reason why tomorrow wasn't a good day to go to town.

Chapter Three

Daisy stood beside the porch railing as David closed the distance to the steps. Warmth infused her body the moment he climbed up. She breathed in the fresh scent of soap and shampoo while resisting the desire to run her fingers through his thick, light-brown hair. "I assume the laptop tucked under your arm means you're ready for me to read your masterpiece."

"From the beginning for continuity."

"Perfect." She settled on the first of two rocking chairs outside the front room.

David sat beside her. "I've rewritten the first page three times since you first read it."

"Because it's the most important, or because you can't make up your mind?"

"Little bit of both." He opened his laptop and placed it on Daisy's lap.

She eyed the screen and read aloud. "*Chapter One. She was thirty-two-years old the day she disappeared without a trace. A prostitute authorities deemed unworthy of investigation. A woman who, in the opinion of many, existed in life's dark underbelly, undeserving of compassion. And yet the measure of a life isn't defined by a profession, but by the character of those left behind. Such is the case of Rose Fowler.*"

Daisy pressed her hand to her chest. "Even if she wasn't my grandmother, I'd already care about her."

"The rewrites paid off." David pushed up. "I'll wait in my camper and let you read the rest without me hovering over you."

Her eyes followed David as he climbed off the porch and disappeared around the side of the house. How had she fallen in love with the man who had first kissed her New Year's Eve but not since? A man perhaps destined to spend his life on the road? Maybe her feelings were more akin to infatuation, inspired by the way he treated her mom and aunt with dignity and respect. She couldn't think about that now.

Daisy set her chair to a gentle rocking motion and resumed reading. The world around her faded as the story drew her in. David's words tugged on her emotions and held her captive through each chapter. Her grandmother's tragic childhood. How as a fifteen-year old she was left alone to fend for herself. The desperation that drew her into prostitution. How Poppy and Pansy survived before and after their mama's disappearance. Their love for each other and their family. Three times tears blurred her vision, forcing her to blink and sniffle.

At the end of the chapter revealing the mysterious safe-deposit key, her heart pounded at the revelation that Curtis was Pansy's biological father. She scrolled to the next page, eager to read David's depiction of Curtis Butler's confession and crime. The page was blank. She pressed the page-down key. Nothing happened. Was the rest of the story in another document? She checked his desktop. Nothing there.

Daisy closed the laptop, dashed to the camper's open door, and stepped inside.

"What's your opinion?"

"It's brilliant." She slid onto the dinette bench across from him and set down his laptop. "But where's the rest of the story?"

"The final chapters haven't been written."

She studied his expression. Was he stalling because he wanted to stay around longer or because doubts about her grandfather's guilt had resurfaced? "I thought you'd come to grips with the truth about Curtis."

"What is the truth, Daisy?"

Was this a trick question? "He admitted killing Rose."

"He claimed she fell but didn't say anything about pushing her."

"Do criminals ever admit their crimes?"

"When cornered or facing death, sometimes they do."

"Not if they're cowards or evil to the core."

"Men like your grandfather who control business empires aren't cowardly. Granted he's cold, but evil?" David propped his forearms on the table. "You're an attorney, so you know subtleties matter. Body language. Facial expressions. What is left unsaid."

"I also understand the meaning of beyond a reasonable doubt."

"Then wouldn't you want me to explore every possibility?"

Daisy thrust her thumb toward her parents' home. "He admitted being in Rose's bedroom, David. The only way she could have fallen and hit her head with enough force to sustain a fatal injury was if someone shoved or slugged her."

"I'm not saying he wasn't in the room."

"Then what *are* you saying?"

"It's possible he's covering for someone."

"Are you serious? The man whose rejection led to his youngest son's suicide? The same man who denied Aunt Pansy's existence because she also failed to meet his standards of acceptability? How could that man have enough heart to protect anyone other than himself?"

"Self-preservation? Guilty conscience? Any number of reasons."

Daisy stared at him for a long moment. "You're not going to let this go, are you?"

"I can't. Journalistic integrity."

Daisy squeezed her eyes shut and mentally replayed the day she and her dad confronted the man she'd first met two months earlier. She pictured her grandfather's demeanor and expression. The words he'd spoken. The sense that something seemed off.

"I suspect somewhere deep down you also have doubts."

Daisy opened her eyes. Had David read her body language? "I admit there was a moment." She turned toward the window and caught sight of the tabby cat charged with keeping the greenhouse rodent free stretched out on the driveway. "What's your next move?"

"Reopen the investigation."

Daisy cringed.

"I could use a partner."

"What are you suggesting?"

He reached across the table and touched her arm. "Help me uncover the truth and find justice for your family."

Daisy's skin tingled beneath his touch. Should she agree because he needed her, or because she longed to spend more time with him? Did the reason matter? Especially since she was desperate for a project to keep her busy. "Similar to Sherlock Holmes and Dr. Watson?"

"More like Sherlock and Mary Russell."

Daisy's eyes widened. "Holmes had a female partner?"

"Different author, a century later. So, are we a team?"

"How could I resist—David Lambert and Daisy Butler, modern-day supersleuths."

He grinned. "Our first decision—should we tell your parents what we're up to?"

"You mean poke a hornet's nest before we find out if it's packed or empty? Although I had hoped the days of keeping secrets from my family had passed." She glanced around the small space. The tiny kitchenette. His bed, neatly made. "We'll tell Mom and let her decide whether or not to tell Dad."

"Now that we're on the same page about the investigation, how about an honest critique on what you read? Don't hold back. I can take plenty of criticism."

"Do you want to hear that you captured my imagination from the first paragraph and held it fast until the last word? Or that the way you portrayed Rose, Mom, and Aunt Pansy reached in and touched my soul?"

"Any constructive feedback?"

"Your writing is brilliant, David."

A smile lit up his face. "Now that we're partners, you'll be a key character in the rest of the story."

Would she also become a key part of his life beyond the investigation? Would he kiss her again?

"Question." David tapped the table. "What do lawyers and authors have in common?"

"Hmm. They provide ample joke material?" Daisy tilted her head. "On a more serious note, they both understand the power of words."

"Indeed they do."

Movement outside the greenhouse caught Poppy's eye. Why was Daisy carrying David's laptop to his camper? Had he finished writing his book and asked her to read it? If she'd known about the winning lottery ticket, would she have agreed to let him write her mama's story? She spun away from the window and spotted Danny at the far end of the building loading plants onto a flatbed cart. Another late delivery meant he would skip supper with the family. Again. She set her garden shears beside a row of boxwoods and walked out of the greenhouse.

Poppy paused beside David's camper. Resisting the urge to knock on his door, she strolled around the side of the house and into the front room. She dropped onto the sofa, lifted her mama's photo off the end table, and stroked her beautiful, flawless face. The day she showed the picture to David, he claimed she favored her mother. Had he spoken out of pity, or had he recognized something she didn't? Or couldn't? The last time she'd looked in a mirror, she'd cringed at the sight of her birthmark. Did she dare take another peek and see if by some miracle the dark color had faded? Why bother? Even if it had lightened, the blemish would still draw stares from strangers.

She set the photo on the coffee table beside the scrapbook displaying her childhood poems—another of her mother's treasures. If Rose had chosen a different way to earn a living, maybe she'd still be alive. On the other hand, if Mama hadn't disappeared, David would never have come into their lives.

Poppy's fingers found a worn spot on the sofa's velvety upholstery. Not surprising given every piece of furniture in the room dated back to her mama's childhood. How many strange men had sat on one of the mismatched wingback chairs before Rose led them to her bedroom? If Danny cashed the check, she could buy a new sofa and maybe a pretty rug and a fancy coffee table.

Caught off guard by the mental musing, Poppy curled her fingers and pressed her nails into her flesh. Was this how money changed people? One small purchase? Then another and another after that until accumulating possessions became an all-consuming quest?

Startled by her vibrating phone, she pulled it from her pocket. Lilly. Her middle child. The one member of her family most susceptible to self-indulgence. "Hey, honey."

"Hi, Mom. How's your day going?"

"Same as always. And yours?"

"Andy and I need to buy a bigger car. You know, with the baby coming and all. The problem is, we don't know how much we can afford."

Could she be any more obvious? "If you're asking for my advice, I suggest you decide based on what you can afford today."

"But...what if...I mean, Dad's going to cash the lottery check, isn't he?"

"My answer hasn't changed since yesterday or all the days before."

A sigh resonated through the phone. "I thought by now he would've made some kind of decision."

"Believe me, honey, I'll call you the moment he decides."

"I hope it's soon." After chatting for a few more minutes, Lilly ended the call.

Poppy leaned her head back and closed her eyes. She and Danny had raised their children to respect the value of family, honest work, and humility. Lilly's unrelenting questioning confirmed his fear and the reason he struggled with a decision. Wealth held the power to undermine everything they'd worked to achieve, and in the process, destroy their family. Much as it had destroyed Curtis Butler's family and led to the death of one son and planted seeds of hatred in the other. One fact remained clear. Danny's choice would have a lasting effect on the people she loved.

Chapter Four

An hour after sunrise, Daisy wandered into the kitchen and found her mom standing at the counter facing the window. "Are you daydreaming or keeping tabs on our squirrel population?"

"Seems we're blessed with a second consecutive day of sunshine." She spun around. "Today's the latest you've slept since New Year's Day."

"Last night David and I talked about the case into the wee hours." Daisy poured a cup of coffee and leaned against the counter beside her mom. "What's going on in your head this morning?"

"A tidal wave of emotions over David's announcement. I still don't understand why he wants to go digging into Mama's case again. Who besides Curtis had a reason to kill her, or as my lawyer daughter and police-officer son would say, a motive?"

"At first, I had a difficult time accepting David's decision. Until I came to terms with the fact that prostitution exposes women to all sorts of dubious characters."

"You read the letters from Mama's clients. They all adored her."

Daisy held up her right hand, her fingers splayed. "Five clients, Mom. What about the men who didn't write to her? How many of them were prone to violent streaks or were emotionally disturbed?"

Her mom gripped her mug and gazed at the dark liquid as if searching for an answer. "I remember once after Mama entertained a client, her lip swelled up. Another time she had a black eye. Both times she told Pansy and me she'd fallen. We believed her."

"She needed you to believe her, to protect you from the truth. The same way you're keeping Dad in the dark about me helping David with the investigation."

"When you think the time's right, I want you to tell him." Poppy set her mug on the counter. "Do you believe Curtis is guilty?"

"I did."

"And now?"

Daisy eyed the hutch and the floral tin holding every lottery ticket Pansy had given as gifts, except the last one. Her dad's birthday present, the mega-million-dollar winner. "A jury should always consider any new evidence before returning a verdict."

"What if David doesn't find any?"

"We'll reconsider everything we already know. By the way, he wants to meet you and me in my room in half an hour. Which means I need to shower and dress."

"You haven't had a bite to eat."

"Not a problem. I'll pull a Pansy and opt for a breakfast of champions." Daisy lifted two cookies from the jar, kissed her mom's cheek, and headed to the bathroom. Thirty minutes after struggling with her own mental tsunami, she stood in the doorway of the room she and Lilly shared while growing up. The same room where her grandmother had earned a living entertaining men.

Her mom leaned on the doorframe beside Daisy.

David walked the small space, then turned in a slow circle between the twin beds. "What can you tell me about this room when your mother slept here, Poppy?"

"Mama always kept it neat and her bed made."

"The brass bed up in the attic?"

"It stood right where you're standing, in front of the window. Those nightstands were on each side of her bed, with matching brass lamps on top."

David eased to the dresser and ran his fingers along the smooth edge and rounded corners "What about this piece?"

"Same place where it was back then. Perfume bottles and the jewelry box where Mama hid the safe-deposit key were on top."

Daisy's mind drifted to the day she and her mom opened the safe-deposit box and found the letter proving that Curtis was Pansy's father. Another dark secret revealed.

David lifted a handheld mirror off the dresser. "Any other furniture in here?"

Her mom shook her head.

"What about a rug?"

"Again, no."

David stepped off the gap between the dresser and walls. "Curtis claimed Rose fell and hit her head on the dresser, which is about four feet, and in my estimation, about the same distance from the bed's footboard to the dresser. With someone facing Rose, a foot shorter."

Cold hard facts. Daisy's attorney instincts kicked in. "Which means if someone pushed her, she'd couldn't have fallen straight back, making it unlikely her head struck the dresser."

"Astute assumption." David dropped to his knees and ran his fingers over a wide spot on the floorboards. He motioned to Daisy. "Come over here and tell me what you see."

She knelt beside him and examined a series of faint blotches. "They appear to be slight discolorations." Daisy gasped as reality struck home. "Oh my gosh, are you thinking they're bloodstains?"

"If those splotches are blood, and if the deputies hadn't taken four days to respond to Poppy's phone calls or dismissed your grandmother's disappearance as a runaway, they might have noticed."

"Unless there's another explanation for the stains. Hey, Mom." Daisy turned and faced a vacant doorway.

David nudged her arm. "She walked away the second you called out to her."

"This is all too much for her." Daisy swallowed as she stared at the splotches. "Let's assume for a moment that those *are* bloodstains and that Rose was the victim of a brutal attack. According to bits of information Dad shared with Mom, Curtis had a violent streak when he drank. That fact, plus his confession about being with Rose when she died, would be enough circumstantial evidence for a district attorney to pursue a murder case."

"On the other hand, a good defense attorney would argue that Curtis lacked a motive to harm the only woman he claimed to have loved, much less kill her."

Daisy sat back on her heels. "The district attorney would counter by presenting the letter that identified Pansy as his child. An inconvenient detail he'd want to keep from ever seeing the light of day."

"Except, the accused is a wealthy man who had the means to provide an ample financial bribe if Rose agreed to secrecy."

"Good point. On the other hand, Curtis confessed that a scandal would have destroyed everything he'd accomplished."

"More circumstantial evidence."

She tilted her head. "How so?"

David lifted off his knees and helped Daisy to her feet. "He never defined what he meant by scandal."

"Score one for the defense." Her eyes drifted to the brown stuffed bear propped on Lilly's pillow. Was it possible she and her sister had spent years sleeping in a room harboring evidence of a murder? "When Lilly, Basil, and I were growing up, Mom told us so many sweet stories about her childhood. How much Rose loved and cared for her and Pansy. The chocolate kisses their mama kept in a jar." A shudder ripped through Daisy. "I can't begin to imagine the pain Mom experienced when she discovered her mother slept with men to feed her little family of three."

"Your mother and your aunt are amazing women who deserve to learn the truth, no matter where it leads."

Poppy's breath came in short spurts as the truth slammed her chest like a giant sledgehammer. Every time her mama allowed strange men to come into her home and onto her bed, she put her life and her daughters' lives in danger. When David published his book, how would readers judge Rose Fowler? As a common hooker who marketed sex? Or a mother who sacrificed everything to put food on the table and clothes on her children's backs?

Too overwhelmed by unchecked emotions to answer any more questions, Poppy had fled from the doorway the moment Daisy asked a question. Her heart raced as she darted through the kitchen and out to the back porch. She hugged her chest as her eyes drifted to her private retreat. What if on that day all those years ago, some kind of emergency had forced her to disobey the rules and rush back to the house? Would Mama still be alive? Or would she have interrupted a killer and lost her own life, leaving Pansy alone in the world?

Poppy dropped onto the bench, longing for the days when she lived in denial, before David showed up on the front porch. Before the possibility that her mother had suffered a painful death became all too real. How would Danny react if he knew David had reopened the investigation? Maybe she shouldn't wait for Daisy to break the news. Except he already had enough to deal with. Perhaps it was best to wait and carry this burden alone until Daisy found the right moment to break the news.

Chapter Five

Exhausted from a restless night, Poppy placed two breakfast plates on the kitchen table and dropped onto her chair. She cradled her coffee mug in both hands and stole a glance at Danny. Should she start a conversation and wait for him to respond? Might as well. "Pansy wants to tape a picture she drew of a bakery and flower shop on a vacant store window across from Willy's house. What do you think? Should I take her to town, or come up with an excuse not to go?"

He dipped his fork into scrambled eggs. "Take her. Just avoid Willy's. As of yesterday the winning number was still posted."

Poppy sipped her coffee and waited, hoping their conversation hadn't come to an end, although Danny seldom had much to say during breakfast.

He gobbled the rest of his food, refilled his coffee, and strode out the back door without making eye contact or uttering another word.

Disappointed, Poppy pushed her plate away, unable to focus. Maybe a few minutes of rest would help clear her brain fog She crossed her arms on the table and laid her head in the crook of her elbow. Within minutes she drifted to sleep. At some point she dreamed she was floating in darkness toward the distant sound of voices. Who was calling out to her? Someone familiar.

A tap on her shoulder.

"Mom, are you okay?"

Poppy's eyes opened. She blinked, lifted her head, and stared at Daisy. "What time is it?"

"A little after nine."

"Oh my gosh. I fell asleep three hours ago." She sat straight up, her neck and shoulders stiff. "Have you eaten?"

"Aunt Pansy and I didn't want to wake you, so we indulged on a breakfast of champions in the front room."

Poppy brushed a strand of hair away from her cheek, then carried her plate to the sink.

Pansy swooped in wearing her sparkly New York ball cap. "Boots wants to go to the thrift store with us." She laid her drawing on the table and patted her fanny pack. "How many cookie jars can I buy with forty-five dollars? After we shop, can we go to Willy's for ice cream?"

How long would Willy's son continue to display the winning numbers? A week? A month? Forever? At some point her family would have to trust Pansy to keep Danny's winning ticket a secret. Not today. "We have plenty of ice cream in the freezer, so we'll skip going to Willy's."

"Okay. Daisy's going with us. When can we leave?"

"As soon as I clean up." After changing clothes, Poppy climbed behind the wheel of the family truck. Daisy sat in the passenger seat, with Pansy and Boots in the back. She eased down the driveway and turned onto the two-lane road. After driving a mile, her brows pinched. "I've counted fifteen cars and trucks since we left home. That's a lot more than normal for way out here."

Daisy nodded. "Maybe an accident rerouted traffic."

Poppy tightened her fingers around the steering wheel and continued counting until she arrived at the wide spot in the road the locals called a town. The tension tightening her neck raced down her spine. Vehicles lined the street and filled every parking spot at the church and Willy's gas station and convenience store.

Daisy exchanged glances with her. "Do you want to turn around and drive back home?"

"It's best to act as normal as possible." Poppy parked on the street a block from the thrift store.

"Come on, Boots." Pansy hopped out, grabbed her dog's leash, and headed up the sidewalk.

"Hold on, Pansy." Poppy caught up with her. "Maddie might not want a dog in her store, sweetie."

"It's okay. He'll be good."

"We need to let Maddie decide."

"She won't mind. You'll see."

Daisy fell in step beside her mom. She nodded toward a real-estate sign planted in front of the stone-and-iron fence guarding the Victorian-style home across the street. "Agnes Watkins' house is still on the market."

"I'm not surprised. Can you imagine anyone from around here wanting to buy it?"

"The mysterious house on the hill we kids claimed was haunted? I'll catch up with you and Aunt Pansy after I take a closer look." Daisy waited for two cars to pass, then dashed across the road.

Poppy grasped her sister's arm as they reached the sidewalk leading to the thrift store. "Do you remember what we said about Danny's winning lottery ticket?"

"Uh-huh. It's our secret." Pansy zipped her finger across her lips. "I won't tell anyone." She pulled away from Poppy's grasp and rushed ahead. The bell over the door jangled as she pushed the door open.

Poppy followed her inside.

Customers strolled along the center aisle.

Maddie slid off her stool behind the checkout counter and pressed her palms together. "Two of my favorite people and one handsome canine."

"It's not a problem for Pansy and me to take him back to the truck."

"No need. I'll keep him up here with me while you two shop. Dogs are such wonderful pets. Mom and I miss our sweet cocker spaniel. Although we still have our cat, when he bothers to show up."

Pansy patted Boots. "You stay here with Miss Maddie while I go find us some cookie jars." She handed over the leash before scurrying toward the last aisle on the right—her favorite starting place.

"You'll be good, won't you, Boots?" Maddie stroked the dog's back, prompting a tail wag.

"You're a good sport." Poppy dropped her keys in her purse. "What's with all the cars parked everywhere?"

"Would you believe people are flocking from all over Georgia to buy lottery tickets at Willy's? Don't they know the chances of another winner coming from the same store is about as likely as lightning striking the same tree twice? I'm not complaining, mind you. Lots of folks are making their way over here. The most business I've had in months. Did you notice the sign's still up across the street? In addition to the house, Agnes's sons are selling every bit of her land."

Poppy hazarded a glance at the house across the street. Had Maddie noticed Daisy walking up the driveway? If she had, she'd want to know why her daughter hadn't returned to New York.

Maddie stepped around Boots and climbed onto a stool. "Without Agnes hanging onto all her land like an old tightwad, maybe newcomers will settle around here and turn our little spot on the map into an honest-to-goodness town."

Relieved Maddie hadn't asked about Daisy, Poppy set her purse on the counter. "I suppose folks who are tired of city living and snarled traffic might want to buy some land and build."

Pansy rushed to the counter and set down a rooster-shaped cookie jar. "I picked out two more." She scurried away.

Maddie grinned. "Your sister is a master at finding treasures."

Pansy returned carrying two glass jars. "Two's marked ten dollars and one's twenty-five." She set her treasures on the counter and fished bills from her fanny pack. "I counted my money and I have enough."

"You know what, honey? Everything is discounted today, so you have more than enough." Maddie returned a ten.

"Goody." Pansy dashed off.

Maddie slid the cash into a drawer. "Is she still dreaming about opening her own place?"

"More than ever." Poppy lifted the lid off the rooster jar and peered inside. "One day we need to find a way to make it happen."

"Your family is amazing. The way you all love and protect each other."

"You and your mother always treated us with respect. Even after you learned how Mama earned a living."

"Rose was my best friend. No one had a right to judge her. She did the best she knew how to take care of you and Pansy. Has David solved her case?"

"He's still working on it."

Pansy returned and plopped a teddy bear on the counter. "I wanna buy this for Lilly and Andy's baby." She handed Maddie the ten.

"The perfect gift from an awesome aunt."

"Me and Poppy are gonna put the picture I drew in my store's window across the street from Willy's house."

"You can count on me to be your first customer. My favorite cake is chocolate with fudge icing."

"I'll bake one special for you." Pansy wrapped her arm around the rooster and teddy bear, then scooted behind the counter and clutched her dog's leash. "Come on, Boots, we've got work to do."

"That's my cue." Poppy lifted the glass jars off the counter. "Thank you, Maddie."

"You and Pansy always brighten my day." The bell over the door jangled as three new customers strolled in. Maddie slid off her stool. "Another busy morning."

Grateful for the distraction, Poppy scurried out and caught up with her sister at the truck.

Pansy set her treasures on the floor, then lifted her drawing and a roll of tape off the dashboard.

Daisy joined them halfway up the side-street sidewalk. "First time I've seen Agnes's house up close."

"While she was alive, no one dared walk up her driveway without an invitation."

Pansy skipped ahead to the window sandwiched between two rundown, shuttered storefronts. She pressed her hands against the glass and peered inside. "Can we go in?"

Poppy pointed to the lockbox attached to the doorknob. "The building's locked, sweetie."

"Who has the key?"

Daisy tapped a realtor's sign propped in the window. "That real estate lady." She snapped a picture of the sign.

"Can we call her tomorrow?" Pansy wiped smudges off the glass and taped her picture beside the realtor's sign. "Now everyone will know 'bout my new bakery."

"Afternoon, ladies."

Poppy startled at the deep male voice. She spun and stood face-to-face with a stranger who was staring at her. She turned away.

"Nice picture." He pointed to Pansy's drawing. "You buying this place?"

"Uh-huh. I'm gonna paint the name on the window."

"Why?" He chuckled. "Did you win the lottery or something?"

Poppy's heart jumped to her throat.

Daisy looped her arm around Pansy's waist. "My aunt has dreamed about opening her own place for years. It takes a long time to save enough money."

"Tell me about it." The man pulled a handful of lottery tickets from his pocket and nodded toward a dinged-up car. "First thing I'll do when I win is ditch that old clunker and buy me a brand-spanking new Corvette. Nice dog." He stepped off the curb.

Grateful for Daisy's quick thinking, Poppy fell in step beside her daughter as she steered Pansy toward the corner.

"I didn't tell that man 'bout Danny's ticket."

Poppy reached for her sister's hand. "Because you're the best secret keeper—"

"And I promised."

"Yes, you did." Poppy pressed her palm to her left cheek as the man drove past. Would she ever find the courage to face strangers without covering her birthmark?

Chapter Six

Daisy lifted off her knees, brushed clumps of clay off her jeans, and peeled off her gardening gloves. Planting tulip bulbs in the middle of what would have been a workday had done little to alleviate her escalating impatience. She climbed onto the front porch, settled on a rocking chair, and gazed across the front lawn to the dense woods separating her family's property from the two-lane road. How many times had she driven down that same stretch of pavement, past the ranch owned by her reclusive grandfather, and wondered what lay hidden behind the dense woods and shrouds of secrecy? Now she knew.

She closed her eyes and mentally replayed yesterday's trek beyond Agnes Watkins' stone-and-iron fence and up her steep driveway. The thrill she experienced when she climbed onto the porch of the house she and her high-school friends had believed was haunted. Peeking through the slit between the dark drapes. Everything looked so normal, almost inviting.

Footsteps striking the porch steps dashed Daisy's mental musings. She opened her eyes.

David approached. "Appears you've been digging *in* the dirt instead of digging up dirt."

Her heart beat a bit faster as she held up her gloves. "Your clue?"

"Plus that clay smudge on your face." He swiped his finger across her cheek.

His touch sent waves of desire surging through her. "Good detective work."

He grinned. "Easy pickings."

She swallowed. Was she that obvious? "What's happening with our *who killed Rose Fowler* investigation?"

David sat beside her. "I reread all those letters from her admirers."

"Anything pop up since the last time we pored over them?"

"More questions." He set his chair in motion. "For example, why didn't Rose open them?"

Daisy matched his rhythm. "My first childhood crush happened when I was in the second grade. Johnny's desk was beside mine. He was a real cutie. On Valentine's day, I couldn't wait to rush home and sift through the my classmate's cards to find the one from him. It was a drawing of a yellow kitten with the words, 'Valentine, you're P U R R fect.' A random card, but in my mind it was personal."

"Cute story. But what does your crush have to do with Rose?"

"I suspect she kept those letters sealed for self-protection."

"Meaning?"

"Based on everything Mom told me, Rose rationalized prostitution as the only way she could earn a decent living. If she had opened and read those letters, the line between client and lover would have blurred. Making her feel cheap and immoral."

"Self-deception is a powerful emotion."

"One that kept me from telling the law firm about my nonexistent relationship with Curtis. Do you suppose the partners would have hired me if they'd known my grandmother was a prostitute?"

"To get access to Curtis, you bet they would have." David stopped rocking. "I identified the two deputies who dismissed Rose's disappearance."

Daisy's eyes widened. "Are you serious?"

He nodded. "One passed away a few years ago. The other guy retired last year and moved out of state. I'm tracking him down."

"After thirty-five years, do you suppose he'll remember enough to shed any light on the case?"

"Hard to say. However, one fact remains clear. At some point, we'll need to question Curtis again. In person."

"We resorted to threats to get past his assistant the three times he agreed to see anyone in our family. Now that Cynthia's in charge of his business, she'll protect him like a moat full of hungry crocodiles."

"Not if we appeal to her business savvy."

Daisy stared at him. Was he delusional? "Her business savvy is the very reason why she'll keep us away."

"At this point, Curtis is the only person who knows what happened. Besides, you're a brilliant attorney and I'm a smart investigator. Together we'll come up with a plan to get past Cynthia."

"Have you ever resorted to breaking and entering?"

"Not yet." David grinned. "Although you'd be a P U R R fect partner in crime."

"Yeah, I would."

The front door swung open.

David inched closer to Daisy. "Seems our Bonnie-and-Clyde future has been thwarted."

Her mom ambled over. "I hope I'm not interrupting?"

"Never." David stood and offered his chair.

She motioned him to sit, then leaned back against the railing. "I love everything about this old house. The creaky wood floors. The rooms Danny added to accommodate our growing family. I rocked all three of my babies to sleep in those chairs. When Basil came along, Daisy and Lilly liked to sit on the front steps and watch the deer grazing over by the woods. Most days Pansy sat with them and made up stories."

Daisy noted her mom's faraway look. "You didn't come out here to reflect on the past or talk about Georgia's deer population, did you?"

She turned toward the railing and ran her finger along a jagged crack in the wood. "Danny wants to talk to you, me, and David tonight after Pansy goes to sleep."

Daisy eased to her mom's side. "Has he made a decision?"

Her mom stared straight ahead for a long moment. "From the first time your dad held you in his arms, he was awed over the life we'd created. At the same time, he was terrified he'd fail as a father. Just as Curtis failed him." She flicked a leaf off the railing. "Every day since, he's worked to protect and provide for our family the best way he knows how." She patted Daisy's hand. "I don't think he's decided what to do with that check."

"Danny's a good man, Poppy." David moved to the railing. "He understands that life-changing decisions are best not made in haste."

Daisy peered around her mom at David's profile—the man who in a few weeks had become important enough to receive an invitation to her dad's private meeting. Maybe her family would give him a reason to stay.

Three hours after supper, Daisy glimpsed Boots sprawled on the floor beside Pansy's bed. Her aunt's faithful companion during the day, her protector at night. She switched off the light and tiptoed from the bedroom. After texting David, she found her mom sitting on a wingback chair in the front room. "Pansy wore herself out painting a verbal picture of her store and the different kinds of cakes she plans to bake."

"Is she asleep?"

"She drifted off a few minutes ago." Daisy sat on the sofa and tucked her foot under her thigh.

"Then it's time." Her mom tapped her phone. A ping followed. "Danny's on his way over."

"So's David."

"Our investigative journalist was a champion during supper—the way his stories entertained Pansy."

"Easy task." David wandered in. "Your sister's the perfect audience." He sat beside Daisy and set his notepad and pen on the coffee table.

"You brought the tools of your trade." Daisy elbowed him. "Are you expecting a newsflash or more content for your book?"

"Investigative journalists worth their salt always show up prepared to add to their stories."

"Speaking of stories, were all those teenage shenanigans you shared with Aunt Pansy true, or were they creations of your writer's imagination?"

"True." David held his finger an inch from his thumb. "With a tad bit of creative embellishment." He winked. "Now that I've bared my soul, how about revealing tidbits from your misspent youth?"

Daisy pressed her index finger to her lips. "Not in front of Mom. She believes I was a model teenager."

David chuckled. "What's the real scoop, Poppy?"

"My firstborn had her moments. One of these days, I'll fill you in. Off the record, of course."

"For my ears only."

Footsteps struck the hall floor. Daisy's dad lumbered in and lowered his six-foot, muscular frame onto the second wingback. He crossed his arms and made eye contact with each of them while tapping his fingers on his biceps.

Daisy's eyes locked on her dad's face. Did his stoic expression mean he'd finally made a decision, or was he still caught in a quandary?

His tapping stopped. His eyes grew lightning fierce. "The woman who brought me into this world believed in two things—expensive possessions and social status. She raised my sisters to take their place among Savannah's privileged class and groomed them to live the same empty lifestyle she valued. Money was the only thing my old man contributed to their upbringing, with predictable results. One of my sisters has been divorced three times and lives with a wealthy man known as a womanizer. The other one has spent most of her adult life fighting a losing battle with alcohol and drug addiction."

He drew in a deep breath and slowly released the air. "My brother Bobby was the best person in our screwed-up family. Like Pansy, he loved everyone unconditionally. I did everything I could to make him feel loved and respected." His voice cracked. "Truth is, I couldn't protect him from Margaret and Curtis Butler's heartless souls."

Daisy's lip caught between her teeth. She had never heard her dad utter his mother's name or witnessed so much pain in his eyes.

"The night Bobby took his own life, I vowed never to let money destroy me or anyone I loved. When I learned about the winning ticket, I considered it a mockery of everything I stand for. How many people have plucked down their last dollar hoping to win?" He pulled the check from his shirt pocket. "If I cash this, will I legitimize a lottery that offers false hope to desperate people?"

Daisy's mom picked at a fingernail.

Her dad stuffed the check back in his pocket and ran his fingers through his thick hair. The gray at his temples had become more pronounced during the past two months. "I can't make a decision one way or the other until I know if this money is a curse or a blessing. Which is why I've called this meeting. I want you three to come up with a list of reasons why I should cash the check as well as reasons why I'd best rip it to shreds."

"Without you?" Daisy leaned forward. "Why the three of us?"

He propped his forearms across his knees. "Your mother knows my heart. You understand all the legal ramifications, and I trust David's objectivity and honesty."

Daisy caught David's eye. His brows arched as if asking a question. Was he seeking her permission? She glanced at her mom. The time seemed right. She nodded at David.

He nodded back, then faced her dad. "Speaking of honesty, there's something you need to know before you include me in this task. I never put words on paper until I know beyond a reasonable doubt they're true. Which is why I've reopened the investigation into Rose's disappearance, and why I've asked Daisy to be my investigative partner."

Daisy's body tensed at the sight of her dad's pointed stare.

"I understand why you need more evidence to prove my old man's guilt." He paused while keeping his eyes glued on David.

Daisy held her breath. Was she seconds away from hearing the word but?

"Fact is, your integrity is another reason I value your input, young man."

David cleared his throat. "In that case, do you mind if I offer an opinion?"

"I'm listening."

"On the surface, excluding Pansy from our should-you/shouldn't-you discussions makes sense. However, I believe her unrestrained insight could prove invaluable."

Daisy's dad remained silent for a long moment. "Point well taken. Include her in the discussions, and inform me when you've completed the task." He lifted off his chair and strode to the bedroom.

"We'll start working on those lists tomorrow." Daisy's mom stood, rushed to the bedroom, and closed the door behind her.

Daisy turned to face David. "Smart move suggesting we include Aunt Pansy."

"I predict she'll come up with the most imaginative reasons for our take-the-money list."

"Is that what you think Dad should do?"

"He's counting on my objectivity—"

"Which means even if you have an opinion, you can't answer."

"You have that right, Counselor."

Daisy propped her elbow on the back of the sofa and planted her cheek on her knuckles. "What's your opinion about being the first outsider Dad has invited into our inner circle?"

David lifted off the sofa and reached for her hand. "Come with me, partner."

"Where are we going?"

"To the kitchen to celebrate my new position in the Butler family with a big slice of Pansy's red-velvet cake."

Chapter Seven

Poppy breathed in the scent of freshly brewed coffee while placing paper and pencils on the table. She had never imagined her kitchen would one day function as a meeting room to discuss the pros and cons of instant wealth. Danny's comment about knowing her heart had unleashed a flurry of conflicting questions. Did he expect her to lean one way or the other? If he did take the money, would he use it to exact revenge against his father?

Daisy wandered in and set her laptop on the table. "The morning Mr. Warner summoned me to the law firm's conference room to promote me to senior associate, I envisioned one day sitting around their fancy conference table discussing big cases. Instead, I'm meeting in my family's kitchen to list reasons Dad should or shouldn't cash a ginormous check. A monumental task, considering his decision will impact my professional future."

"At least David comes to the table without a stake in Danny's decision."

Pansy dashed in and laid her sketchpad and box of colored pencils on the table. "I'm ready." She poured a glass of orange juice while Boots sprawled on the floor beside her chair.

The back door swung open. "Good morning, ladies." David breezed in clutching his notepad. He sat beside Daisy. "Coffee smells enticing."

Poppy fixed him a cup, then settled across from him and stared at the blank paper lying on the table. She'd never led any kind of meeting. Didn't matter. This was her kitchen and Danny was her husband. "I suppose we should begin this meeting with reasons why Danny shouldn't cash the check." She picked her pencil off the table and wrote 'against' across the top of the paper.

When Daisy opened her laptop, Pansy opened her sketchpad and began drawing. David cradled his coffee cup in both hands. No one spoke.

Poppy drummed her fingers. "Someone has to go first." She made eye contact with David, hoping he'd take the hint.

He cleared his throat. "I've investigated more than one crime triggered by arguments over money. I'm not suggesting that would happen to your family—"

"Crimes, no." Lilly's last phone call played in Poppy's mind. "Squabbles and disagreements, definitely. Money tends to change people and not always for the better." What if Lilly and Andy's babies grew up privileged and spoiled? Would they turn out like Danny's sisters?

"There's also the issue of anonymity," added Daisy. "If word leaked about a windfall fortune, scammers and opportunists would swoop on our family like a flock of hungry vultures spotting a deer that lost a battle with a car."

A chill skittered up Poppy's spine as she imagined a heartless criminal kidnapping her grandson and demanding millions for his safe return. "Another reason to reject the money. Potential kidnappers."

Pansy tilted her head. "Basil's gonna be a policeman. He'll protect us from bad people."

Daisy nodded. "Good point, Aunt Pansy, especially if no one found out our family had money."

After the team added three more reasons to their don't-cash-the-check list, David clicked his pen. "Before we go too far down a rabbit hole, I suggest we switch topics and discuss valid reasons why Danny *should* cash the check."

"I suppose we are becoming a bit morbid." Poppy released a long sigh. "We could give most of the money away."

Daisy tapped her keyboard. "This morning I researched charities and identified a dozen excellent choices."

"Eleven dollars a month." Pansy exchanged her green pencil for a brown one. "People on TV ask us to send money for sick kids in hospitals and old people who don't have enough food to eat. Sometimes they want money for dogs and cats locked up in cages."

"Here's an idea," added David. "The Butler family could start their own charity, a foundation of sorts."

"Giving to charity would eliminate every item on our negative list—" Poppy exchanged a knowing glance with Daisy. "Except one."

Daisy rolled her eyes. "The family squabble initiated by my sister."

Poppy nodded. "We'd never hear the end of it."

"You know Danny better than anyone, Poppy." David leaned back and laced his fingers behind his neck. "If he decides to cash the check, how do you suppose he'd want to spend the money?"

Poppy's gaze shifted to one of Pansy's drawings on the wall behind David. "He'd want to help people who need a hand up instead of a handout. People like his brother Bobby, or young girls whose families die in car crashes and leave them all alone in the world."

"We can build a town." Pansy set her pencil on the table. "Like Ray built in *Field of Dreams*. All those baseball players living in the cornfields came out to play. Then the cars came. We could build houses and a school where kids wouldn't tease other kids or call them names. Everyone would buy cakes and cookies from my bakery."

David snapped his fingers. "That's what I call creative, out-of-the-box thinking."

Poppy stared at her sister for a long moment. Leave it to Pansy to come up with a totally outlandish idea. At least adding it to the list would add a bit of humor. Following another hour of brainstorming, Poppy compared the two lists. "We've come up with more take-the-money than don't-take-the-money ideas."

"We can name our town Roseville." Pansy closed her sketchpad. "Mama would like that."

Poppy's eyes darted to her sister. How long would she cling to that crazy idea? "We don't know what Danny will decide, sweetie."

Pansy jumped up. "I'm gonna tell him about my idea—"

"Wait." Poppy grabbed her sister's arm. "We need to give him our list without trying to influence him one way or the other."

"Cause it's his money?"

"Yes."

"Can we give it to him now?"

"If you promise not to say anything."

"Cross my heart." Pansy traced an x on her chest then zipped her thumb and finger across her lips. "I won't say a word."

"All right then." Poppy stood and stretched. "Let's go find Danny."

Daisy closed her laptop as her mom and aunt strode out the back door. "Leave it to my aunt to come up with a crazy idea."

"You have to admit it was the most creative." David flipped his notepad closed. "Based on our discussion, which decision do you hope your dad will make?"

"From a personal perspective..." Daisy trilled her lips. "If he takes the money, I'll become my family's full-time attorney. If he doesn't, I'll have to find another job. I suppose I could beg Michael to take me back. Except New York is a long way from home—" She glanced at David. "And the people I love."

"You could open your own office and represent everyday folks."

"My expertise is corporate law." Daisy tapped her finger to her chin. "Although defending innocent victims does have a certain appeal."

"Speaking of victims." David pulled his phone from his pocket and tapped the screen. "My contact located one of the deputies who investigated Rose's disappearance. He moved to St. Augustine Beach after he retired."

"Do you suppose he'll talk to us?"

"Only one way to find out." David placed a call and pressed the speaker icon. The man answered.

When the conversation ended, Daisy locked eyes with David. "I'm surprised he agreed to talk to us."

"That's the only way he can discover what we know."

"Good point. We should keep tomorrow's meeting to ourselves until we find out if anything comes of it."

"I agree." David pocketed his phone moments before Daisy's mom returned without Pansy.

"How did Dad react to our the list?"

"Typical Danny." She plopped onto her chair. "He stuffed it in his pocket and continued loading plants onto the truck."

"What did Pansy do?"

"She kept her promise."

"Good for her." Daisy leaned back. "Chances are Dad has already made up his mind and wants a reason to validate his choice."

David nudged Daisy's arm. "Danny's too practical to give us an assignment laced with an ulterior motive."

"He's also never been faced with this kind of decision." Daisy caught her mom's eye. "Who do you think is right, me or David?"

She hesitated for a long moment. "Maybe the truth is somewhere in between. I suppose it's possible your dad is leaning one way more than the other. On the other hand, I doubt he would have asked David to join us if he'd already decided."

"Good intuition, Poppy." David slid his pen behind his ear. "The truth often lies somewhere in the middle."

Daisy stared at David's profile. "Does that logic normally apply to cold cases?"

"Most of the time, yes it does."

Chapter Eight

Trapped between Danny's indecision and Lilly's impatience, Poppy stood on the back porch clutching a plate of cookies. Twenty-four hours had passed, and not only had Danny failed to say a word about the list, he'd also insisted on eating last night's supper alone in the greenhouse.

She eyed the empty space where David parked his truck. Had he and Daisy left to chase down a lead? So many unanswered questions about her mama's disappearance and her family's future remained. No matter the consequences, she needed to talk to Danny.

Poppy eased to the porch steps and froze at the bottom. The greenhouse shimmered in the late-morning sun. Inside, Danny sat with his back to the window, hunched over the junkyard door stretched across two filing cabinets that served as his desk. Was he paying bills or ordering supplies? Maybe this wasn't a good time to interrupt him. Besides, waiting a bit longer wouldn't make that much difference.

She averted her eyes and meandered through the backyard to her private retreat. Inside, she set the cookies on the bench and lifted the trunk lid. Her old scrapbook bulging with newspaper clippings featuring Curtis's family lay beside her month-old work in progress. She hadn't added a single item to her new scrapbook since she'd pasted Pansy's birthday card to Danny on the second page.

A thin manila envelope peeked out between the scrapbooks. The envelope she'd kept hidden until a few weeks ago when she'd shown it to David and Daisy. Poppy lifted the envelope and removed the yellowed newspaper clipping. Her fingers traced the front-page photo of Rose Fowler beneath the headline, *Prostitute Disappears Without a Trace.* After that edition hit the streets, she and Pansy had hidden in their home to avoid curious stares and questions, until they ran out of food and were forced to go to town.

Poppy slipped the article back in the envelope and placed it under her new scrapbook. She'd survived a lot of heartache and drama since her mama died, thanks in large part to Danny. Somehow she had to pull herself together and find the courage to talk to him. She closed the trunk, grabbed the cookies, and forced her legs to carry her out of her retreat and across the backyard. Her pulse accelerated the second she stepped inside the greenhouse. Breathing deeply to slow her heart beat, she squared her shoulders and headed straight to his office hidden behind a massive ficus tree. "I brought you cookies."

"Dessert before lunch?" He looked up from the stack of papers. "I'm guessing there's more on your mind than satisfying my sweet tooth."

No use trying to hide her intentions; he knew her too well. She set the plate on his desk. "We need to talk."

His eyes probed her face. "Lilly called again, didn't she?"

Poppy failed to suppress a sigh. "Thirty minutes ago." She dropped onto a metal folding chair across from Danny and eyed the framed profile photo of her unmarred cheek—taken when she was pregnant with Daisy. Such a happy time.

Danny caught her eye. "Do you want to talk about Lilly, or is something else on your mind?"

"Actually, I've been wondering if you've had a chance to look at our list of pros and cons?"

"I read them." He broke eye contact, plucked a cookie off the plate, and took a bite.

Poppy crossed her leg and pumped her foot. Was he stalling because he'd made a decision, or because he hadn't? Or maybe the list fell short of his expectations. She counted to twenty. Then thirty. No matter what he thought about the list, she had to discuss the real reason she'd brought him cookies. "Lilly invited us to supper Sunday." The words spilled out.

Danny stared at her. "Did you accept?"

Poppy uncrossed her leg and plucked a marble paperweight off the desk—his Father's Day gift from years earlier. She fingered the inscription—*Best Dad Ever*. "Not yet."

Danny polished off the cookie. After brushing crumbs from his fingers, he rounded his desk and held out his hand. "Come with me."

Her brows pinched. Where? Why?

"Please."

She set down the paperweight and accepted his hand. Her fingers entwined with his as he escorted her past rows of colorful annuals. Was he moments away from revealing his decision? Her pulse raced again.

Danny stopped at the center aisle. He released Poppy's hand and swept his arm in a wide arc. "Look around you and tell me what you see."

How did he want her to answer? "A successful business?"

"Which we built from scratch with hard work and plenty of sweat. It's given us everything we've needed to live a comfortable life and raise well-adjusted, productive children."

Was he trying to tell her the family didn't need the lottery winnings?

"Even if I planned to give all the money away, cashing that check could undermine everything you and I have accomplished. Especially with Lilly. You know she'd expect a big chunk of cash."

Poppy caught her lip between her teeth. He was right about their middle child. Lilly had always envied celebrities and their lavish lifestyles. And unlike Daisy and Basil, she had pressured her dad to claim the winning ticket. "You've decided, haven't you?"

"Our family's future is at stake, which is why I need more time to weigh all the pros and cons." He stooped and picked a petal off the concrete. "Call Lilly and tell her we're not available Sunday."

Poppy's stomach churned as her eyes followed Danny's trek back to his desk. How much longer did he need? A day? A week? A month? Would he ever decide? She peered down the center aisle. The greenhouse tabby stretched out on the warm concrete, a docile creature until called to duty by the scent of an unwelcome rodent. Six weeks ago, she was the same as that cat—satisfied with an easy, predictable life. Then in one day a random lottery ticket had turned her life upside down.

Maybe she should persuade Danny. Contradictory thoughts erupted and collided in her head. If he tore the check to bits, he'd dishonor Pansy's gift. On the other hand, what would happen if he took the money? Either choice promised to create havoc for the family she loved.

Poppy focused on the cat licking its paw. Maybe one day she would discover the heart of a lion lurked inside her chest. Until then, she had to wait and trust the man who shared her bed to make the best decision for their family's future.

Chapter Nine

Daisy's anxiety escalated tenfold as David exited Interstate 95 and followed directions to their destination. "I hope this guy remembers enough to make our trip worthwhile."

"And is willing to level with us." David turned into a parking lot a half block from the beach. With his notepad in hand, he circled to the truck's passenger side and opened the door. "Are you ready, partner?"

"As ready as I'll ever be." Daisy stepped out. The gentle rush of waves rolling onto shore perked her ears as she breathed in the salty sea air. "I love the smell of the ocean."

"Is this your first trip to St. Augustine?"

"It is."

He closed and locked the door. "In the spring we should come back and explore Old Town."

"More investigative work?"

"Hopefully we'll have solved this case before then."

Did that mean he planned to stay around for a while? Maybe until he finished writing the book?

David pressed his hand to her back.

A tingle surged up her spine. "By spring we'll be ready for a break."

"More than ready." He escorted her across the parking lot and into the restaurant.

The hostess greeted them with a smile. "Table for two?"

"We're meeting a gentleman—"

"Oh, yes. Mr. Jenkins is waiting for you." She led them to a table on the awning-shaded veranda. A man with thinning salt-and-pepper hair and a gray moustache cradled a bottle of beer.

"Officer Jenkins?"

"The one and only."

"I'm David Lambert and this is Daisy Butler, Rose Fowler's grand-daughter."

"Name's Brad." The man motioned them to sit.

David pulled out a chair for Daisy then settled beside her.

She pushed her sunglasses up. "Thank you for agreeing to meet with us."

Brad's eyes shifted from her to David. "Every year the chance someone would show up to question Rose's disappearance grew less likely. At some point, I put the incident out of my mind." He held up his beer. "I don't normally drink at noon."

"Liquid courage?"

"Something like that." Brad motioned to the waitress. "I asked her to take your drink orders but hold off on lunch to give us time to talk."

After ordering, David set his notepad on the table. "You were one of the two deputies who investigated Rose's case?"

Brad scowled. "Cover-up is a more accurate description."

Daisy cringed. Maybe she should have ordered something stronger than sweet tea. A Texas margarita would've fit the bill. "Covered up how?"

"Your grandmother had a lot of johns—"

"We prefer to call them clients."

"I would too, if she was my kin. Anyway, her clients were influential men who had a lot to lose if anyone discovered their extracurricular activities."

Like Curtis Butler.

Brad turned toward the railing separating the restaurant from the beach. "When the first call about her disappearance came in, my partner and I were told to ignore it."

David clicked his pen. "Who gave the order?"

"Our chief deputy. When the calls kept coming, he ordered us to follow up but dismiss the case as a runaway."

"No matter what you found?"

"Even if we discovered a mountain of evidence." Brad faced Daisy. "A lot of folks knew how Rose earned her living. They also recognized that she was a good mother to her two daughters. Before we showed up at her house, I had my suspicions. When we walked into her bedroom, I suspected foul play."

The waitress set two tall glasses of tea on the table, then walked away.

David reached for his glass. "From evidence or hunches?"

"Both. First, the room was in perfect order. Clean. Neat. Bed made. According to her oldest daughter—" Brad eyed Daisy. "What's her name?"

"Poppy."

"Oh yeah, and her sister's Pansy. Is everyone in your family named after flowers?"

"Family tradition."

"Interesting. Back to Rose. Both daughters claimed they hadn't touched anything. In my opinion, the room looked too perfect, as if someone had staged it. Also, none of your grandmother's personal belongings were missing. Would a woman leave voluntarily without packing a bag?"

Daisy shook her head. "Not a chance."

"Good investigative instincts." David sipped his tea. "You mentioned evidence."

"The first clues were a faint disinfectant odor and the remnants of a stain on the floor. When I pointed it out to my partner, he claimed the stain and smell were most likely from dog or cat urine."

Daisy tilted her head. "Rose didn't have pets."

"Didn't matter. We stuck to that explanation."

David opened his notepad. "Despite what you observed, why did you ignore the facts?"

"You have to understand. My partner had a sick wife and was two years from retirement. I was a rookie with a new wife and a baby on the way. Neither one of us could afford to tick off our boss and risk getting canned. So yeah, accepting the stain as something other than foul play came easy." Brad took a long swig of beer. "What I found beside the floorboard is a different story." He fell silent.

"Look." David planted his arms on the table. "We're not here to judge you or to cause you problems. We just want to find out what happened to Rose."

Brad sucked in air, then released a long sigh. "What I'm about to show you is proof of at least one crime—mine for suppressing evidence." He slid his hand into his jean's pocket.

Daisy's eyes widened. Her heart pounded against her ribs. Was Brad seconds from cracking the case wide open and proving her grandfather's guilt?

Brad pulled his fisted hand from his pocket and held a tiny evidence bag inches above the table. "No one other than me and, my partner, who died six years ago, and whoever left this, knows it exists." He unclenched his fingers. An object fell from the bag and landed on the table with a sharp clink. A gold shell casing rolled to a stop beside Brad's beer.

Daisy gasped.

"Nine millimeter." Brad tapped the table. "From a small handgun."

David lifted the casing with his pen. "Fingerprints?"

"Never checked."

"Mind if I keep this?"

Brad's eyes narrowed on David.

"You know the statute of limitations applies to your evidence suppression."

"Yeah. But not for murder. Any chance you'll solve the case?"

"This casing might help."

"Then take it."

David slid the casing back in the evidence bag and pocketed the evidence. "Your boss was obviously protecting someone. Any idea who?"

"You'd have to ask him. Last I heard, he's still somewhere in Savannah." Brad wrote on a napkin and pushed it across the table. "That's his name."

David pocketed the napkin.

"He's in his eighties, so maybe he'll come clean. I've told you everything I know, and now I'm starving." Brad motioned to their waitress. After ordering, he eyed Daisy. "Are you also an investigator or just along for the ride?"

Would the ex-cop freak if she revealed her profession, especially after he confessed to his deception? Best not to find out. "I'm David's partner." Perhaps she should change the subject before he asked another question. "What keeps you busy now that you're retired?"

"Fishing. Playing with the grandkids. Little bit of volunteer work here and there."

"What kind of volunteer work?"

"Finding jobs and safe places to live for paroled first offenders, to keep them from landing back in jail."

Daisy's eyes drifted to a seagull swooping toward the surf. "I imagine it's more satisfying to help people than to arrest them."

"At least the successes offset the failures and make the effort worthwhile." Brad propped his arm across the back of the chair beside him. "What attracted you to Rose's case, David?"

"Pansy Fowler's imagination."

While David shared how the story Pansy mailed him had roused his curiosity, Daisy focused on a young man straddling a surfboard far offshore. The only person brave or crazy enough to endure the cold water. He must be a tourist visiting from up north, maybe as far away as Canada. She watched him float in the gentle surf. How long would he wait for a ride-worthy wave?

The surfboarder paddled vigorously ahead of a swell, then sprang to his feet and rode the wave a few yards. A lot of effort for little payoff. He attempted to ride two more swells before carrying his board out of the water and wandering up the beach to a new spot. Was that what she and David were doing? Waiting to catch a big wave, and hoping to ride it to victory?

During the remainder of lunch, Daisy listened while David and Brad discussed sports, life in sunny Florida, and last year's hurricane season. After finishing a slice of key-lime pie, David handed Brad a business card. "If anything else comes to mind, please call." He paid for their meal then escorted Daisy to his truck. "Your mom never mentioned Rose owning a firearm."

Daisy pulled her sunglasses down. "Years ago she told me her mom was terrified of guns."

David removed the secured shell casing from his pocket. "When do you want to tell your family about this?"

"Dad's already stressed to the limit."

"So you want to wait?"

"In a sense I'm their attorney, so they'd expect me to level with them."

"Then you want to tell them?"

Daisy puffed her cheeks and blew out air. "I don't know. Maybe it's best to wait for the right moment. In the meantime, you keep the casing."

David pocketed the evidence then backed out of the parking space. "Now that we've completed our first investigative interview, what's your reaction to our new venture?"

Lilly's ringtone chimed. "Hold that question." Daisy pulled her phone from her purse. "Hey, sis."

"Do you have any idea what's going on with Mom and Dad?"

Daisy's brows pinched. "What are you talking about?"

"Mom turned down my invitation to supper Sunday. Is something wrong, or is she avoiding me because Dad won't make a decision?"

Daisy eyed a flock of seagulls soaring toward the shore. "They both have a lot on their minds."

"Basil won't take sides, and Mom will go along with whatever Dad decides. That leaves our future up to me and you—"

"The decision isn't ours to make, Lilly."

"Do you have any idea how millions of dollars would change all our lives?"

"Believe me, I do. So does Dad. Which is why he's weighing all the pros and cons before making a decision."

"Maybe Andy and I'll pop over Sunday and talk to him."

"Bad idea—"

"Is that your lawyer or oldest-daughter opinion?"

"Both." Daisy pressed her fingers to the back of her neck. "Try to understand that we need to trust Dad to do what's best for our family"

"Based on his insane idea that money destroys families?"

"Lilly, please."

A sigh resonated. "I don't mean to come across as greedy or insensitive...I just want what's best for *my* family."

"We all do." Daisy ended the call and dropped her phone in her purse.

David braked at a red light and glanced at her. "Based on your side of the conversation, I'm guessing your sister's patience is wearing thin."

"I love her to pieces." Her eyes followed a high-dollar sports car speeding through the intersection. "But, sometimes she's exasperating."

"Family dynamics." David glanced at her. "Back to my question."

"About today's joint venture?"

"Yeah?"

"When Brad dropped that shell casing on the table, the anticipation of discovering new evidence evoked new hope inside me. The potential to solve the case—"

"You got caught up in the excitement, didn't you?"

"Way more than I expected."

Chapter Ten

Fifteen minutes before supper, Daisy strolled into the kitchen and savored the onion and garlic scents wafting across the space where her mother and aunt were busy working. "Meatloaf?"

"Uh-huh." Pansy looked up from mashing potatoes. "Danny's favorite."

Daisy eyed her mom. "Special occasion or food to soothe the soul?"

She set a tomato on a cutting board. "I talked to your dad earlier today. He read our list."

Definitely the latter. "Did it help?"

"He seems more confused than ever." Her mom cut the tomato into chunks and scraped them into a salad bowl.

Daisy moved plates from the cabinet to the table. Now seemed as good a time as any. "Lilly called me this afternoon. She wanted to know the real reason you and Dad declined her invitation."

Her mom set the salad bowl on the table. "What'd you tell her?"

"That you had a lot going on in your minds."

Pansy plunked the bowl of mashed potatoes beside the salad. "I wanna give Lilly and Andy the teddy bear for their baby. When can we invite them to supper?"

"In a couple of weeks." Daisy's mom transferred the meatloaf from the oven to a serving platter.

David breezed in and patted his belly. "Smells like another melt-in-your-mouth supper."

Pansy poured tea into five tall glasses. "I fixed the potatoes with lots of butter."

David grinned. "Your mashed potatoes are as good as your cakes."

"'Cept with no sugar." Pansy giggled. "That would make 'em sweet potatoes."

David elbowed her. "Good one, Pansy."

Footsteps struck the back-porch floorboards. The head of the household lumbered in and headed straight to his chair. The rest of the family plus one took their seats, bowed their heads, and waited for Poppy to say grace. Pansy's exuberant *amen* at the end of the prayer signaled the official start of another Butler family supper.

After filling her plate and salad bowl, Daisy tuned out David and Pansy's playful banter. What role would she play tonight? Loving daughter who shielded her parents from grim news? Or attorney who understood clients deserved to know the truth, no matter how painful? She stole glances at both parents. Her dad remained laser-focused on his food while her mom picked at her supper and offered an occasional comment. Everything seemed normal, at least for the moment.

Daisy settled into daughter mode until Pansy speared a tomato and pointed it at her. "Where did you and David go today?"

So much for normal.

Her mom glanced at David then eyed Daisy. "I was wondering the same thing...not that it's any of our business. Unless of course, you want to tell us."

Daisy fidgeted. Pansy opened the door. Now she had to gather the courage to step through. She squared her shoulders and shifted from daughter to attorney mode. "David located one of the deputies who investigated Grandmother Rose's disappearance."

"That's good news." Her mom's eyes widened. "Right?"

Daisy nodded. "This morning we drove to St. Augustine to meet him."

Her dad set his fork on the table. "How much did he remember?"

"Enough." Daisy maintained eye contact with her dad while relaying Brad's comments about the chief deputy's orders to dismiss the case.

His jaw tightened. "Then your trip was pointless."

"Not exactly." Daisy caught her mom's wide-eyed expression. "Deputy Jenkins gave us a piece of evidence he'd kept hidden for years."

Her dad's eyes narrowed. "What sort of evidence?"

She'd poked the hornet's nest, so nothing short of the truth would do. "A shell casing he found in Grandmother Rose's bedroom the day he and his partner showed up to investigate."

Pansy's head tilted. "What's a shell casing?"

"It's a sleeve for a bullet."

"Did someone shoot Mama?"

A gasp escaped from Daisy's mom. She bolted to her feet and dashed out the back door.

Her dad lifted off his chair and leaned on the table, his eyes lightning fierce. "No matter how long it takes or where it lands, you and David uncover the truth and bury the coward who stole your grandmother's life."

"We will." Daisy's shoulder and neck muscles drew taut. "I promise."

"I'll hold you to it." He straightened and dashed out.

Daisy's shoulders slumped. Had she made a promise she couldn't keep? She faced David. "Now what do we do?"

"Find that chief deputy and drill him for answers."

Sweat ran cold between Poppy's shoulder blades as she stumbled across the back porch. Danny caught up with her at the screen door. He slid his arm around her waist and guided her down the steps. They made their way across the yard to her private retreat. She entered the dark space and dropped onto the bench.

Danny pulled the chain to illuminate the overhead light then settled beside her. "Are you okay?"

"A couple of days ago, David noticed a discolored spot on Mama's bedroom floor." She squeezed her eyes shut to summon memories of the day her mother disappeared. "If someone had shot Mama, wouldn't Pansy and I have heard a loud bang?"

"Depends on the gun."

She leaned back and opened her eyes. "Why do you think Curtis paid off our mortgage and sent me and Pansy money after Mama disappeared?"

"Guilty conscience? A warped sense of responsibility?"

"Do you believe he's guilty?"

"If Rose was shot, and if my old man didn't pull the trigger, he for darn sure knows who did."

"Our family's been burdened with secrets far too long." Poppy released a long sigh. "All those years ago, when you secretly discovered I was clipping newspaper stories about your family, what did you think I was doing with them?"

"Creating some sort of record."

"I wanted to believe my scrapbook would help our children understand their heritage. Truth is, I kept it secret from everyone except Daisy."

"You've always had high hopes for our firstborn."

Poppy pressed her hand to her cheek. "The day we attended Daisy's graduation from law school, I wore that floppy hat to hide my birthmark. You shielded me from prying eyes as best you could."

"Only because all those strangers made you uncomfortable."

She blinked and eyed the ancient trunk holding her scrapbooks. "A couple weeks ago, I started a new scrapbook. I'm calling it 'Danny Butler's Family Legacy.'"

"A more appropriate title is 'Poppy and Danny Butler's Family Legacy.'"

"What is our legacy, Danny? A family torn apart by a troubled past or blessed by a bright future?"

He slid his arm around her shoulders and pulled her close. "Do you want me to ask David to stop the investigation?"

"Mama's waited thirty-five years for the truth to come out." She leaned into him and drew strength from his muscular arms and familiar scent. "We've come too far to give up now."

Danny remained silent for a long moment. "Daisy needs to focus all her attention on the case."

"Meaning?"

"I'll hold off on a decision about the lottery check until she and David solve the crime."

"We have no idea how long that will take, and you know Lilly will keep pressing you for a decision."

"Call her in the morning and accept her supper invitation."

"Are you sure?"

"Positive."

"You know she'll hound you for an answer."

"I'll make her understand."

Poppy stared at the dim light cast by the overhead bulb. Although she had no doubt Danny would try to talk sense into their middle child, mountains of reservations about his ability to succeed consumed her. She closed her eyes and sent up a silent prayer asking God to help the man she loved find the right words.

Chapter Eleven

J olted awake by her phone alarm, Daisy switched on the bedside lamp and squinted. The moment her eyes adjusted to the light, she swung her legs over the side of the bed and padded toward the closet. As her focus drifted to the discolored spot on the floor, a shiver cascaded down her spine and raised the hairs on the back of her neck. How many thousands of times had her feet touched what David believed was the remnant of her grandmother's blood? Proof a crime had taken place? She filled her lungs, donned her robe, and tiptoed out to the front porch.

Cold air nipped her cheeks and released a crop of goosebumps, forcing Daisy to pull her robe tight across her chest. Maybe she should have grabbed a cup of coffee before braving the pre-dawn chill. Except she needed time alone to sort through her emotions. How much longer would her future remain suspended in a time warp? If she and David failed to solve her grandmother's case, would her dad postpone a decision about the lottery check indefinitely?

Movement at the edge of the lawn drew Daisy's eye. A family of deer, barely visible in the moonlight, emerged from the woods. Maybe she needed another project. Something that would keep her busy but wouldn't distract from her role as David's investigative partner. She sat on the top step, wrapped her arms around her shins, and let her mind wander to a litany of possibilities. By the time the sky morphed from inky black to pale gray, she had settled on a decision. Eager to set her plan in motion, she raced to her room and made a phone call.

Five hours after the sun peeked over the horizon, Daisy glanced at David sitting in the passenger seat, pleased he'd agreed to come with her. She turned onto the driveway across from the thrift store, eased past the elaborate stone-and-iron fence, and parked beside Agnes Watkins's front porch. A round turret extended past the Victorian's second story to a cone-shaped roof. "From the outside it seems the house is in decent shape."

"At least from a distance." David scooted to the driver's side and opened the door.

They climbed onto the porch extending from a bay window across the front and around the side of the house. Daisy fingered a paint chip on an intricately carved wood column that supported the roof sheltering the wide space. "I imagine Agnes spent a lot of time sitting out here keeping an eye on her land."

"How much property did she own?"

"Everything from a mile back all the way to Curtis's ranch."

"That's a lot of acreage."

"Rumors are she inherited it all from her husband's family. If her sons accept my offer, I'll own this beauty."

"You were brave to make an offer without seeing the inside."

"Based on everything I know about Agnes's penchant for perfection, I'm confident the entire house is well maintained." Daisy removed two keys from under the doormat. She pocketed one and unlocked the stained-glass front door with the other. Inside the foyer, the sweet scent of lavender permeated the stale air.

David sniffed. "What's that sickly-sweet smell?"

"Agnes's signature cologne."

"She must've bathed in it."

"You didn't have to see her to know she was close by. A clue her sense of smell had known better days." Daisy strolled into the living room and pulled back the dark drapes shrouding the windows. Sunlight streamed in and lit tiny particles of dust floating in the air.

David swept his arm in a wide arc. "Does all this furniture stay with the house?"

"Everything in and out of sight."

"I hope you're fond of antiques."

"They're not my favorite style." Daisy mentally pictured Michael Warner's parents' Southampton mansion—the clean lines and sophisticated luxury. "I'm more of a contemporary kind of gal." She eyed the antique area rug holding center stage in front of the fireplace. "Although, I could opt for eclectic and keep a few pieces. I'll donate what I don't want to the thrift store."

She meandered across the foyer and opened French doors leading to a parlor. Similar to the living room, elaborate crown molding wrapped around the high ceiling. "Based on the wall color, fragrance isn't the only fondness Agnes had for lavender. "

"You could call this the grape room." David hiked his foot on the hearth. "The house has two fireplaces?"

"Three, counting the one on the back deck."

"Impressive." He pointed to the landscape above the mantel. "Nice painting."

"At least Agnes's art selection is superior to her fragrance choice." Daisy ran her fingers across the top of a mahogany desk set in front of a bay window. "I'll definitely keep this beauty." She propped her hip on the corner of the desk and caught David's eye. "When I move in, we could work on Rose's case from here. Fewer interruptions."

"Lambert and Butler, investigative team extraordinaire."

"What do you suppose nosy neighbors would say about our collaboration?"

"Speaking of nosy neighbors." David nodded toward the window. "Your first houseguest."

Daisy spun around. Maddie had made it halfway up the driveway. "More like a curious neighbor who can't wait to see Old Agnes's inner sanctum." She scooted to the foyer and opened the front door.

"That's one steep driveway." Maddie climbed onto the porch. "Perfect for cars but near impossible for foot traffic. Which is likely why Agnes planned it that way." She stopped and took a deep breath.

"Are you okay?"

"I just need a second to let my pulse return to normal." Moments later Maddie stepped inside. She sniffed, then scrunched her nose. "If I didn't know better, I'd swear old Agnes was running a secret lavender factory in here. It'll take weeks to air the place out."

David chuckled. "She definitely left a lasting impression."

"In more ways than one." Maddie turned in a slow circle. "Are you looking to buy the place, Daisy, or are you simply satisfying your curiosity?"

How much should she reveal, given she hadn't told her parents about her offer? "Despite the overpowering aroma and the fact that it belonged to Agnes, this house is a good investment."

"Then you are buying it. Does that mean you're moving back to Georgia? Not that anyone could blame you for leaving New York. I mean, all those people and the traffic must be a nightmare. What about your job?" Maddie snapped her fingers. "You're fixing to open an office here and bring a little bit of New York to our neck of the woods, aren't you? As far as I know, the closest attorney is clear over in Savannah, so you'd have a ready-made business."

"Don't go jumping to conclusions, Maddie."

"Whatever you do, I'm happy to have you as a neighbor. Are you keeping all this furniture?" Maddie strolled into the living room and lifted a figurine off an end table. "I'm surprised Agnes's sons didn't take all her stuff. Although those boys were always a couple of aces short of a full deck. I'll be happy to sell any pieces you don't want on consignment." She set down the figurine and faced David. "Are you still working on Rose's case?"

"Every day."

Daisy opened a window, emitting a waft of fresh air and sending dust particles into a swirl. "Actually, David and I are working the case together."

"Good for you." Maddie snapped her fingers. "Wait. Are you two a couple or just business partners? Poppy would've told me if you had a romance going, so I'm guessing you're partners. Which makes sense. Do you mind if I snoop around upstairs?"

"Be my guest." Daisy suppressed a giggle as her across-the-street neighbor dashed to the second floor. "After eyeing this house for years, she finally gets a look inside. How many tickets to tour Agnes's mysterious hideout do you suppose I could sell?"

"Depends on how many people live in a ten-mile radius, and how long it takes the rumor about a New York lawyer moving in to spread."

"I'm guessing a week." Daisy strolled back to the parlor.

David followed and pulled the French doors closed. "What's your take on Maddie's assumption that you're setting up a law office?"

Daisy lifted a vase off the mantel. "If Dad cashes the check, it could work to my family's advantage."

"Meaning?"

"A recipient who wanted to remain anonymous would hire the best law firm to manage the money. Right"

David nodded. "A prestigious New York firm that hired a smart-as-a-whip, southern-born attorney would definitely fit that bill."

"Exactly, not that I'm bragging. However, I am smart enough to let a few well-chosen comments lead Maddie to the same conclusion. Of course, I'd respond with a non-denial denial."

"Which she wouldn't buy."

"You catch on fast."

"There is one little problem. Once the rumor about you setting up shop circulates, potential clients are likely to come knocking on your door."

Daisy set the figurine back on the mantel. "A situation I'll deal with when and if the time comes."

"There is one more fact to consider." A smile lit David's eyes. "A proper law office needs a good investigator."

Did he want a legitimate reason to stick around for a while? "Do you know someone who might qualify?"

"I think I can recommend a well-qualified candidate."

Her heart skipped a beat. Maybe opening a local office wasn't such a bad idea.

Footsteps and creaking stairsteps broadcast Maddie's return. She knocked on the door.

Daisy motioned her in. "What do you think of Agnes's taste?"

"There's a ton of expensive furniture and lots of knickknacks upstairs. With all the new traffic stirred up by the winning lottery ticket, I could sell everything you don't want for a pretty penny. For now, I need to return to the store and relieve Mom. We'll talk about a deal and your new law office later." Maddie waved over her shoulder as she headed to the front door.

David snapped his fingers while hiking his foot on the hearth. "Step one in your set-the-stage plan with Maddie is accomplished."

"Which makes solving Rose's case more urgent than ever." Daisy peered out the window at the driveway that divided into two stretches of pavement. One section curved in front of the house and bordered the woods. The other continued straight and led to a free-standing garage. The perfect spot to park a camper...if Agnes's sons accepted her offer.

Chapter Twelve

Three minutes into her call with Lilly, Poppy drew in a deep breath and slowly released the air. She peered out the front-room window and moved her phone from one ear to the other. "Believe me, honey, your dad hasn't made a decision."

"But he's close. Why else would you change your minds about coming for supper Sunday?"

Poppy pinched the bridge of her nose. Why couldn't she make her middle child understand? "Just as I told you two minutes ago, we want to spend time with you and Andy."

"Should I bake Dad's favorite dessert or yours? I'll fix both. I have so many ideas and plans to share with you, Mom. Oh my goodness, it's almost two. I have to run. I don't want to be late for my doctor's appointment."

"Lilly—"

"We'll talk lots more Sunday. I love you, and tell Dad I love him too." Lilly ended the call.

Poppy huffed and brushed her fingers through her hair. "Why does she refuse to listen?"

"Your tone can only mean one thing." Daisy wandered in. "You were talking to my sister."

Poppy spun away from the window. "I tried to tell her your dad hasn't made a decision about the check."

"Let me guess, your middle child only heard what she wanted to hear."

"She's convinced he'll decide by Sunday."

Daisy plopped onto the sofa. "I don't envy you and Dad, especially given Lilly's pregnant-lady hormones."

Poppy settled beside her and crossed her leg over her knee. "No doubt she'll stretch your dad's patience to the limit."

"Won't be the first time or the last." Daisy tucked her foot under her knee. "Forget my sister for the moment. I have some news."

"About Mama's case?"

"Not exactly. I've been thinking about the bonus I earned for landing Curtis's account."

"A well-deserved reward for a job well done."

"That's debatable. Anyway, years ago you told me that this house and the land were the only physical assets Rose passed on to you and Pansy."

"Both have provided our family everything we've needed to raise a family and enjoy a good life."

"A lot of happy memories live within these walls." Daisy stretched her arm across the back of the sofa. "Which is why I decided to invest a portion of my bonus in real estate."

Poppy's eyes widened. "You bought a house? Where? In Savannah?"

"Much closer to home. Yesterday I made an offer on Agnes Watkins' home. This morning her sons accepted."

"Oh my gosh." Poppy uncrossed her legs and pressed her hands to her chest. "When do you plan to move?"

"My offer's all cash, so in a week or two."

Poppy's brows drew together. "I'm delighted we'll practically be neighbors, honey, but what will you do if your dad decides not to cash the check? You've worked hard building your career, and Agnes's house is a long way from a good-size town and potential corporate clients."

Daisy hesitated, as if debating how to respond. "I could commute, or rent the house to Lilly and Andy."

Poppy tilted her head back and stared at the ceiling.

"What are you thinking, Mom?"

"When you were growing up...all those pictures I showed you of your dad's family...did I make success seem too important?"

"I chose to study law because it fascinated me, not because of anything you said or did. Besides, I could always hang out my shingle as a general-practice lawyer."

"Same thing happened in that movie *Doc Hollywood*." Poppy straightened her neck and eyed Daisy's blank expression. "It's the story about a young doctor on his way to Hollywood to interview for a fancy plastic-surgeon job. Until his car breaks down in a little town needing a doctor."

"Let me take a wild guess. He chooses love and small-town life over living in a big city and earning a boat load of money."

"It's a romantic comedy."

"Aunt Pansy wants us to build a town so people will come, and you're suggesting I consider *Doc Hollywood* when making a career choice." Daisy rolled her eyes. "You watch way too many movies."

"I just want you to be happy, honey."

"You're a treasure, Mom." Daisy squeezed Poppy's hand. "And I love you."

Footsteps struck the hall floor as David strolled in from the back of the house. "Is this a private meeting?"

"Mom and I are talking about real-estate investments, career choices, and movies with the potential to imitate real life."

"Sounds intriguing. Mind if I join you?"

"Be our guest."

David settled on a wingback chair. "Did your real-estate discussion include Agnes's house?"

She nodded. "Agnes's sons accepted Daisy's offer this morning."

A knowing glance passed between David and Daisy.

"You already knew, didn't you?"

"Daisy told me a couple hours ago."

"After I move in, David and I plan to work the case from there."

Poppy suppressed an involuntary smile. For weeks she'd noticed the subtle glances her daughter and David had exchanged during supper, and Daisy's dreamy-eyed expression when she talked about him. The way he kissed her daughter when they all stayed up to usher in the new year. They seemed to care for each other. If they spent more time alone, would their relationship grow into an honest-to-goodness romance? Poppy failed to stifle a giggle. Same as *Doc Hollywood*.

Daisy nudged her arm. "What has you tickled?"

"A scene from the movie we talked about. Enough talk about Hollywood. I think David would prefer to talk about the case."

"Actually, that's why I came in." He crossed his ankle over his knee. "I located the chief deputy who dismissed Rose's case as a runaway. He and his wife live in an assisted-living facility in Savannah."

Poppy scooted to the edge of the sofa. "Did you talk to him?"

"Not yet. I'm counting on a surprise visit from your daughter and me to shake details loose."

"Same ploy district attorneys use when questioning suspects," added Daisy. "Don't give them time to fabricate a story."

Poppy's shoulder muscles tightened. "When do you plan to ambush the guy?"

"Tomorrow morning." David fingered his sneaker. "I already broke the news to your husband."

"How'd he respond?"

"Typical Danny style. He nodded and walked away without commenting."

"He trusts you."

"Danny's a good man."

"So are you, David." Had Daisy taken her hint, or was she ignoring the comment. "Well, it's time I leave you two alone and go fix us some lunch." Poppy meandered to the kitchen as reality struck home. Tomorrow David and Daisy would face the man who could hold the key to solving her mama's case and forcing Danny to make a decision.

Chapter Thirteen

Daisy's heart pounded as their destination came into view. "Assisted living *and* memory care. Did you know?"

David turned onto the driveway. "That the chief deputy might have dementia? I figure we have a fifty-fifty chance he's okay."

"Not the best odds."

"Or the worse." He pulled into a parking space. "Are you ready for Team Lambert and Butler's first serious investigative work?"

"How do you plan to get past whoever's functioning as the gatekeeper, partner?"

"Charm and subtle persuasion."

"Was that how you convinced Mom to let you in the door the first day you showed up on my parents' front porch?"

"And the second day." He grinned while stuffing his notepad in his jacket pocket.

"Does that approach always work?"

"Has so far."

"All right, then." Daisy shouldered her purse, hoping to keep her anxiety at bay. "Let's go turn on the charm."

They made their way to the front walkway, entered the tastefully decorated lobby, and approached an attractive woman sitting behind a desk.

She looked up. "Welcome. How may I help you?"

Would David notice her name badge and call her by name?

"Your facility is impressive, Ms. Reynolds."

Yeah, he noticed.

"The fresh flowers are as lovely as you are."

Daisy suppressed a giggle. Talk about charm.

The woman's face lit with a smile. "Thank you. We do our best to make our residents and guests feel at home."

"I can tell." David pocketed his keys. "It's no surprise Hank Bennett chose to live here."

Daisy peered at David's profile. Smooth transition.

"Oh yes, Mr. Bennett, our resident chief deputy. Are you family?"

"I'm an investigator. It's been years, so it's possible he won't remember me."

"His mind is as sharp as a switchblade. I can't say the same for his wife. Although most days she remembers he's her husband." Ms. Reynolds pointed to a log book. "After you sign in, I'll escort you to the lounge. Mr. Bennet is there every morning with his pals."

Daisy's pulse accelerated as she signed under David's name. So far so good.

The woman turned the log book back around. "Mr. Lambert, Ms. Butler, please come with me." She escorted them to a large room furnished with sofas and easy chairs. "As usual, Mr. Bennett is entertaining his friends with stories about his active-duty days."

David nodded toward four men sitting around a card table. "Does he always wear a red shirt?"

"That's his favorite. Enjoy your visit." Ms. Reynolds spun around and left them alone.

Daisy leaned close. "Lucky guess or good investigative work?"

"He's the only one talking." David pressed his hand to her back as they approached. "Chief Deputy Bennett, I'm David Lambert and this is my associate Daisy Butler. We'd appreciate a few minutes of your time."

"Whatever you're selling, I'm not buying."

"I can't imagine someone pulling a fast one on you, sir."

"You're a smart young man. So, is this a social or an official visit?"

Daisy eyed the man—still muscular despite his advanced age. David handed him a business card.

The chief read the information, then pocketed the card. "Excuse me, fellas, seems this young man is investigating one of my cases." He led Daisy and David out to a patio and a glass-top table shaded by an umbrella. "Which case are you investigating? The one about the fourteen-year-old kid who took his grandfather's truck for a joyride? He crashed into a car driven by a fugitive wanted for murder. That kid grew up and became one of my sharpest deputies. As far as I know, he's still working."

"Amazing how a single incident can change the direction of one's life." David cleared his throat. "We're interested in a case dating back three-and-a-half decades."

"That's a long time ago."

"True. However, based on everything I've heard about you, I suspect Rose Fowler's disappearance is still fresh in your mind."

The chief's cheek twitched. "Who have you been talking to?"

"One of your former deputies."

"Brad Jenkins."

Daisy bristled at the chief's smug expression.

"Brad knows the truth about that hooker—"

"I suggest you choose your words carefully, sir." David's tone screamed a warning. "Ms. Butler is Rose Fowler's granddaughter."

"Sorry, ma'am, I don't mean any disrespect. Fact is, there wasn't a shred of evidence hinting of foul play. Which made it obvious that your grandmother ran off with one of her johns."

Daisy forced her anger into submission while mentally transitioning from granddaughter to defense attorney. She smiled at her witness. "A logical deduction. However, if there had been the slightest bit of evidence, might you have come to a different conclusion?"

"Of course. My department always followed the facts."

Unless they proved inconvenient. "That's good to know." Daisy tilted her head. "How would your department respond if evidence came to light years after the incident?"

Hank's eyes narrowed to a slit. "Why are you asking?"

David slid his hand into his pants pocket, withdrew clenched fingers around the evidence bag, and held his fist an inch above the table. "This surfaced a couple days ago." He uncurled his fingers. The shell casing landed on the glass with a sharp clink.

The chief's nostrils flared.

"The day you sent your deputies to investigate Rose Fowler's disappearance, Deputy Jenkins found that on her bedroom floor. He kept it under wraps to avoid losing his job." David scooped the casing off the table and slipped it back in his pocket. "We're not looking to create problems for him or you. We just want to know who you were protecting."

"What makes you think I was protecting anyone?"

"Why else would a reputable chief order deputies to quash an investigation?"

Hank leaned back, as if struggling to distance himself from any semblance of the truth. "Rose Fowler serviced a number of well-connected men. An investigation would have destroyed reputations and ruined careers."

Daisy's body tensed. "You knew a crime had taken place, didn't you?"

"I'd been given orders."

"By whom?"

"People a lot higher up the food chain."

She forced her escalating anger into submission. "Is Curtis Butler one of those people?"

He stared at her for a long moment. "You're related to him, aren't you?"

"He's my grandfather."

"In that case, you need to ask him."

"We did. He claimed Rose died from an accidental fall."

"Then why are you questioning me?"

"The shell casing proves otherwise."

"That's an assumption, not a fact." The chief shifted his gaze to David. "What drove you to investigate this case after all these years?"

"Rose Fowler's family deserves to know the truth."

"You want to know the truth?" His tone screamed of contempt. "A woman engaged in a dangerous profession disappeared at the hand of people who had the power to destroy lives."

Daisy crossed her arms on the table and locked eyes with the chief. "You know who those people are, don't you?"

"My family knows nothing about the case. I can't stop you from digging into the past, but if either of you believe I'd put my children and grandchildren at risk to satisfy your morbid curiosity, you're insane. I suggest you do yourselves a favor and don't contact me again." He pushed off his chair and stalked back inside.

Daisy unfolded her arms and drummed her fingers on the table. "Are you thinking what I'm thinking?"

"That Curtis is likely one of those powerful people? Yeah. Which means we have no choice other than confronting him."

"How do you propose slipping past his gatekeepers?"

"His bodyguard or Cynthia?"

Daisy envisioned the woman Curtis had trusted to manage his business. "The bodyguard's a piece of cake compared to Cynthia."

"We'll devise a foolproof plan."

"Breaking and entering is out of the question."

"What happened to your sense of adventure?" David stood and pulled out Daisy's chair.

"The only way I ever want to see the inside of a jail is to visit a future client." As they entered the lounge, Daisy caught a glimpse of Hank talking to his friends. So much for checking on his wife. "Do you suppose he's telling them about us?"

"You can bet he's spinning some kind of wild story."

After thanking Ms. Reynolds and signing out, they returned to David's truck. "Before we leave Savannah, is there someplace you want to go?"

"How about a different kind of adventure?"

"I'm game."

Daisy searched her memory for directions. Twenty minutes later they parked in front of a grand, three-story, brick house. The gate extending from the wrought-iron fence to the driveway stood open. Rose bushes lined the brick, inlaid concrete leading to a free-standing garage. "Curtis Butler's Savannah home."

"Proof that an impressive façade fails to reveal the chaos inside."

"The one time Mom and I drove by here, my grandmother—who I'd only seen in pictures—was clipping roses. The moment she spotted us, we drove on."

"I'd say it's time she becomes acquainted with one of her granddaughters."

Daisy kept her gaze firmly planted on the front porch. "She might not know she has grandchildren."

"All the more reason to walk up that driveway."

"Do you suppose she'll welcome us or call the cops?"

"Number-one question. Do you want to find out or sit here and play a guessing game?"

"Let's go before I come to my senses and back out." Daisy swung her door open.

"Right answer." He dashed around the front of the truck and joined her on the driveway.

She clung to David's arm as they walked past three expensive cars and made their way to the front porch.

Moments after she rang the bell, a thin, middle-aged woman wearing a maid's uniform responded. "May I help you?"

Daisy plastered on her best smile. "We're here to visit Mrs. Curtis."

"She's entertaining guests and doesn't wish to be disturbed. Who should I tell her is calling?"

Daisy hesitated. Should she reveal her identity? No reason not to. "Her granddaughter." She fished a business card from her purse and handed it over.

The woman stared at Daisy then eyed David. "Who are you?"

"David Lambert. I'm writing a book about the Butler family."

"I'll give Mrs. Butler the message. You have a nice day now." The woman's face paled as she backed away, then closed the door.

"At least we know my grandmother's housekeeper didn't know her boss had a granddaughter."

"I doubt Mrs. Butler shares personal information with the hired help."

Daisy glanced over her shoulder as they made their way back to the truck. "What are the chances she'll reach out to me?"

"Do you expect an answer, or is your question rhetorical?"

"The fact that I'm an attorney might pique her curiosity enough to make her call me."

"Definitely rhetorical."

"Whatever happens, at least she'll discover she's a grandmother. Although I doubt she'll consider that good news."

"After we update your parents on our visit with the chief deputy, do you plan to tell them about our detour?"

"We need to keep this little adventure private. Unless my grandmother decides to acknowledge my existence."

"Wise decision."

Chapter Fourteen

A memory struggling to find its way to the surface sent Poppy rushing to Pansy's bedroom, the space she had shared with her sister when their mama was alive. She peered out the side window framing the driveway. Before Danny built the greenhouse and had concrete poured, the gravel surface extended beyond the house.

Poppy squeezed her eyes shut. The memory broke free—dashing with Pansy to the mailbox at the end of the driveway. Their daily adventure meandering past the woods to collect the mail. Except every other week when their mama assigned them other chores and made the trip herself. Was that little detail significant or simply a coincidence?

Poppy opened her eyes, spun around, and sidled to the wall of shelves displaying Pansy's ball-cap collection and assorted treasures. She lifted the figurine wearing a red gown, one of her sister's latest thrift-store finds. A sudden urge compelled her to set the figurine back in place. She dashed out to the hall and placed a stepstool underneath the overhead attic door, then lowered the pull-down stairs and climbed up. Light from windows on each end of the room cast a dim glow across the space. Poppy pulled a chain illuminating the single bulb hanging from the rafters.

The floorboards creaked beneath her feet as she strode toward her mother's leather suitcase. She knelt down, unfastened the straps, and lifted the lid. A red dress lay on top—one of a dozen her mama wore before kissing her daughters and sending them to their refuge. Poppy stroked the satiny-smooth fabric then pressed the bodice to her birthmarked cheek. She closed her eyes as another memory surfaced. The hours she and Pansy spent in their little house pretending their mama was a beautiful princess who would one day meet a handsome prince and take them to live in a big castle. A dream she'd held in her heart even after that older boy forced her to face the truth about how her mother earned a living.

Another memory surfaced. How many times had she regretted the day when Pansy's bout with nausea sent her racing back to the big house for help? The strange noises she heard coming from her mama's bedroom. The door cracked open barely enough to peek in. The shocking bolt of electricity racing through her body as she watched her mama in bed with that man on top of her. How she backed away and escaped to the backyard, vomiting until nothing was left to heave. That was the day the image of her mother as a princess shattered into a million pieces.

Had her mama worn a bright blue dress the day she disappeared? Or was it green? She swallowed past the tightness in her throat. That day, someone stole Rose Fowler's life and robbed her grandchildren of the one opportunity to know the only grandmother who would have loved them.

Poppy's heart ached as she carefully folded the red garment and placed it back in the trunk. She pushed off her knees, strode to the brass headboard leaning against the opposite wall, and ran her palm along the curved top. She understood why men desired her mother. She was a beautiful woman with soft skin and silky hair.

A question formed and sent a shiver racing through Poppy's limbs. Was the man who fathered her the same man who killed her mother? Her eyes drifted to a stamped envelope lying on the floor. She stooped to pick it up. A birthday card from Maddie, her mama's closest childhood friend.

Why had the memory of trekking to the mailbox suddenly surfaced? Poppy pocketed the card and climbed down the ladder. She pushed the overhead door closed then meandered to the front porch to wait for David and Daisy to return from Savannah. After they solved the case, would she find the courage to bury the painful images and relish the memory of her mama's loving and gentle spirit?

An hour after settling on the rocking chair and summoning childhood memories, the crunch of gravel announced the investigative team's return. Poppy dashed off the porch and met them at David's parking space. "Any luck?"

"David and I confirmed one fact." Daisy slid her arm around Poppy's shoulders as they strolled toward the porch and sat on the steps. "The chief deputy is definitely protecting someone. The million-dollar questions are who and why?"

"I remembered something that might be important." Poppy shared her mailbox memory.

David pulled his notepad from his pocket. "Did Rose insist on going to collect the mail the same day and time every two weeks?"

"Saturday afternoon. I know because that was also the day Mama fixed us pancakes, with smiley faces for Pansy."

"Do you remember what Rose did or how she acted when she returned from the mailbox?"

Poppy closed her eyes and dug deep. An image surfaced. "I think she headed straight to her room and closed the door." Her eyes popped open. "Maybe she brought a letter or package in the house she didn't want me and Pansy to see. We never opened mail addressed to Mama, so it could have been a letter from a client. Except, how would one of those letters show up like clockwork?"

David chuckled. "Your daughter isn't the only family member with keen investigative instincts."

"Do you think the mailbox incident means something?"

"Consistent patterns are never random. So yes, you've provided an important bit of information."

Poppy's chest puffed. "Maybe after all these years, I've remembered something to help find justice for Mama."

Daisy nudged her arm. "It seems our investigative team has expanded to Lambert, Butler, and Butler."

Chapter Fifteen

Two days after confronting the chief deputy, Daisy sat across from David at his camper's dinette and eyed three names on his laptop. "Potential witnesses?"

"All had a connection with Curtis, and two are definitely higher up the food chain than the chief deputy."

"After thirty-five years, you're fortunate to have found that many who are still alive."

"Seems luck is on our side."

"It's about time." Daisy set her phone on the table. "Who's target number one?"

"The district attorney when Rose disappeared."

"Another surprise visit?"

"Not this time. I took a shot at calling his private number."

"How'd you dig up that detail?"

"I have my sources. When I explained that I had information about Rose Fowler's murder, dead silence. Thirty seconds later he agreed to meet us."

"When?"

"In an hour."

A rolling sensation rippled through Daisy's chest. If the man knew too much...was it possible they'd walk into an ambush? "Where?"

David reached across the table and grasped her hand. "I'd never put you in danger. We're meeting at a public place."

"Was I that obvious?"

"We've spent time together nearly every day since we met." He smiled. "So yeah, I'm tuned into your expressions."

"Some investigator you've hooked up with. Although—" She tilted her head. "For a lawyer whose prior experience involved corporate contracts and profit sheets, I'm a doggone good partner."

"In every way imaginable."

His hand squeezing hers awakened every nerve ending in her body. If she slid next to him, would he kiss her, the way he had on New Year's Eve, but with more passion?

"Your phone's vibrating."

Daisy blinked. "What? Oh." Talk about terrible timing. She plucked her phone off the table. Leave it to her brother to interrupt the most inopportune times. Maybe she should ignore him. Except Basil didn't normally call unless he had something important to say. She pressed the speaker icon. "Hey, knucklehead."

"Back at you, noodle-noggin." Their pet names made her smile. "What's up?"

"Are you alone?"

"I'm with David." She pressed the speaker icon and pushed the phone across the table.

"Hi, Basil. How's your training going?"

"Two more weeks and I'll qualify as one of Georgia's newest law enforcement officers."

"Any idea where you'll end up?"

"I'm considering the sheriff's department. More authority, broader jurisdiction, and they're hiring."

"I've worked with a lot of deputies over the years. Good choice."

"Thanks."

"I'll give you back to your sister." David pushed the phone toward Daisy.

"Hmm. I might be forced to ditch Knucklehead and address you as Deputy Basil."

"And obligate me to call you Counselor Daisy instead of noodle-noggin? Just keep calling me knucklehead."

"That's a relief." She pulled the phone closer. "So, did you call to chat or pester your big sister?"

"Lilly called me a few minutes ago. She said Dad's planning to reveal his 'should-he-or-shouldn't-he-cash-the-check' decision with her and Andy Sunday night."

Daisy rolled her eyes. "Our sister is delusional." She explained the supper invitation and Lilly's reaction.

"Typical Lilly. What's the real scoop about Dad's decision?"

"He'll decide after David and I solve Rose's case."

"Hey, David, did you and my sister form a new partnership? Lambert and Butler— investigative and legal services for hire?"

"Best investigative duo in Georgia. If we add Deputy Butler to our roster, we'd have one kick-butt team."

"Two Butlers and a Lambert." Basil chuckled. "Or maybe two Lamberts and a Butler?"

Daisy fidgeted. Had David noticed the heat escaping her ears and attacking her cheeks?

"Hey, Basil." David grinned. "You made your sister blush."

Yeah, he noticed.

"My solemn duty as her little brother."

Hoping to maintain a smidgen of dignity, Daisy initiated an exaggerated eye roll. "You two are hilarious."

"Gotta run, noodle-noggin. Class is about to start."

"If the subject is 'how to annoy your sister,' you'll ace the test."

"Hey, I could teach that one. Keep me updated on Lilly's clueless drama."

"Will do, knucklehead." Daisy pocketed her phone. "Basil's right about Lilly. She's in for one big disappointment."

"Hopefully, we're not."

Her brows raised. Not disappointed about what?

"Our interview with the DA."

"Right." Fearing her cheeks were seconds from turning fire-engine red, Daisy slid off the bench and hastened to the door. "Are you driving?"

David slung his satchel over his shoulder "If you want me to."

"Doesn't matter...I mean yes, you drive." *Get a grip.*

Following a forty-five minute drive along country roads, David turned off the pavement. Four motorcycles, two pickups, and one high-dollar sportscar parked on the gravel fronting a single-story windowless building. The B's in 'Bud's Bar and Grill' flickered.

"I can't believe a former district attorney would choose this location."

"It makes sense for a man who needs anonymity." David pulled beside the sportscar. "Do you want me to check it out first?"

"I wouldn't be much of an investigative partner if I let a rundown building freak me out."

"All right then, let's do some crackerjack investigative work."

Daisy stepped onto the gravel. "Good thing I didn't wear heels." She slid her hand around David's bicep as they climbed two steps and walked into the dimly lit space. The scents of greasy food and stale beer churned her stomach. Country music played in the background. Four burly men gathered around a pool table turned and gawked. Two men sitting at the bar spun toward them. The bartender nodded in their direction. Daisy leaned close to David. "I'm the only female in here."

"Which is why everyone is staring at us." He led her past the bar to an occupied booth at the far end of the room. "Lawrence Baker?"

The elderly man held a glass half-filled with amber liquid and motioned to the bench across from him.

David scooted in beside Daisy and set his satchel on the seat. "Thank you for agreeing to meet us."

"Would you like a drink?"

"No thanks."

"Suit yourself." Baker lifted his glass and took a long sip. His diamond-studded ring made it obvious he'd arrived in the expensive car. "Now that you're here, what do you want to know?"

David removed his notepad from his satchel. "Everything you can tell us about Rose Fowler."

Baker remained silent for a long moment. "To start off, you need to understand what was going on in my life back then. I was dealing with a contentious divorce and running behind in my campaign for a second term as county DA." He eyed Daisy. "You're related to Rose, aren't you?"

"I'm her granddaughter."

"You favor her."

"So I've been told. In case you're wondering, I know how she earned her living. So you don't need to sugarcoat your story."

"Good to know." Baker set down his glass. "A friend put me in touch with CD, a procurer who served an exclusive clientele. He set me up with Rose."

David made a note. "Were CD his initials or his first name?"

"In his line of work, real names weren't prudent."

"Thus an alias." Daisy leaned forward. "Do you know what kind of car CD drove?"

Baker's brow scrunched. "What do you know about him?"

"Nothing, except we heard that Rose was recruited, so to speak, by a man driving a white Cadillac."

"Rumor was he bought a new caddy every year." Baker fell silent for a long moment. "Rose was young and beautiful. More importantly, she lived off the beaten path."

Daisy drew back at the sight of his faraway stare.

"She treated me more like a suitor than a paying customer. The second time I called on her and every time after, I took her flowers. I suppose that was my way of rationalizing an illicit relationship. When she disappeared, even if I'd suspected foul play, I couldn't risk becoming embroiled in a scandal." He blinked as if returning from his own private journey. "Why are you investigating her disappearance after all these years?"

David exchanged glances with Daisy. "Her family wants to discover the truth." He turned back toward Baker. "Evidence of a murder recently surfaced."

"The guy who killed her deserves punishment."

Daisy's brows furrowed. Did he know something? "Why do you assume her killer was a man?"

Baker stared at her as if she'd asked the most outrageous question. "Her customers were men. Don't you think it's logical one of them was the culprit?" Baker downed the rest of his drink. "If you came here hoping to find answers, you'll leave with two facts. First, I didn't kill Rose Fowler. And second, CD lined a lot of pockets with substantial amounts of cash. Which means the chance of you identifying the guilty party is a longshot at best. Protecting reputations comes at a hefty price."

David clicked his pen. "Were Chief Deputy Jenkins' coffers among those CD fattened?"

"Did he investigate Rose's disappearance?"

"He wrote it off as a runaway."

"Then draw your own conclusion."

Daisy laced her fingers and studied the former district attorney's features. Coming face-to-face with one of her grandmother's clients raised a question. Was it possible? "I'm curious. When did your relationship with my grandmother begin?"

His nostrils flared. "If you're thinking that either of Rose's daughters were mine, you're mistaken. Even though I never laid eyes on them, I knew they existed."

Daisy imagined her mom and aunt hiding in their refuge, protected from the reality of their mother's occupation. "Did she talk about them?"

"One time when I asked about the drawing hanging in her living room."

"My grandmother loved her daughters."

"She was a good-hearted woman." Baker's brows gathered in. "If I hadn't been a public servant subject to scrutiny...there's no use focusing on what might have been." His brows straightened. "If you don't have any more questions—"

"Just two." David poised his pen over his notepad. "First, how did you schedule appointments with Rose?"

"All contacts were arranged through CD. That way none of her clients ever crossed paths."

"Second, how did you pay for her services?"

"Hundred dollar bills in secured envelopes mailed to a P.O. box."

"Risky."

"Also untraceable. Now if you'll excuse me, I have a long drive home, and I prefer not to drive after dark."

David pushed a business card across the table. "If you think of anything else that might help us solve the case, please call."

Baker pocketed the card, slapped a twenty on the table, and headed to the exit.

Daisy's eyes followed him until he reached the door. "At least he gave us a clue about Rose's trip to the mailbox every other Saturday. CD most likely left her cash payments. Her clients would have assumed the same thing. It's possible Curtis interrupted a robbery gone wrong. But then why would he cover it up? Unless the perpetrator blackmailed him to keep quiet, or he was terrified word would leak about his own clandestine activities."

David propped his elbow on the table, rested his chin on his knuckles, and grinned. "Amazing."

"What?"

"You'd have given District Attorney Baker a run for his money, Counselor."

"Are you saying my theory has merit?"

"At this point all theories are on the table. For now, do you want to stick around and recruit a couple of new clients?"

Daisy peered around David. "What about that guy wearing the red bandanna and leaning on his pool cue? Do you suppose he's an out-of-work laborer killing time, or a pool hustler who's itching for a fight?"

"Do I have a third choice?"

"He's a closet millionaire, a lottery winner who prefers to spend time riding his bike and hanging out with his buddies."

"Hmm. Think I'll go with option three."

"Good choice. I suggest we ditch this joint and find a place that stirs rather than suppresses the appetite."

"While enjoying dinner, we'll celebrate little victories."

And pretend we're on a date.

Chapter Sixteen

A half mile from her middle child's home, Poppy clutched a tin filled with Pansy's chocolate-chip cookies and peered out the truck's passenger window. How long after they arrived would Danny tell Lilly and Andy that he hadn't made a decision? The first few minutes? An hour? Would he wait until they finished supper?

Poppy's pulse accelerated as the house came into view. Daisy had still lived in New York the last time they'd visited Lilly's home, before she was pregnant with their first grandchild. Before Pansy gave Danny a lottery ticket that had one chance in untold millions to win. Before she and Daisy unlocked the safe-deposit box and read the letter naming Curtis Butler as Pansy's biological father.

Danny turned onto the driveway and parked at the edge of the carport.

How would Lilly react to her dad's revelation? Would her reaction sway his decision one way or the other?

The passenger door opened.

Poppy blinked.

"Do you need a minute?"

"I'm ready." She breathed deeply to slow her pounding pulse and accepted Danny's hand.

Lilly swung the door open seconds before they reached the porch. "We're so excited you're here." Her face beamed as she patted her tummy. "Jonah—that's the name we picked for your grandson—is extra bouncy today." She linked arms with Poppy. "I'm dying to show you what I bought for his room."

Poppy caught Danny's eye.

He nodded. "You go on while I catch up with Andy."

Obviously he didn't intend to break the news first thing. She handed the tin to Lilly. "Pansy's cookies."

"She's such a sweetheart." Lilly set the tin on the living-room coffee table, then led Poppy down the hall and into a bedroom. "Isn't that the most gorgeous crib you've ever seen?" She stroked the railing. "It's Italian, and when Jonah's older, it will convert to a toddler bed." Lilly pointed to the matching dresser. "Both cost a pretty penny, but only the best for our baby."

A knot formed in Poppy's belly. How many thousands of pennies? Had her daughter accumulated mountains of credit-card debt based on an assumption?

"I also ordered the most darling rocking chair. The furniture is a bit big for this little room, but they're perfect for our new home."

Poppy stared wide-eyed. "What new home?"

"The one I've picked out. It's gorgeous and big. Five bedrooms and four bathrooms. Perfect for our growing family. Our lease is up next month, so as soon as Dad gives me my share of the lottery money, we'll buy it with cash."

Her share? How much was she expecting? Should she break the news now?

Lilly pressed her palms together. "After we move, I'll ask Aunt Pansy to help me paint a mural in our baby's new room. Something sweet. Maybe zoo animals or a beach scene. Do you remember how much fun Daisy, Basil, and I had when you and Dad took us to Tybee Island? Maybe I'll buy a vacation house on the beach that's big enough for our entire family."

Poppy winced. "You're getting a little ahead of yourself, honey—"

"Same thing Andy said, but it's all so exciting." Her face flushed. "We'll talk more during supper. I fixed Dad's favorites and two desserts. You go relax with Dad and Andy while I get everything ready." Lilly dashed out.

A pain erupted in the back of Poppy's throat. Why hadn't she tried harder to make Lilly accept the truth? She trudged to the living room and tuned into Andy sharing details about his current carpenter job.

Danny caught her eye. "Did Lilly tell you our grandson's name is Jonah?"

"She did." Poppy settled on the gray sectional sofa adorned with red and white throw pillows and eyed the seascape highlighted by a pale blue sky peeking between billowing clouds.

Andy propped his arm across the back of the sofa. "What'd you think of Lilly's choice of baby furniture, Poppy?"

How should she respond? Even though her son-in-law had always come across as levelheaded, he'd grown up in a big family that struggled to make ends meet. Had he bought into Lilly's grand ideas and extravagant purchases? "She has good taste." Not to mention expensive.

Lilly peered around the corner. "Supper's on the table."

Relieved she wouldn't have to say more, Poppy followed the tomato and onion scents to the kitchen. Two elaborate cut-glass candle holders adorned the table. Another extravagant purchase or a garage-sale find?

"Meatloaf and mashed potatoes." Danny sniffed. "Smells delicious."

"Especially for you, Dad." Lilly pointed to a chair. "You sit across from me, Mom."

Danny pulled a chair out for Poppy, then sat between her and his daughter.

Following Andy's blessing, Lilly passed a bowl of green beans. "Not fresh from a garden but almost as good as Mom's." The moment all four plates were filled, she faced her dad. "Did my talented husband tell you that he's starting his own construction company?"

Andy cleared his throat. "It's just an idea—"

"—Which we plan to act on soon."

Poppy caught Danny's eye. Would he say something now?

He broke eye contact and pointed his fork at Andy. "Your idea or Lilly's?"

Andy exchanged glances with his wife.

Lilly responded with a half shrug. "Mostly mine, but he's onboard. Did I mention that Friday was my last day at work?"

Poppy cringed. "Maybe you should have waited a bit longer, honey."

"Don't worry, Mom. I didn't breathe a word about the lottery ticket." Lilly cut a piece of meatloaf. "I'm over the moon about being a full-time mom. There's so much I need to accomplish before Jonah arrives. First thing I plan to do…"

While Lilly prattled on, Poppy's chest tightened as if an elephant had pinned her against a wall. Why didn't Danny speak up? Had he decided to cash the check without telling her? Was he testing Lilly? By the time everyone had swallowed their last bite, she could no longer contain herself. "Your dad has something to tell you and Andy."

Danny wiped his face with a napkin, then faced his daughter. "The last time you talked to your mother, what did she tell you about my decision?"

Lilly tilted her head. "That you hadn't decided?"

"Good, you remember. Do you also recall what I've always said about money?"

"That wealth messes up families. But that was before you won the lottery. I've read lots of magazine stories about rich people who have big houses and are plenty happy…" Lilly's voice trailed off. Her eyes shifted to her mom then back to her dad. "What are you trying to tell me?"

Danny pushed his plate away. "No amount of money is worth destroying our family."

"You didn't cash the check, did you?" Lilly's face paled. "But you're going to, right?"

Danny's eyes remained trained on his daughter. "I don't know." His calm voice defied his flared nostrils and tense jaw.

Lilly's face paled. "Please, Dad, you have to. Mom?" Her eyes pleaded. "Make him understand."

Understand what? That her daughter's outrageous purchases and extravagant visions were proving him right? "Your dad will do what he believes is best for all of us."

"What's best is cashing that check." Lilly whipped around toward her husband. "Andy?"

He reached for his wife's hand. "It's not our decision, sugar pie."

Lilly's gaze shifted back to Danny. "When will you decide?"

"After David and Daisy solve your grandmother's case."

"That could take a long time." Lilly's chin quivered. "If I'd known…I don't feel so well."

Andy stood and pulled Lilly's chair away from the table. "Excuse us." He slid his arm around her shoulders and led her out of the kitchen.

Danny drummed his fingers on the table. "How much of the phantom money has our middle child already spent?"

Poppy slumped back in her chair. Was his question rhetorical?

"Did she say?"

He expected an answer. "She bought a special crib and dresser for Jonah?"

"Is special your definition of outrageously expensive?"

"She didn't tell me how much they cost." Poppy's shoulders curled forward. "I should have forced her to accept reality."

"You tried to tell her."

"Maybe I didn't try hard enough."

"She only heard what she wanted to hear."

Footsteps announced Andy's return. "Sorry for the disruption. Sometimes pregnancy nausea pops up out of nowhere." He dropped onto his chair.

Poppy placed her hand on Andy's arm. "Is Lilly okay?"

"I suspect she's down for the night."

"Well, one thing is certain. The mother of my grandson doesn't need to face a table full of dirty dishes in the morning." Poppy withdrew her hand. "You two clear the table. I'll load the dishwasher."

When they finished kitchen duty, Andy brushed his fingers through his hair. "Do you want to stay for dessert?"

Danny removed his keys from his pocket. "I think it's best we head on home."

"Lilly doesn't mean to disrespect you, Danny. She's just become caught up in the prospect of wealth."

He grasped his son-in-law's shoulder. "You're a good husband, Andy."

"Thank you for understanding."

"Go tend to your wife while we let ourselves out."

A gust of cold air sent a shiver through Poppy as she and Danny trekked through the carport and climbed into the family truck. Twenty-four hours ago he'd remained on the fence. Had Lilly's pleas moved him closer to ripping the check to shreds? Poppy pressed her fingers to the back of her neck to ease the onset of a killer tension headache.

"I understand tonight wasn't easy for you." Danny placed his hand on her thigh. "No matter what I decide, your support means the world to me, sweetheart."

A lump forming in her throat rendered Poppy speechless. She squeezed Danny's hand and swallowed as her shoulders relaxed, and the pain began to subside. Deep down she grasped one all-consuming reality. Somehow her family would find a way to survive whatever decision he landed on.

Chapter Seventeen

D aisy sauntered behind Pansy's chair at the kitchen table and placed her hands on her shoulders. "Good morning."

"I've been awake a long time."

"So I see." She peered over her aunt's head at her sketchpad open to a drawing of a glass case displaying an array of cakes. "Awesome picture. The detail is amazing."

"It's my new bakery. Can we call the real-estate lady today and tell her we wanna buy that store?"

Daisy's mom closed the dishwasher. "We should wait a bit longer, sweetie."

"What if someone else buys it?"

"That won't happen." Daisy squeezed her aunt's shoulders. "Because I already bought it for you."

"You did?" Her mom's eyes bulged as she dropped onto her chair. "When?"

"The same day I made an offer on Agnes's house. At a bargain-basement price, mind you." Daisy sat beside her mom. "Lucky for me her sons were eager to sell."

Pansy closed her sketchpad. "Is the key still in that lockbox?"

"Not any longer."

"When can we go inside?"

"If Mom has time, the three of us could drive over this morning."

"Can we?" Pansy's face beamed. "Please?"

Poppy shrugged. "We might as well."

"Goody." Pansy bolted from her chair and dashed to the hall with Boots scampering behind her.

Daisy eyed her mom's wide-eyed expression. "I'm sorry for catching you off guard."

"I know you want the best for your aunt, honey. But do you believe she's ready to manage a business?"

"Not without a lot of help. But ready to live her dream? Absolutely."

Her mom released a sigh. "She has waited a long time."

"We'll figure out the next steps."

"Before we do anything, you need to clue your dad in. He doesn't need any more surprises."

"I'll break the news now." Daisy wrapped two cookies in a napkin, then made her way to the greenhouse and approached her dad's makeshift office. "Do you have a minute?"

He pushed his laptop aside. "What's up?"

She pulled up a chair and placed the cookies on his desk.

"A gift or a bribe?"

"Depends." She laced her fingers and shared the news.

Her dad eyed her for a long moment.

She held her breath.

"You did a good deed, Daisy."

She released the air and unlaced her fingers. "It seemed appropriate to spend some of my bonus from landing Curtis's account to help the daughter he rejected." Pansy racing from the back porch to the driveway caught her eye. "It seems our favorite baker is ready to check out her new store." Daisy stood. "Thank you for your support, Dad."

"As Pansy said, 'money isn't bad if it's used to help people.'"

"Sometimes she's the wisest person in our family."

"Because she has a pure heart." He snatched a cookie off the desk. "You didn't need a bribe."

"What bribe? The cookies are a gift." Daisy tapped the paperweight. "For the world's best dad." Understanding her dad found responding to compliments awkward, she scooted to the exit and on to the family truck.

During the ride to town, Pansy talked a blue streak about the different kinds of cakes she planned to sell. The moment Daisy's mom parked in front the vacated stores, Pansy hopped out and dashed to the door. "My picture's still taped to the window."

Daisy followed and slid the key into the lock. The door groaned as she pushed it open and stepped inside. Cobwebs, stale air, and layers of dust attested to the years the space had been abandoned. "Welcome to Pansy Butler's future bakery and flower shop."

Pansy blew a layer of dust off a counter, triggering a sneeze.

Daisy's mom pulled two tissues from her purse and handed one to her sister. "It'll take a heap of work to fix this place up." She ran her finger along a crack in the front window. "You should hire Andy to do the work." Her brows gathered in. "With the baby on the way, he and Lilly need lots of extra money."

Was there something her mom wasn't telling her? Had her sister loaded up credit cards believing she was weeks away from a gigantic financial windfall? "Good idea. I'll call him tonight."

Pansy meandered to a tattered curtain stretched across a doorway leading to the back of the store. She pulled it aside and sneezed again. "Where do those stairs go?"

"To an apartment." Daisy's mom blew her nose. "The widow who last had a business here lived upstairs."

"Is it your apartment now, Daisy?"

"This entire building now belongs to us."

"After I open my bakery, can I live up there?"

Daisy slid her arm around Pansy's shoulders. "It's best to take one step at a time. Beginning with fixing up the main floor."

"We've gotta go to the thrift store and buy lots of things I'm gonna need for my bakery." Pansy dashed to the front door and out to the sidewalk.

Daisy linked arms with her mom. "I do believe we're going shopping."

"Should we tell Maddie about your investment?"

Willy waved from his front porch across the street. "Are you ladies sightseeing?"

Pansy stepped to the curb. "Daisy bought the whole building. I'm gonna open a bakery and flower shop."

"Good for you, Daisy. It's about time someone put all that space to use."

Daisy leaned close to her mom. "We'll definitely clue Maddie in."

Pansy skipped ahead and cut the corner.

"Thank you for making my sister happy, honey."

"Buying the store was the easy part. Figuring out how to turn it into a functioning bakery will take a lot of work." Daisy patted her mom's hand. "I'm curious. Is there more to your suggestion that I hire Andy than helping out your son-in-law?"

She sighed then explained Lilly's extravagant purchases and the scene during supper.

"I can only imagine Dad's response."

"Chances are your sister pushed him a step closer to destroying the check."

"I can't say I blame him."

The bell over the thrift-store door jangled as Pansy rushed inside. Daisy and her mom followed close behind.

Maddie greeted them, her brows raised. "Is Pansy right about you buying those buildings across from Willy's house, Daisy?"

She nodded. "They're good investments."

"Well, I declare. You just might bring a bit of prosperity to our little patch of land. Who'd have ever thought we'd have a bakery right around the corner?"

A customer approached the counter carrying a full shopping basket. After adding up the items and bagging the purchases, Maddie climbed onto her stool and aimed her thumb over her shoulder. "Folks are excited about buying Agnes's possessions. How soon before you decide what you want to keep and what you want to sell, Daisy?"

"Basil, David, and Dad will move everything Saturday."

"That soon?" Maddie nodded toward the right. "I'd best finish clearing out that aisle."

Pansy scurried from the far side of the store and set two glass cake platters on the counter. She lifted the cover off one. "These'll look pretty in my store." She elbowed her sister. "This one is like Mama's favorite."

"They look expensive, sweetie. Do you have enough money?"

Pansy pulled bills from her fanny pack and counted. "Is thirty-three dollars enough?"

"Tell you what, Aunt Pansy." Daisy set her purse on the counter. "Since cake plates qualify as necessities, I'll pay for them out of our equipment budget."

Pansy's head tilted. "Do you have one of those?"

"I do now."

"Can I shop for more equipment?"

"Yes, but I'll have the final decision about what qualifies as necessary."

"Okay." Pansy dashed off.

Daisy's mom touched her arm. "Never in my wildest imagination would I have guessed that you and my sister would one day become business partners."

"Sometimes life takes unexpected detours."

"Speaking of unexpected—" Maddie leaned close. "Have you heard about that reporter who's been snooping around? He's asking all kinds of questions about the winning lottery ticket."

Daisy exchanged glances with her mom then trained her eyes on Maddie. "What kind of questions?"

"How many tickets did Willy sell? Did mostly locals buy them? Has anyone around here been acting unusual? He asked me who bought Agnes's house, I told him you did, with bonus money from your New York law firm."

"How did he respond?"

"He asked, 'what firm?'" Maddie shrugged. "I told him I didn't know. Folks have been asking when you're fixing to set up your office."

Daisy's mom stared at her. "What office?"

"Our friend jumped to her own conclusions about me setting up shop, Mom."

Maddie's eyes widened. "If the lawyers at your law firm changed their minds, they're missing out on a good opportunity."

Pansy rushed back and set a pink ball cap and a dog bowl on the counter.

Grateful for the distraction, Daisy tapped her aunt's arm. "I don't think those qualify as equipment."

"That's why I'm buying them with my money." Pansy fished bills from her fanny pack and set them on the counter. "I'm all done." She carried her personal purchases and one cake platter toward the door.

"I do believe our shopping trip has come to an end." Daisy plucked the lidded cake plate off the counter. "One more question, Maddie. When did that reporter last come snooping around?"

"An hour before you walked in."

Chapter Eighteen

Maddie's revelation about the snooping reporter played in Poppy's mind as she carried three place settings to the table. Danny assumed the guy was simply fishing for a story. Which made sense. Still, the thought of another stranger poking into everyone's business didn't sit well.

"You forgot plates for Daisy and David." Pansy pointed to the empty space across from her sister.

"They're not eating supper with us tonight."

"Is David Daisy's boyfriend now? Did they go on a date?"

"David's still her special friend, sweetie. Tonight they're making Daisy's new house ready for her to move in."

"Is David gonna move there too?"

"Just Daisy."

"Oh." Pansy nodded toward the floor beside the cabinet. "Boots likes his new doggie bowl."

Her dog yawned and rested his head in her lap, his tail slapping the kitchen floor.

"When I open my bakery, I'm gonna bake special cookies for dogs. Do cats like treats?"

Leave it to Pansy to lighten the mood. "I think they prefer mice."

Danny lumbered in from the back porch. "Who prefers mice?"

Pansy giggled while stroking her dog's muzzle. "Cats."

"Indeed they do." He washed his hands before taking his place at the table opposite Pansy. "Do I smell baked fried chicken?"

"The healthy way to fix it." Poppy transferred the chicken from the oven to a platter. After setting the main course on the table, she took her seat, closed her eyes and returned thanks. Following Pansy's enthusiastic 'amen,' she peered across the table. Tonight was the first time since the week before Thanksgiving that she faced two empty chairs. A sinking sensation invaded her chest. What if David decided to move his camper to Daisy's driveway? It made sense, considering they were working on her mama's case together. How could she adjust to the old norm after all the excitement and drama of the last few months? Maybe she needed a new project to distract her.

"There's an apartment over my bakery." Pansy spooned green beans onto her plate. "I'm gonna live there."

Danny's brows arched as he eyed Poppy.

She shrugged. "Pansy and Daisy have a lot to do before we talk about a move."

Pansy slipped a piece of chicken to Boots. "Daisy has a budget for my new store. We're gonna buy a fancy baking oven." In between bites she rattled off a long list of items she would need for her store.

Poppy marveled at her sister's accuracy. Had she and Daisy talked, or had Pansy come up with the list on her own? Either way, her sister never ceased to amaze her. One minute she came across as a delightful child and the next as a knowledgeable woman.

Halfway through supper the doorbell sent Boots scrambling from the kitchen.

"I'll get it." Pansy dashed after him. Moments later she returned with a man walking beside her. "Jason Jones is a reporter. He wants to ask us some questions."

Poppy automatically pressed her hand to her birthmarked cheek. Sweat erupted and ran cold between her shoulder blades. Was he the reporter who'd been snooping around? Would her husband throw him out and raise suspicion? Oh, that he would remain calm.

Danny pushed off his chair, towering over the stranger. "We'll talk in the front room. My wife and sister-in-law will join us momentarily."

The moment Danny led the stranger out of the kitchen, Poppy scooted close to Pansy, keeping her voice low. "Do you remember what to do if Mr. Jones asks about the winning lottery ticket?"

Pansy planted her hands on her hips. "How come everyone always asks me that question? I know that man might try to trick us. Danny won't let that happen."

A twinge of guilt pricked Poppy's conscience. Had the family spent a lifetime underestimating her sister, or had the promise of a fulfilled dream enhanced her confidence? "You're right."

"I know, so let's go." Pansy pushed up and scooted toward the front room.

Poppy followed.

Mr. Jones had settled on the sofa. Boots sat on his haunches with his tail flat on the floor a foot from the unexpected guest. Danny hiked his hip on a wingback armrest, his arms folded across his chest.

Pansy plopped onto the other wingback.

After praying for the courage to face the stranger without covering her cheek, a calm washed over Poppy. She settled on the chair beside Danny and laced her fingers in her lap.

The reporter stared at her for a long moment.

She refused to look away while willing her jaw to remain unclenched.

The man blinked. "Like I was telling your husband, people are curious about the secret lottery winner. Who can blame them? It's the biggest amount of cash ever won in our state." He jabbed his finger toward Pansy. "I hear you give lottery tickets as gifts."

Boots rose to all fours and growled.

Jones flinched.

Pansy leaned forward. "Come here, Boots."

Her dog barked once, then lowered his tail and padded to Pansy.

"Dogs have a sense about people." Pansy stroked his head. "I don't think he likes you."

"He most likely smells my cat."

Danny cleared his throat. "About your question, my sister-in-law also gives us beautiful hand-drawn cards."

"I see." The man eyed Pansy then turned back toward Danny. "Rumors are your oldest daughter recently came into some money."

"A bonus from her law firm." Danny's tone remained calm, his words measured. "If you came here hoping to discover who won the lottery, you're barking up the wrong tree."

"Perhaps you're right." Jones paused for a long moment. "Do you mind if I ask one more question?"

Danny held up a finger. "One more."

"Are you related to Curtis Butler?"

Poppy's mouth went dry. Had Maddie told him about David's investigation? Did it matter one way or the other?

Danny's features grew rigid. "Why are you asking?"

He shrugged. "Editorial curiosity. His family is well known in Savannah's elite circles."

Danny's jaw remained tense. "Curtis is my old man."

"He's worth millions." Jones's brows gathered in as he glanced around the room. "Why do you live here?" His tone hinted of curiosity.

"Where I choose to live is none of your business." Danny rose to his feet. "Now that you've asked one last question, and considering you've interrupted our supper, I'll show you to the door."

"Thanks for your time." Jones pushed off the sofa and cut a wide path around Boots.

Pansy gripped her dog's collar. "It's okay. He's gonna go now."

The second the front door closed, Poppy rushed to Danny's side. "Do you think he suspects something?"

"Doesn't matter. The man's nothing more than a nuisance."

"I need to warn Daisy."

Pansy scurried to the hall. "See? No one has to ask me that question anymore."

Danny's brow pinched. "What question?"

"If I remember what to do when someone asks me about your winning ticket."

"You're right." Danny's facial muscles relaxed. "Because you're the best sister and sister-in-law in the world."

Pansy's face beamed. "Papa Curtis would be proud of me, wouldn't he?"

Tension crept up Poppy's spine. How would Danny respond? With the truth or what Pansy deserved to hear?

Danny slid his arm around his sister's shoulders. "He'd be proud as a peacock."

The tension gripping Poppy's shoulders released. Sometimes a little lie was the only compassionate response.

The moment they returned to the kitchen Poppy called Daisy. No response. She left a message, hoping her daughter would hear it before Jones confronted her.

Chapter Nineteen

Daisy closed the flaps on box number fourteen, then swept the back of her hand across her brow and dropped onto the antique sofa in her new living room. "That takes care of the first floor."

David stacked the box on the pile lined up along the window wall. "By the time we finish upstairs, Maddie will have enough furniture and miscellaneous items to fill one, maybe two aisles."

"A windfall for Rose's childhood friend."

"At least that friend convinced you to place everything on consignment."

"Whatever profit I make will go toward Aunt Pansy's bakery renovation."

David sat beside her. "Did Andy agree to take on the project?"

"Every weekend until it's finished. Other than the parlor desk and the dining room table—" She tapped her foot on the antique area rug. "That's the only downstairs piece I'm keeping."

"None of those are what I'd call contemporary."

"I know." Daisy ran her fingers along the sofa's brocade upholstery. "But they're likely worth a fortune, and the rug's intricate pattern will contrast nicely with the contemporary furniture I ordered."

"Have you settled on eclectic?"

"Wise choice, don't you think?"

He chortled. "You're asking a guy who spends most of his time living in a camper not much bigger than a closet for a decorating opinion?"

"Don't you have a home base?"

"A studio apartment furnished with basic essentials. A bed for sleeping and a table and chair for eating and writing."

"Rather bare bones, wouldn't you say?"

"It's cheap and convenient. A place to hang out and write between investigations."

Daisy leaned her head back. Should she ask if he'd identified his next case? Did she want to know?

"Have you given more thought to your future?"

"I need a lot more time before lighting that match." She eyed the elaborate crown molding. "Agnes lived here bitter and alone for years after her husband died and her sons moved out. Metaphorically speaking, these walls are crying out for sunshine and cheer."

"You could throw a big party or charge admission to satisfy local residents' curiosity."

"Better to offer free admission."

David nudged her arm. "Did you just move closer to lighting that cigar?"

"Enough with the investigative probe." Daisy yawned, pushed off the sofa, and headed to the stairs. "Time to tackle the second floor and discover what's hidden in Agnes Watkins' closets."

"Hopefully no skeletons or anything that bites." David grabbed a package of boxes and followed her up the stairs.

At the landing Daisy strolled into the first room on the left and switched on the light. An elaborate, crystal chandelier illuminated the space filled wall-to-wall with heavy Baroque-style furniture. "Talk about overkill. I'm surprised the floor hasn't caved in."

David set the boxes beside the bed. "Based on the lingering lavender scent, I'm guessing this was Agnes's bedroom."

Daisy lifted one of the perfume bottles off a dresser. "Proof positive." She pulled a top drawer open. "Is snooping around in someone's private space akin to exercising a search warrant?"

"Only if we expect to find a crime worth investigating."

"Years ago my friends and I believed this house was haunted. Which made sense since Agnes's scowl scared the dickens out of little kids. Does that qualify as a crime?"

"Maybe against humanity."

Daisy emptied the first drawer and opened the second. "Before I turn this into my bedroom, I need to pull everything out. Including those five-hundred-pound drapes and every inch of carpet."

"Fresh start?"

In more ways than one. "Totally." She pointed to the chandelier. "But I'm keeping that beauty."

"Good decision."

After boxing clothes and linens worth selling at the thrift store and bagging the rest as donations, David wheeled a portable file box out of the closet. "This looks interesting." He stooped and lifted the lid.

Daisy knelt beside him and leafed through several dozen file folders. "These are leases for her rental properties. Some for land and others for dwellings." She sat back on her heels. "Why do you suppose her sons opted to sell everything she owned, especially since her rentals represent a fair amount of income?"

"Maybe they want to be done with everything connected with their scowling mother. Or immediate cash is more enticing than owning land and property they'd have to manage."

"Whatever the reason, whoever buys the property will eventually need these."

"Your first duty as an all-purpose attorney?"

Daisy playfully planted her hands on her hips. "Are you reverting back to investigative mode?"

"Yeah, how am I doing?"

"Not bad for an amateur."

He laughed. "Retaliation for my all-purpose remark."

"You catch on fast." Daisy slapped the lid on the file box. "For now, I suggest we stuff the one discovery that comes close to qualifying as evidence back in the closet and check out upstairs-room number two."

"Lead the way, Counselor."

David pressed his hand to her back as they headed to a bedroom facing the front of the house. He flipped on the understated chandelier. "This room comes close to qualifying as your style."

Daisy peered around the space. "No knickknacks or personal items. This must be her guest room, which means no one ever slept in here.

Except perhaps the resident ghost. Do you suppose they fly in or arrive in vehicles?"

He pointed to the window. "Seems we're about to find out."

Daisy peered out at headlights drawing closer. The porch light cast a glow on the car as it rolled to a stop. A man climbed from the driver's side. "At least it's not a phantom guest."

David's brows drew in. "I recognize that guy."

"Do you know him?"

"Personally? No. His reputation? Yeah. He's an independent journalist who sells scandalous stories to the highest bidder."

"Should we ignore him?"

"He won't give up until you face him head-on. Just be careful." David led the way downstairs and opened the front door as the reporter cleared the top step. "How can we help you?"

The man squared his shoulders and peered around David. "Are you Daisy Butler?"

"I am."

"Name's Jones." He lifted his chin and handed her a business card. I talked to your parents earlier, and I'd appreciate a few minutes of your time."

Daisy gripped David's arm. Had they tried to call and warn her? She forced her expression to remain neutral. Why had she chosen tonight to place her phone on silent? What had he gleaned from her parents? Or from Pansy? Should she call her mom now? That would rouse all sorts of suspicion. "We'll talk on the porch." She led Jones to a round wrought-iron table, motioned to a chair, and sat across from him. David stood behind her with his hands on her shoulders.

Jones glanced at David, then at Daisy. "I hear you've recently come into some money."

How much did he know? *Take control, go on the offense, and find out what he knows.* She crossed her arms on the table and eyed his smug expression. "Is snooping into citizens' personal finances your forte?"

"I go where stories take me."

"Are you aware that I'm an attorney from an influential New York law firm?"

"Who earned a fat bonus."

Bingo. "Well then, it seems you've answered your own question."

He mirrored her posture. His eyes probed. "Do you believe a local bought the winning lottery ticket?"

She held his gaze. "Attorneys deal with facts, Mr. Jones. As far as I know, no one from around here has given the slightest indication of instant wealth."

His eyes remained locked on hers. "One more question. Your grandfather is worth millions. Why do your parents live in that old house?"

Careful, he's fishing. "Do you question everyone's lifestyle?"

"You're not going to answer, are you?"

"Your query is irrelevant."

Jones stared at her for a long moment. "You're good at what you do, Ms. Butler. So am I. You folks have a pleasant evening." He stood, pivoted toward the front steps, and returned to his car.

The moment he backed down the driveway, David leaned close to Daisy. "Impressive moves, Counselor."

She puffed her cheeks and released a long stream of air. "Do you suppose he'll come back?"

"After you stood toe-to-toe with him?" He squeezed her shoulders before settling across from her. "Unless he still smells a story, he'll give everyone a break and move on."

"Speaking of breaks, we're due for one."

"What do you suggest?"

"Let's walk over to Willy's and buy a couple of beers."

"Great idea." David pulled his pinging phone from his belt clip. "A text from Lawrence Evans."

"Curtis's former attorney?"

David nodded. "And Cynthia Evans' ex. He agreed to meet with us tomorrow afternoon."

"In that case." Daisy slid her chair away from the table. "Let's add chips and cheese to our order."

"To celebrate your audacity and our progress or to satisfy a snack craving?"

"Does the reason matter?"

"Not a bit."
"Then both."

Chapter Twenty

A gentle breeze tousled Daisy's hair as she and David sauntered along the wide path shaded by massive Spanish moss-draped trees in Savannah's Forsyth Park. The space seemed more appropriate for lazy strolls than clandestine encounters. "At least Curtis's former attorney opted for a better meeting place than the DA."

"He doesn't know we're investigating Rose's disappearance."

Daisy eyed a jogger rushing past them "What *does* he think we're doing?"

"Collaborating on a story about Curtis's business empire."

"That's not totally inaccurate."

A couple holding hands smiled at them as they strolled by. Did they think she and David were a couple? Why wouldn't they? She fought the desire to reach for his hand and intertwine her fingers with his. How would he respond if she did?

"That's him." David pointed to an elderly gentleman standing at the decorative fence encircling an elaborate two-tier fountain holding center stage in a circular patio. "The guy with the leashed golden retriever."

They sidled over. David stood beside their target. "Thank you for agreeing to meet us, Mr. Evans."

The man stared straight ahead. "You understand, Mr. Lambert, that I'm here voluntarily and everything I tell you is off the record."

"As we agreed."

Daisy eyed the man's thick salt-and-pepper hair, neatly trimmed white goatee, and starched white shirt. How would he respond if he discovered the real reason for their meeting?

David patted the dog's head. "What's his name?"

"Bailey. After George from *It's a Wonderful Life*. My wife's favorite Christmas movie." His jaw twitched. "The woman I'm married to now, not Cynthia." He peered around David and caught Daisy's eye. "I knew Curtis had a son. Finding out he has a granddaughter came as quite a shock."

Did he have a clue that Curtis had two sons? "Until a couple months ago, I doubt he knew I existed."

"Curtis always held personal details close to the vest. I understand you're an attorney for the Warner Law Firm."

Daisy hesitated. Had David told him?

"I did a little checking before agreeing to this meeting."

How much checking? She swallowed. "I was."

"Until you landed the Butler account?"

He obviously did more than a little checking. "I decided to go out on my own."

"Smart move. Big law firms pay well with a lot of perks, but they also demand too much personal sacrifice." Evans broke eye contact with Daisy and faced the fountain. "You're here to learn about Curtis."

David nodded. "What's your history with him?"

"He and my father were fraternity brothers at Princeton. They remained close friends for years. That's how I landed the position as Curtis's personal attorney straight out of law school."

"Was he your only client?"

"No, but my most important one for the nineteen years I represented him."

David leaned on the fence. "What's the story about your ex and her association with Curtis?"

"I married Cynthia a few years after my first wife died. I was forty-three; she was eighteen years younger and ambitious. Curtis hired her on my recommendation."

"When?"

"Twenty-nine years ago." Evans curled his fingers around the fence railing. "Six months later she confessed to a year-long affair with a younger man. Turned out I was nothing more than a first-class ticket into the Butler empire."

David swatted a fly away from his face. "Was Cynthia the reason you're no longer Curtis's attorney?"

"She gave him an ultimatum. Fire me or lose her."

Daisy exchanged glances with David. That meant Cynthia Evans wasn't on Curtis's payroll when her grandmother disappeared, but Lawrence Evans was. She transitioned into investigator mode. "Were your ex and Curtis emotionally involved?"

"If you're asking whether or not they had an affair, the answer's no. Cynthia was too smart to become entangled in a physical relationship. She had a much bigger prize in mind."

Daisy pictured the woman's demeanor and air of authority the few times they'd interacted. "Managing the Butler business empire?"

"It took her years, but she finally achieved her objective." Evans paused. "Curtis was hard-nosed and driven, as if he had something to prove to the world."

Daisy's mind drifted to the day her grandfather revealed how his father had threatened to cut him out of his will and destroy him if he refused to follow in his footsteps. In essence Curtis had been bullied and bribed into joining the Butler empire.

Evans uncurled his fingers and lowered his hands to his side. "Other than my father, Curtis had few close friends and an apathetic relationship with his wife and daughters."

David spun around. "What do you know about Rose Fowler?"

"Was she that prostitute who disappeared?"

"Without a trace thirty-five years ago."

"I read about her. Other than that, nothing."

David slid his hands in his pockets. "Were you aware that Curtis had a long-term extra-marital affair?"

"I knew he had frequent clandestine meetings. Hold on." The man's brows pinched. "Are you suggesting that woman was Rose Fowler?"

"Not suggesting, Mr. Evans. Stating."

He faced David, his eyes fierce. "You requested this meeting under false pretenses—as an investigator and not an author."

"Not entirely. I *am* writing a book, and Curtis is big part of it. So is Rose."

He glared at David. "Are you claiming that Curtis was involved in that woman's disappearance?"

Daisy bit her lip to stop the rush of words threatening to escape. How much would David reveal?

"The question is, do you believe Curtis was capable of hurting someone?"

"Emotionally or financially, without a doubt. But physically?" Evans spun back toward the fountain. "If he was cornered or threatened—I wouldn't rule out his capacity for violence."

Daisy gripped the fence to steady her trembling fingers. Why couldn't or wouldn't the man who for years had offered legal counsel to her grandfather defend him now? "Do you know if Curtis owns guns?"

"Wealthy people require protection from predators and potential enemies, Ms. Butler."

"Is that a yes?"

"He kept pistols at the Savannah house and at the ranch." Evans fell silent for a long moment, as if mentally debating his next move. "You need to contact Curtis's former housekeeper." He removed his phone from his pocket and tapped a message.

David's phone pinged.

"I texted her name and address to you."

David read the message. "Why her, and what can she tell us?"

"After she abruptly left her job, she reached out to me for legal advice."

"About?"

"Attorney client privilege. Any additional information will have to come from her. Now if you'll excuse me, I'm meeting a friend for lunch."

David extended his hand. "Thank you for taking the time to talk to us."

"I hope you find what you're looking for." He released David's hand and nodded at Daisy, then walked away.

Her eyes followed him as he strode back the way they had come. "If my instincts are correct, Lawrence Evans knows more about my grandfather's past than he's legally able to reveal."

"Your instincts are spot-on." David glanced at his phone. "Perhaps a surprise visit to one Elsie Harrison will fill in some blanks."

"You mean now?"

"Can you think of a better time?"

Go on a wild goose chase or hold hands in a romantic park? While preferring the latter, time was a-wasting. "I suppose now's as good a time as any." Had her tone hinted of disappointment?

"At least we'll enjoy the park on the way back to my truck."

Yeah, he'd caught her tone.

An hour later David pulled onto a driveway and parked in front of the single-car garage attached to a modest home in Jessup. Islands of lush shrubs accentuated the manicured front lawn.

Daisy nodded toward the drawn blinds in the front windows. "Doesn't appear that anyone's home."

They made their way to the front door. David rang the bell. No response. He rang a second, then a third time. "Either she's ignoring us, or you're right about her not being home." He scribed a note and placed it along with his business card in the mailbox. "If she's curious, she'll reach out."

"And if she doesn't?"

"We'll give her a week, then make another surprise visit."

Chapter Twenty-One

A t noon, Daisy stood at the railing on her front porch and watched her brother, David, and her dad load the last piece of furniture onto the rental truck, before Basil pulled the door closed. She spun around and eyed the windows, now free from drapes and needing serious washing. Thank goodness she'd had the sense to hire a professional cleaning crew. She glanced at her watch. They were due to arrive in one hour.

Basil moseyed over. After guzzling a full bottle of water, he swiped the back of his hand across his mouth. "Old Agnes had a thing for heavy furniture."

Daisy elbowed his ribs. "Too much hard labor for you, knucklehead?"

"Heck, no." He flexed his biceps. "Best workout I've had all week, and we're only half done. So, when are you moving in?"

"Tomorrow afternoon."

"You bought yourself a nice house, noodle-noggin, despite Agnes's ghost roaming the halls, searching for little kids to terrorize."

"You're hilarious." Daisy tapped her finger to her chin. "Although I could file for an eviction notice."

"Better to hire some kick-butt ghostbusters."

Pansy dashed out the front door. "Me and Poppy have lunch all set up in Daisy's new dining room."

"Come on, sis, I'm famished." Basil linked arms with Daisy and followed David and their dad inside. They strolled through the empty living room and under the arched entry to the antique dining room table. He leaned close to Daisy. "Which chair do you suppose Agnes's ghost has claimed?"

She ignored him and tuned into Pansy dictating seating arrangements.

"Daisy, you and David sit on that side."

Basil nudged Daisy. "Beware of ghosts *and* Cupid."

Heat curled up Daisy's neck and warmed her ears. Would her little brother ever outgrow his proclivity to embarrass her? Determined to stop the warmth from invading her cheeks, she initiated an exaggerated eye roll and sniffed. "Sandwiches and oatmeal-raison cookies. Perfect lunch for our hardworking crew and one annoying little brother."

Basil laughed. "Annoying but lovable. Right, Aunt Pansy?"

"Uh-huh. When are you gonna get your badge and let me ride in your police car?"

"You mean sheriff's car. Soon."

"With the lights and siren on?"

"For a block or two."

As her family plus one settled down and shared a meal, an involuntary smile spread across Daisy's face. Despite an uncertain future, her decisions to move back to Georgia, buy this house, and help Pansy achieve her dream warmed her heart. And working on her grandmother's case with David was an added bonus. His playful barbs with her brother made him seem like family. What had her college roommate said? That any man she agreed to marry would have to pass muster with her brother and her dog? So far David was batting a thousand. So why hadn't he kissed her since New Year's Eve? Maybe he found living a few yards from her parents' home too intimidating. After all, he was a gentleman. Daisy stole a glance at David's profile. Would moving his camper to her driveway make a difference? Unless he wasn't romantically interested. Except, the way he smiled at her seemed as if he had feelings for her.

"—earth to Daisy." Basil snapped his fingers.

She blinked. "What?"

"Welcome back from wherever you roamed off to."

Daisy's ears heated up again. "Is there a question lurking somewhere in your brain, knucklehead?"

"Yeah. Do you want to keep the table and chairs on the front porch or send them to Maddie's?"

"Keep them."

"In that case we're ready to move the truck to the thrift store." He grabbed a cookie and dashed out.

"Time to get back to work." David pushed up and followed Daisy's dad and her brother to the front door. The three most important men in her life, working together to help her.

Pansy packed the remaining cookies in a plastic container. "I'm gonna take these to Maddie's and help unpack Agnes's treasures." She dashed past Daisy and out the front door.

"How many of those treasures do you suppose will end up displayed in Aunt Pansy's room?"

"Three for sure." Her mom dropped paper plates into a trash bag. "Maddie's payment for her help."

"The barter system is alive and well."

Her mom linked arms with Daisy. "Helping you move reminds me of the first day you left for college."

She patted her mom's hand. "This time I'm only moving a few miles away, and you have an open invitation to visit whenever the mood strikes." They moseyed to the staircase and sat on the second step. "David and I met with Curtis's former personal attorney yesterday. The one who represented him when Rose disappeared."

"And?"

"Curtis kept guns in Savannah and at the ranch." Daisy paused. "He believes under the right circumstances, Curtis is capable of violence."

Her mom drew in a deep breath. "Did I ever tell you about the one time Curtis beat Danny?"

Daisy shook her head.

"It happened on a Sunday at the ranch. Bobby wanted to ride one of his father's horses. Danny knew that wasn't a good idea, but he didn't want to disappoint his brother. So he asked his father for permission. When Curtis claimed his horses were too valuable to let an idiot ride, something snapped inside Danny. He accused his father of treating his youngest son worse than a rabid dog, much less another human being. That's when your grandfather slugged his oldest son and screamed that a kid as stupid as his half-wit brother couldn't possibly have come from him. If Rose confronted Curtis with proof about Pansy being his daughter…why wouldn't he have reacted with a gun instead of his fist?"

"True, except any defense attorney would point out one glaring complication. Curtis loved Rose."

"A crime of passion?"

Daisy nudged her mom's arm. "Now you sound like a proper defense attorney."

"I've watched a lot of old *Law and Order* episodes. Do you suppose we'll ever find out what happened the night Mama disappeared?"

"David and I won't give up until we do." Footsteps struck the front porch. "Maybe my cleaning crew has arrived." Daisy swung the front door open and stood face-to-face with Jason Jones. "You don't give up easily, do you?"

Her mom inched beside Daisy.

The man nodded at her. "Nice to see you again, Mrs. Butler."

Daisy crossed her arms. "What do you want, Mr. Jones?"

"Do you mind if we sit on the porch?"

"We can talk here."

"Suit yourself." He peered around the porch. "What's this house worth? Quarter mil, maybe more?"

"What I paid is a matter of public record. If you're so all-fired eager to find out, look it up for yourself."

"I will." He thrust his thumb over his shoulder. "I just talked to your brother-in-law."

Andy's first weekend working to restore Pansy's store, and he's accosted by a nuisance reporter! "What's your point?"

"Your so-called bonus must've been fatter than a miser's secret bank account. Or was that a story to hide the true source of your sudden windfall?"

Daisy's mom stepped forward. Her eyes narrowed. Her chin lifted. She jabbed her finger on the journalist's chest. "If you're accusing my daughter or anyone else in my family of lying, you'd best go back to that rock you crawled out from under and leave us alone."

Daisy stared wide-eyed at her mom.

The man's facial muscles went slack.

"Now if you'll excuse us, I'm helping my *lawyer* daughter move into her new home." She slammed the door shut, most likely missing the guy's nose by inches.

Silence, followed by receding footsteps.

"Way to go, Mom. Maybe that man will think twice before he pokes another mama bear."

Her mom tapped her fingers on her chest. "I'd always hoped the heart of a lion lurked inside here. Today I found out what made it tick."

Daisy wrapped her arm around her mom's shoulders. "You're a lion with a mighty roar when it counts."

Chapter Twenty-Two

An hour after the guys drove the second truckload down Daisey's driveway Poppy crossed the street and headed into the thrift store. She found Maddie standing at the top of the middle aisle. "Did you fill that entire row?"

"To the brim. Pansy asked if she could pick out furniture as one of the three items she earned for helping. I said yes without thinking. All I have to say is, I hope she has a big bedroom."

"Oh dear. What did she choose?"

"That huge dresser from Agnes's bedroom. She claims it once belonged to a princess."

"Proof my sister has a vivid imagination."

"And good taste. That dresser's worth a fortune." Maddie scooped a gum wrapper off the floor. "That annoying journalist came snooping around earlier. He asked all kinds of questions about Andy fixing up that store. The nerve of some people. I told him to bug off and mind his own business."

Poppy's chest puffed. "That makes two of us who put him in his place." She explained. "I think I left him speechless and shocked the dickens out of Daisy."

Maddie laughed. "Wish I could've seen that man's expression. Maybe now he knows it's best not to make southern ladies as mad as old wet hens. If he has half a brain, he'll figure out he's wasting his time poking around in our neck of the woods. If someone from around here suddenly had all that money, we'd for sure know about it. I mean, how could anyone keep that kind of news secret?"

Poppy's shoulders tensed. Should she respond? Would silence arouse suspicion? She couldn't lie. Except Danny hadn't cashed the check, so technically they didn't have the money. Get a grip and act like a lion instead of a kitten. "It wouldn't be easy, that's for sure."

"Doggone near impossible."

Pansy bounded up the aisle and held out an antique vase. "This'll look real pretty in my new store, soon as Andy gets it all fixed up."

"Great choice, sweetie." Poppy's shoulders relaxed, relieved their family's secret was safe. At least for now.

Pansy spun around and meandered back the way she'd come. Halfway down the aisle she glanced over her shoulder. "I almost forgot to tell you. Danny's ready to go home. He's out by the truck."

Maddie nudged Poppy. "Come on, I'll walk you out."

As they made their way toward the back of the store, Poppy eyed shelves artfully arranged with Agnes's possessions. "Looks as if everything's ready to sell."

"Thanks to Pansy, everything's in place. But ready for prime time? Hardly. Nothing's priced. Willy offered to take care of customers until Mom and I finish tackling that task."

"I wouldn't know where to begin."

"Can you believe Mom has become an expert at online research? She says it helps keep her mind sharp."

"Good for her." When they arrived at the back door, Poppy embraced Maddie. "Thank you for letting Pansy participate."

"Honey, your sister was the hardest working member of the crew, so I should thank you. With the right people to help run the business side, Pansy's bakery will end up a big success."

Who were those people, and how would Daisy find them? Maybe Pansy's 'build a town idea' applied to her bakery. Build it, and help would come. Poppy shook her head at the irrational thought while stepping out into the cool night air. She eyed the dresser in the back of the family truck. Big was an understatement. No way it would fit without moving furniture out of Pansy's room. They'd deal with that challenge tomorrow morning. After all, tonight was date night.

An hour after parking the truck in the driveway, Danny—smelling of soap and shampoo—settled on the arbor swing beside Poppy. He poured top-shelf bourbon into two glasses. "Glad that move is behind us."

"All except Pansy's new furniture."

"I have no idea why she picked that piece." He sipped his drink. "Did Maddie tell you about Jason Jones questioning Andy?"

Good, he was in the mood to talk. "She wasn't the only one he pestered." Poppy relayed the confrontation at Daisy's.

Danny patted her knee. "I'm proud of you for taking a stand." He fell silent and set their swing in motion.

Poppy's heart warmed as she rested her head on his shoulder. For the moment, all seemed right with the world.

The porch light cast Daisy and David's shadow on the driveway as they sat side by side on the top porch step. She breathed in the scent of manly sweat mingling with the remaining trace of shampoo. "The way you worked hard to help move all of Agnes's stuff across the street was above and beyond the call of duty."

"A small price to pay for your family feeding me for nearly two months."

She imagined sitting beside him on the porch every evening after supper, discussing her grandmother's case without interruptions. Unless a nosy neighbor happened to stroll up her driveway. Daisy fingered a crack in the wood. Starting tomorrow, she'd have to prepare her own meals. Why not cook for two instead of one? The time seemed right to make a bold move. "I've been thinking. Since we're working Rose's case from here...it would probably be more convenient if you didn't have to drive over every day or whenever a new lead came our way."

"Are you inviting me to move my camper to your driveway?"

"That seems to make the most sense. Right?"

"What do you suppose Maddie would think about your business partner living a few feet from your back door?"

Did he care, or was he looking for a reason to reject her proposal? "Does it matter?"

"Not to me. What about you?"

"We'd likely start a few rumors. At least they'd be more interesting than the gossip Agnes stirred up. Even better, we could drum up business for Butler and Lambert—Crackerjack Investigative Services."

"You mean Lambert and Butler." David elbowed her arm. "Unless you decide to hang an attorney-for-hire sign on your front porch."

"So what's your answer? Stay parked in my parents' driveway or move here and find out how nosy neighbors react?"

David's arm brushed her shoulder as he leaned close. "I'll take my chance on the nosy-neighbor scenario."

Daisy's pulse quickened. "I'll break the news to Mom after church."

"For now I'm in serious need of a shower." He pushed off the step. "Reserve that parking spot until tomorrow afternoon."

"You've got it." A warm sensation washed over Daisy as her eyes followed David to his truck. After he backed down her driveway and drove away, she plodded past her now empty living room, except for the area rug. She climbed the stairs and switched on the light in the master bedroom. The chandelier cast a warm glow on the newly revealed wood floors. A little buffing here and there and they'd be as good as new. She breathed in the fresh air devoid of even a hint of lavender. The only remaining trace of Agnes was the file box stashed away in the closet.

Daisy turned off the light and wandered through both dark bedrooms facing the backyard. They'd have to remain empty for a while. With her commitment to help Pansy set up her bakery, she'd have to watch her expenses. Especially if it took a couple more months to solve Rose's case, or if her dad decided not to cash the lottery check.

After changing into pajamas, Daisy moseyed to the guest room—the one space that remained as Agnes had left it. At least she had a place to sleep for the next few nights. She turned on the bedside lamp and opened the window a crack to emit a whiff of fresh air. Daisy lay back on the bed and closed her eyes. Visions of David danced in her head. Enjoying a cup of coffee on the front porch while watching the sun rise. Eating a meal she'd prepared at her dining room table. Sitting beside him on the back-porch swing.

An involuntary smile spread across her face. She'd use every feminine ploy she could drum up to transition their relationship from investigative partners to lovers.

Chapter Twenty-Three

Unfamiliar chimes accentuated by sunlight streaming into the guest room nudged Daisy's eyes open. Had she changed her alarm ring? She blinked to clear the fog in her head and plucked her phone off the nightstand. Nine-thirty. The chimes sounded again. The doorbell. Her pulse quickened. Had David shown up early? She brushed her hair away from her cheek, then crept to the window and peered down at the driveway. A sigh of relief escaped. Lilly's car, not David's, was parked beside the front porch.

Daisy scurried to the first floor, pulled the door open, and nodded toward the living room. "Give me a minute." Following an urgent trip to the powder room, she returned and embraced her sister. "You're my first official visitor."

"I brought you a housewarming gift." Lilly handed Daisy a ceramic pot holding an orchid.

"Gorgeous flower. Thanks, sis. I haven't had my morning caffeine fix. What about you?"

"If you have decaf."

Daisy escorted her sister to the kitchen and set the orchid on the windowsill before searching through her selection of coffee pods. "We're in luck. I found one." She placed the pod in her coffee maker. "You're up early, even for Sunday. Are you going to church with Mom?"

Lilly shook her head. "Andy's working on Pansy's store all day, so I'm skipping church. I'd always imagined Agnes's house as dark and creepy."

She ran her fingers over the marble countertop. "I never would've guessed she had a bright and cheery kitchen."

"You should have seen this place before we moved a truckful of stuff to the thrift store. It was a museum specializing in antiques and knickknacks permeated with lavender." Daisy set Lilly's coffee beside a bowl of sugar, then popped in a French-roast pod. "One thing's certain. Except for her choice of perfume, old Agnes had expensive taste."

"Rumor was she had more money than she could spend in a lifetime." Lilly added sugar to her coffee, then sipped while wandering around the kitchen and peeking into cabinets. "Your cupboards are mostly bare."

"Until I moved here, I lived in college dorms and a New York apartment the size of my new living room. Not much space for kitchen supplies."

Lilly opened a cabinet filled with china. She removed a dinner plate and ran her finger around the gold rim. "Fancy dishes."

"That entire set was stored in Agnes's china cabinet. I figured, why not put them to use." Daisy added sweetener to her coffee. "Are you ready for the grand tour?"

Lilly shrugged. "Sure."

So much for her sister's enthusiasm. "We'll start in the den." After escorting Lilly through the entire first floor and the covered deck off the kitchen, Daisy led the way up the stairs and into the master bedroom. "This room was so full of heavy furniture the floors groaned under the weight."

Lilly meandered to the window overlooking the side driveway. "If you ask me, this big house is overkill for one person."

Daisy crossed her arms and stared at the back of her sister's head. What was it with her snarky tone? Was she envious or were her hormones on overload? "You're right. Although, the parlor downstairs will function as investigation central for me and David." She sidled to her sister's side. "He's moving his camper to my driveway later today."

"Makes sense." Lilly wiped a smudge off the window. "Did Mom tell you I quit my job?"

"Why so soon?"

"Because..." Lilly's voice faltered. "I'm in big trouble, Daisy."

Daisy's heart jumped to her throat. "What's wrong? Is baby Jonah okay? Did you and Andy have a fight?"

"Nothing like that." She hesitated.

"It's not a good idea to keep a lawyer in suspense, even if she is your big sister. So spill it."

Lilly heaved a long sigh. "I was counting on Dad cashing the lottery check before the bill came in."

Daisy's eyes narrowed. "What bill?"

"My new credit card. The one Andy doesn't know about. I needed it to buy baby furniture." Tears pooled and rolled down Lilly's cheek.

"Goodness gracious." Daisy slid her arm around her sister's waist. "Is that all you're worried about?"

Lilly swiped her fingers across her cheeks. "Andy's always extra careful with our money. He never charges more than we can afford to pay at the end of the month. He'll never understand."

"That you needed to furnish the nursery? Don't be a silly goose. Of course he'll understand."

Lilly pulled away and trudged to the front window.

Daisy's brow pinched. Something didn't seem right. She eased beside her sister. "Tell me what's really going on."

"If you loan me the money until Dad cashes the check, I won't have to tell Andy."

"You do understand that Dad is as likely to tear it up as he is to cash it. Besides, Andy's earning extra money every weekend for the next month."

Lilly's chin quivered. "It won't be enough."

Her sister's trembling voice and downcast eyes triggered a tightness in Daisy's chest. "How much did you spend?"

Lilly's lower lip caught between her teeth. "Twelve."

"Twelve what?"

"Grand."

Daisy gasped. "How on earth could you spend that much money on baby furniture?"

"I wanted the best—"

"A couple thousand I could understand. But twelve? That amount of cash would furnish ten nurseries. You're right, Andy will have a hard time understanding." Daisy spun around, leaned against the wall, and slid to the floor. "That doesn't mean you shouldn't tell him."

"If you loan me the money, even if Dad doesn't cash that check, I promise I'll pay you back every penny. Unless—" Lilly dropped beside Daisy, her eyes wide. "Did you spend your entire bonus on this house?"

"Of course not." Daisy clamped her lips tight to prevent another cutting remark from rolling off her tongue. "You're my sister, so I'll loan you the money. But only after you tell Andy what you've done."

"I can't."

"You have to."

"Why?"

Daisy clasped Lilly's hand. "Because I love you and Andy too much to let that big of a deception destroy your marriage."

"He'll never forgive me."

"There you go being a silly goose again. Andy's a great guy. Not only will he forgive you, he'll be relieved you trusted him enough to level with him."

"I suppose you're right."

"There's no supposing about it."

Lilly sniffled. "I'll tell him tonight."

"In that case, I'll write you a check tomorrow."

"I um—" Lilly swallowed. "There's one more thing."

Daisy stared at her sister's profile. "Don't tell me there's another secret credit card."

She shook her head. "Just the one. The thing is...I don't want Mom and Dad to know what I've done."

"This is between you, me, and your husband. No one else needs to know."

"You're a good sister, Daisy."

"At one time or another, we've all made poor decisions." Daisy leaned her head against the wall. "The first day I interviewed with the law firm, the partners knew I was Curtis Butler's granddaughter. I wanted the job too much to tell anyone that I'd never met the man."

"At least that secret ended up making instead of costing you money."

"If Michael hadn't extended me a modicum of grace when I finally fessed up, my failure to reveal the truth would have cost me my job *and* my reputation."

"I don't know what I'd do if you weren't here to help me."

"We're family, and we always help each other."

"Maybe one day I can do something to help you." Lilly closed her eyes and pressed her palm to her tummy. The hint of a smile curved her lips. "Until then, no matter what happens—even if Dad never cashes that check—I promise to be happy with the love Andy and I have for each other and the life we've created."

Daisy squeezed her sister's hand and swallowed the lump rising in her throat. Mere words seemed inadequate for the moment. She remained silent as conflicting thoughts about her own future tap-danced across her brain and played havoc with her emotions.

Chapter Twenty-Four

After the last hymn of Sunday's service, Daisy leaned close to her mom and whispered. "Can you and I talk for a few minutes?"

Her mom's brow pinched, then released. She turned to her sister. "Will you wait on the front steps for us, sweetie?"

Pansy fingered her mother's gold cross necklace hanging an inch below her neck. "After you and Daisy talk, can we go get ice cream at Willy's?"

"Absolutely."

As soon as the last row emptied and the aisle cleared, Daisy propped her arm across the back of the pew.

Her mom's head tilted. "Do you have news about Mama's disappearance?"

"Sort of, but not exactly." How should she explain? "Now that David and I have teamed up to solve her case, we need to follow up on leads with a moment's notice. With me living away from home—"

"David's moving his camper to your driveway, isn't he?"

Daisy shot her mom an incredulous look. "This afternoon, and how did you know?"

"I didn't." She placed her arm over Daisy's. "Have I told you recently how proud I am of everything you've accomplished in just a few short years?"

"As far back as I can remember, you've encouraged me to reach for the moon and stars."

"I recognized your potential early on." Her mom paused as a faraway look clouded her eyes. "Everything that's happened to us since David showed up on our front porch has reminded me of what's most important. Family and the love between a man and a woman. The kind of affection and loyalty that endures through a lifetime of peaks and valleys."

"You're describing the kind of relationship you and Dad have."

Her mom nodded. "The day Danny proposed, I knew that he didn't love me. I also accepted the fact that I needed him to feel normal. During the early months of our marriage we settled into a comfortable routine. We worked as a team to start our family's business. Little by little I could tell his affection for me was growing. Then I became pregnant with you, and for the first time, the man whose bed I shared told me he loved me."

"With all his heart, and that you'd be together forever."

"His exact words." A smile sent a sparkle to her mom's eyes and a glow to her cheeks. "That was the moment I understood that Danny accepted me for who I am."

"Because you're a beautiful woman inside and out, Mom."

"In my family's and God's eyes."

Daisy's heart ached for her mom. After all these years, the stares and taunts from her mother's past continued to affect her self-esteem. She touched her mom's birthmarked cheek "Your natural beauty shines through to everyone who knows you."

"Thank you for your kind words."

"They're more than kind, Mom." Daisy pulled her hand away from her mom's cheek. "They're true. You are a beautiful woman."

Her brow knitted then released, as if for a brief moment, she accepted the truth. She broke eye contact with Daisy. "About David's move, did you invite him, or was it his idea?"

"I invited him."

"Good."

"You approve?"

"Why wouldn't I?" Her mom patted Daisy's hand. "You two need time alone to discover if your relationship has the potential to blossom into enduring love."

"Not only are you a treasure, you're the smartest woman I know." Daisy embraced her mom. "If we wait much longer, Pansy's likely to take off for Willy's on her own."

Poppy stood and linked arms with her daughter. "After we indulge in ice cream, I'll take Pansy to check out Andy's work and find the right moment to explain why David's moving out of our driveway."

"Great idea."

Twenty minutes later, while her mom and aunt crossed the side street, Daisy ambled to the free-standing garage at the end of her driveway. The perfect spot for David's camper. She stepped inside, swept away cobwebs, and switched on the overhead light. After locating an electrical outlet, reality crept in. The man whose touch sent rivers of desire coursing through her body was about to set up camp fifteen feet from her back door.

Daisy touched steepled fingers to her lips and summoned memories of the moments they'd spent alone. His smile when their eyes met. Their light-hearted bantering. The way he sometimes winked at her. He clearly enjoyed working the case with her, and he valued her opinions. Maybe he was waiting for her to make the first move before pursuing more than a friendship. Especially after Michael Warner had shown up on her front porch a few weeks after Thanksgiving, and then sent her an expensive Christmas gift.

Daisy meandered to the front of the house and sat on the porch steps. A squirrel skittered across the driveway the same moment a hawk swooped low. How many more animals lived in the woods surrounding her house? Maybe she should buy a dog, or better yet rescue a stray. The perfect choice if her dad cashed the check and she set up a proper law office to manage the estate. What if he didn't? The thought of moving away from her new home didn't sit well. Could she earn a living practicing general law miles away from a major town? The question lingered until her eyes were drawn to David's camper backing up the driveway. She jumped off the step and rushed to his truck. "It's obvious you've had plenty of practice with that maneuver."

"A time or two."

His smile sent a warm sensation surging through her. What excuse could she use to invite him into her home? With nothing more than coffee, a loaf of bread, and a jar of peanut butter on hand, she couldn't offer him a meal.

"Where do you want me to park what Pansy refers to as 'my house on wheels'?"

"Straight back to the garage. There's an outlet inside the door."

"Thanks. By the way, I come bearing gifts from your mom and aunt." He handed Daisy two picnic baskets. "They're loaded to the brim."

Mom to the rescue. "The quintessential southern housewarming gift. After you're settled, why don't you join me for a picnic-style supper?"

"How could I refuse such an intriguing offer from my number-one partner?"

Daisy grinned. "You mean the brilliant, fascinating woman who will allow you to use her office?"

"That's the one."

David winked, then backed into place.

Daisy carried the baskets to her kitchen and peered inside. David wasn't kidding. She wouldn't have to grocery shop for a week. Eager to express her gratitude, she pulled her phone from her pocket and pressed her mom's number.

"Hi, honey."

"You and Pansy are the best mom and aunt in the world." Daisy lifted a container of meatloaf from the first basket. "How did you get all this ready since church?"

"Pansy and I fixed everything yesterday. Before we talked this morning, I'd already planned to ask David to deliver the baskets to you."

"Seems my cheerleader-turned-Cupid is using food instead of arrows to spark a romance."

"You know what they say about the way to a man's heart."

Daisy lifted the lid off a container of cookies and breathed in the succulent, chocolate scent. "I do have one little problem. After enjoying your delicious meals and Pansy's desserts every day since Thanksgiving, David will find my cooking skills sorely lacking."

"Don't underestimate the power of candles, compliments, and a dab of perfume."

A giggle escaped. "My mom, the romantic. Who knew? Although the way you shooed us kids away during your Saturday-date nights with Dad should have clued me in." Daisy bit into a cookie. "If Pansy keeps me supplied with her baked goods, maybe David won't notice my culinary deficiencies. Speaking of Pansy, how'd she take the news about David leaving?"

"She asked if David's your boyfriend now. By the way, the dresser from Agnes's bedroom is now in her room."

"Are you serious?"

"We moved her old dresser out to make a space. Your dad and David had a time guiding it through the doors." She paused. "Danny just walked in. He needs my help. Call me tomorrow?"

"Will do." After emptying all the goodies and changing into jeans and a sweater, Daisy repacked a basket, carried it from the kitchen, and paused beside the dining-room table. Too formal. She strolled to the empty living room and stopped in front of the fireplace. The perfect setting for a casual picnic. She set the basket on her area rug, lit a fire, and waited. How should she act when David arrived? As if she was his friend and investigative partner or a woman who wanted more? Much more.

Twenty minutes after her mental debate began, the front-door chime unleashed a fluttering sensation in her chest. She smoothed her sweater and rushed to pull the door open.

David strolled in carrying a bottle of wine and a corkscrew in one hand and two wine glasses in the other.

"Another housewarming gift from Mom?"

"A gift, yes. But not from your mom. I bought the glasses yesterday at Maddie's. The wine's from Willy's—a decent label for an off-the-beaten-path convenience store."

The fluttering intensified as Daisy breathed the fresh scent of soap accentuated by a hint of musky cologne. "Perfect for a fireside picnic." *And intimate conversation.*

The fire crackled as they settled on the area rug with the picnic basket between them.

David uncorked and poured the wine, then clinked his glass to hers. "To new beginnings."

What did he mean? "And discoveries." She sipped. Should she begin the conversation or wait?

"I left a message for Elsie Harrison, Curtis's former housekeeper."

Was Rose's disappearance what he meant by new beginnings? "Hopefully, she'll call you back."

David's eyes probed. Uh-oh. Had her tone reflected her disappointment? He tilted his head. "It's Sunday and I'm enjoying a glass of wine with a beautiful woman, so enough talk about the case."

Yeah, he'd read her tone. Good. She took another sip. "Are you hungry?"

"For food, not yet. For glimpses of pre-lawyer Daisy Butler, beginning with your college years, you bet."

"Hmm, what does the investigative journalist want to know?"

"To begin, did you keep your nose buried in law books every waking moment, or did you carve out time for fun?"

"I had my moments." Following a lively exchange about college shenanigans and dating experiences, David's smile evaporated. He broke eye contact, fell silent, and polished off his second glass of wine.

A log split and released a flash of miniature sparks.

Daisy stared at the golden liquid in her glass. Had a painful memory crept into his mind? She waited.

David refilled his glass. "There was one relationship." He swallowed a mouthful. "I met Shannon in my senior year during spring break. She was the most uninhibited, exciting woman I'd ever known."

A typical college romance or something else?

"Five weeks after we spent that first night together, we flew to Vegas." He swallowed another sip. "Following three days and nights of partying, gambling, and heavy drinking, we ended up in a cheesy wedding chapel."

Daisy's body froze. Was he married?

"The next morning Shannon realized she'd made a huge mistake." David's tone hinted of anguish. "A week later, she had the marriage annulled."

Did he still love her? "You must have been heartbroken."

"At first. Until I came to my senses and realized that our relationship was fueled by lust and intense physical gratification." His gaze seemed drawn to the flickering flame. "I've never told anyone about that weekend. Not even my mother."

Daisy's heart swelled. He trusted her enough to share an intimate detail from his past.

"You need to know." David's eyes found hers. "Because I'm falling in love with you, Daisy. It's just...we've known each other for such a short time, and there's Michael."

How could she reassure him and let him know she understood without coming on too strong? "I never had feelings for Michael like I have for you." She reached across the picnic basket and placed her hand on his arm. "The first time you touched my hand, my heart nearly jumped out of my chest. That was the moment I began falling for you. I also know that enduring relationships need time to blossom and grow."

"Thank you for understanding." David stroked Daisy's cheek with a tenderness that released ripples of desire. How long before he kissed her a second time? A few more hours? A few days? It didn't matter. She'd wait however long he needed to share his heart with her.

Chapter Twenty-Five

For the first morning in weeks, Poppy prepared breakfast for three instead of five. She sat alone in her kitchen, cradled her coffee mug in both hands, and peered at the empty chairs across the kitchen table. Life had officially returned to normal in the Butler household. At least for the moment. She sipped her coffee and glimpsed Pansy's sketchpad lying open to her newest drawing—an array of cakes in a display cabinet. For years her sister's vision seemed as far-fetched as one of her lottery tickets actually winning. But now—

Startled by Daisy's ringtone, Poppy pressed the speaker icon.

"Hey, Mom. How are things going?"

"I'm curious about your plan after Andy finishes his weekend project."

"Uh-oh, Aunt Pansy must have given you and Dad an earful during breakfast."

"Her bakery is all she's talked about since we left church yesterday, and Andy's making good progress. If her dream doesn't come true, her heart will break."

"Why the anxiety, Mom? I promised I'd help her turn her dream into reality."

Needles of guilt pricked Poppy's conscience. "I didn't mean to doubt you, honey. It's just that Pansy deserves to reach her full potential despite her limitations."

"What do you say we start our conversation over?"

"Good idea." Poppy flopped back in her chair.

"Hey, Mom."

"Good morning, honey. Are you enjoying your new home? Did you and David eat supper in your dining room or out on the front porch?"

"Thanks to your basketful of goodies, we enjoyed a scrumptious picnic in front of the fireplace. We talked for hours until the fire burned out." Daisy paused for a long moment. "David gave me permission to share something he told me."

Poppy fidgeted, her eyes wide. "I'm listening."

Daisy relayed the story of David's whirlwind college romance and short-lived marriage.

Painful memories of Danny's past released a heavy sensation in Poppy's chest. "Rejection is a punishment that lingers far beyond the moment it's delivered. Recovery takes time, especially for a man."

"Last night included the most emotionally gratifying moments I've ever experienced. Not because David and I connected physically, which we didn't. But because we shared intimate details about our deepest feelings."

Poppy pressed her hand to her chest. In one night Daisy and David had connected on a level she and Danny had taken years to even come close to achieving. "Do you know how blessed you are to have experienced that level of intimacy this early in your relationship?"

"Beyond anything I'd ever imagined." Daisy giggled. "It seems time rather than my culinary skills is all I need to capture David's heart. Although, I could use a few cooking lessons from you and Aunt Pansy."

They continued chatting until Pansy rushed in. "We'll have to continue our chat later. Your dad needs my help in the greenhouse."

"Thanks for listening, Mom."

"Call me any time, honey." Poppy ended the call, then retrieved her straw hat and made her way across the backyard. Inside the greenhouse, Danny motioned her to join him at a worktable set along the side. She strolled over and eyed a blooming rosebush holding centerstage. "That's the most beautiful shade of coral I've ever seen. Is it a new variety?"

"New and exclusive." He fingered a leaf. "For the past two years, I've worked to create something special."

"Oh my gosh, Danny." She touched her fingertip to a petal. "Is this *your* hybrid?"

"It is." A smile lit his face and sent a twinkle to his eyes. "I've named it the poppy rose."

Tears of intense joy pooled and spilled down Poppy's cheeks. The man who seldom displayed emotion had secretly toiled to create a flower to honor her. "Other than our three children, this is the most beautiful gift you've ever given me."

Danny wiped the tears from her cheeks. "Come with me." He held her hand while carrying his gift to a marble pedestal he'd set beside the front entrance.

Poppy pressed her hand to her chest. "I wondered why you brought that home from Maddie's."

He placed the rosebush on the pedestal. "My tribute to the beautiful woman who captured my heart all those years ago deserves a place of honor."

Mere words seemed inadequate to express her appreciation. Poppy laced her fingers behind Danny's neck and gazed deep into his eyes. "I love you, sweetheart."

He kissed her, and for the first time in her life, she believed she was beautiful.

Grateful for the close bond she shared with her confidante, Daisy smiled at the photo she'd set on her desk—her mom's profile as she kissed her cheek the day she left for college. Hopefully, one day her mother would see past her birthmark and realize she was a beautiful woman.

Her phone pinged a text from David. "*Good morning.*"

She posted a smiley face. "*Want some coffee?*"

"*Would love some.*"

"*Meet me in the kitchen.*" Daisy pocketed her phone and met David at the back door. "I hope you're hungry."

He strolled in and sniffed. "Do I detect Pansy's cinnamon crumb coffee cake?"

"Warmed up and ready to enjoy." She prepared two cups of coffee. "Do you want to indulge in the dining room or on the front porch?"

"Which do you prefer?"

"Since I'm wearing my favorite sweatshirt, I think the porch."

"Perfect spot to share some good news."

Daisy removed the coffee cake from the oven, then grabbed plates and forks. "About Rose's case?"

"Yeah." David carried the coffee cups. "Elsie Harrison returned my call a few minutes ago."

Daisy's brows raised. "Curtis's former housekeeper?"

"She agreed to meet with us at her house tomorrow."

"That's great news." They moved to the front porch and settled at the wrought-iron table. "Did she give you a clue about what she might tell us?"

"Not a word. Although I had the distinct feeling she had thought long and hard about reaching out to me."

"She must know something." Daisy plated and served the coffee cake.

"I've learned that household staff often knows a great deal about their wealthy clients' private lives." He tasted his slice. "Pansy could make a fortune selling this. How are plans to kick-start her bakery coming along?"

"I'm working on it." Daisy's fork stopped halfway to her mouth the moment a truck turned onto her driveway. "That's Andy."

"Is he working on Pansy's project today?"

"I don't know." She set down her fork as her brother-in-law and sister stepped out and climbed onto the porch. "Lilly must have told him," Daisy mumbled. She stood and embraced her sister, then Andy.

David offered Lilly his seat. "Maybe I should leave."

Lilly dropped onto the chair. "You're practically family, so you might as well stay."

Andy stood behind his wife. "Lilly explained why she asked you for a loan." He placed his hands on her shoulders. "We talked, and I want to trade my labor for whatever amount of money you give her."

Daisy's focus shifted to Lilly's downcast eyes, then to David. "Will you take Andy to the kitchen and fix him a cup of coffee and a slice of coffee cake while Lilly and I talk?"

"Glad to." David clasped Andy's shoulder. "You're in for a treat, pal."

The moment the men walked inside, Daisy propped her forearms on the table and leaned close to her sister. "Was working for free Andy's idea or yours?"

Lilly picked at a fingernail. "He insisted."

"Because he's noble and he loves you." Daisy stared at her sister. What decision would she make if given a choice? "Do you want me to accept or decline Andy's offer?"

"He's paying a guy to help him." Lilly made brief eye contact, then looked away.

"That's not an answer."

"It's not right for Andy to work all those extra hours and not get paid because I made a foolish decision." Lilly laced her fingers over her belly. "You should decline, and if you loan me the money let *me* work off the debt."

Good for her. "Come with me." Daisy escorted her sister into the parlor. She removed a check from her desk's top drawer and handed it over.

Lilly stared at the check. "When did you write this?"

"The day you admitted what you'd done."

"How did you know I'd keep my promise to confess to Andy?"

"Because Mom and Dad raised us to do what's right."

"If I'd remembered what they taught us, I wouldn't be in this mess." Lilly folded the check and slid it into her jeans pocket. "About me working off the debt, what do you want me to do to pay you back?"

"I'll devise a plan we can both live with. For now, are you ready to indulge in a slice of Aunt Pansy's soon-to-be famous coffee cake while you tell your sweet husband about your decision?"

"You're the best sister ever, and yes, I'm ready to let Andy know I'm taking responsibility for my actions. The coffee cake is an extra bonus to satisfy my pregnant-lady appetite."

Daisy laughed as she wrapped her arm around Lilly's shoulders. "I couldn't ask for a better little sister."

Chapter Twenty-Six

Tuesday morning while David drove, Daisy read aloud his notes about Rose's case the best she could. "You weren't kidding about your handwriting, or should I say scribbling."

"Would you believe those scrawls are the Lambert version of shorthand, Counselor?"

"Ladies and Gentlemen of the jury, the witness claims to have mastered his own stenographic style. I ask you, is he stating a fact or attempting to defend poor penmanship?"

David chortled. "Guilty as charged. However, I can read my own writing. At least most of the time."

"And when you can't?"

"I rely on my memory." He turned onto Elsie Harrison's driveway and parked behind an older-model SUV.

Daisy eyed the open blinds at the front window. "After all these years, what are the chances she'll remember anything important?"

"Time for Lambert and Butler to go to work and find out."

"Unless our witness needs an attorney." Daisy handed over his notepad. "In which case, we'll become Butler and Lambert." She grinned, pushed her sunglasses to the top of her head, and climbed out.

The moment they stepped onto the porch, an elderly gentleman opened the door. "My wife is waiting out back." He escorted them through the house and out to a backyard any professional gardener would claim with unabashed pride. A pitcher of lemonade, four glasses, and a plate of cookies lay on a glass-top table. "Mr. Lambert and Ms. Butler are here, dear."

A thin woman with short white hair motioned them to sit. "It's such a lovely morning for a chat." Her smile crinkled her nose and deepened the lines around her eyes. "How about a glass of lemonade?"

Daisy nodded. "Yes, please. Did you bake the cookies, Mrs. Harrison?"

"They're store-bought but soft and delicious. Please call me Elsie. First names are much more personal, don't you think?" She handed Daisy a glass of lemonade. "Are you related to Curtis Butler, or is your last name a coincidence?"

"He's my grandfather."

Elsie swept her arm in a wide arc. "Thanks to your grandfather, I've had all the time in the world to tend to my garden." She poured a glass for David. "After you left us your note, Harold and I had quite a debate about whether or not to call you."

Her husband drummed his fingers on the table. "My wife is mighty persuasive when she gets a hankering to do something. She convinced me enough time has passed."

Daisy sipped her lemonade. Enough time to reveal incriminatory information or share useless gossip? "How long did you work for Curtis?"

Elsie wrapped her fingers around her glass. "I was Mr. Butler's live-in housekeeper every Tuesday through Saturday for twelve years. At his ranch, not his Savannah house. Although one time I worked there a couple of days to help Mrs. Butler prepare for one of her fancy parties. Her regular housekeeper claimed to have come down with the flu. After working for Mrs. Butler for half a day, I suspected the woman might've been faking illness to avoid her boss's unreasonable demands."

David opened his notepad. "What else did you learn about the family during those years?"

"The family? Not much. Mr. Butler was another story. He was a hard-nosed businessman who kept a strict schedule. Other than bigwig politicians and other rich people, he seldom had visitors. Except for his annual Memorial Day events when hundreds of guests rubbed elbows. You should've seen the lawn all gussied up. The big white tent. All those fancy tables and chairs." She paused. Her brows pinched. "I found it odd that his wife and daughters never attended and rarely came for a visit. And their sons only showed up a few times. I remember Bobby. He was such a sweet boy, and his big brother...what was his name?"

"Danny." Daisy swallowed. "He's my dad."

"You're blessed to have such an attentive father, Daisy. The way he looked after his little brother was a sight to behold." Elsie's head tilted. "Whatever happened to Bobby?"

Daisy exchanged glances with David. Should she reveal the truth? That he'd taken his own life after the man she'd worked for rejected him during a party in his Savannah home? Best to keep that bit of news private. "He passed away a long time ago."

"Such a loss." Elsie swatted a fly buzzing the cookies then covered the plate with a napkin. "Too many fine young people die before their time. But, I suspect you're more interested in finding out what happened the night Rose Fowler disappeared, than hearing about Mr. Butler's family."

Daisy's eyes widened. How much did she remember?

David clicked his pen. "We're all ears."

"Well." Elsie leaned forward. "First you need to know that Mr. Butler's chauffeur drove him wherever he needed to go. Savannah. The airport. It didn't matter. I suppose it was because he'd rather work than waste time sitting behind the wheel. The one exception was every Friday afternoon at three-thirty like clockwork. That's when Mr. Butler left the ranch alone in his fancy sportscar. Three hours later he'd come home and go straight to his bedroom." Elsie paused. "Except that one night."

David jotted a note.

Daisy caught her bottom lip between her teeth. Her mom had never mentioned Rose entertaining a man every Friday.

Elsie's eyes seemed to glaze over. "When he hadn't returned by seven-fifteen, I thought maybe he'd been tied up in traffic. I couldn't relax until I knew he was okay, so I waited by my bedroom window—the one that faced the driveway between the house and the garage. Seven-thirty came and went. I figured there had to be a reasonable explanation. Still, I couldn't help but worry. Then, a few minutes before eight, Mr. Butler drove up and parked in the garage. Needless to say, I thought everything was okay."

Elsie poured herself a glass of lemonade and took a long sip. "Until a big black car pulled beside the garage. After Mr. Butler climbed into the back seat, that car took off lickety-split across the backyard. I ran to the other window and watched it drive all the way to the edge of the woods. After the headlights went off, no matter how hard I tried, I couldn't see what was going on. At some point that car drove back to the driveway and let Mr. Butler out. Then it took off."

David poised his pen over his notepad. "What kind of car was it?"

"All I know is it had four doors and dark windows so I couldn't see who was inside." She hesitated.

"Had you seen the car before that night?"

"Not as far as I can remember. But then, most cars look alike. Except, there was something about that car." She squeezed her eyes closed for a brief moment, then shrugged. "Whatever I saw is long gone from my memory."

David made a notation. "What happened after the car left?"

"Nothing. Until the next day when Mr. Butler called me to his office. I was as jittery as a mouse in a roomful of hungry kitties. During all those years, he barely acknowledged my existence, much less invited me to join him in his private space."

"What did you do?" asked Daisy.

"What could I do? I walked into his office. He was leaning against his desk, smiling. Not one of those I'm-glad-you're-here kind of grins. But a sinister look under a cold-as-ice stare. That's when I knew he'd noticed me watching out the window the night before."

Daisy cringed. "Did he ask questions or offer an explanation? Or threaten you in any way?"

"That depends on what you'd call a threat. Mr. Butler told me he no longer needed my services. Talk about a shocker. But then he picked a check off his desk and dangled it in front of me. He said, 'I trust paying off your mortgage will satisfy your curiosity and secure your discretion.' I couldn't believe it when he handed over a hundred grand *more* than I needed to pay off our house and cover the taxes. Harold and I debated for a month whether or not to cash what we called hush money. Even though I assumed I'd witnessed something sinister, I had no idea what. So we figured, why not cash it?"

David peered at Daisy for a split second, then turned back to Elsie. "Did you happen to read or hear anything about Rose Fowler?"

"Who?"

"She was a woman who entertained men for a living until she disappeared thirty-five years ago."

"Oh my word." Elsie gasped. "Do you think Mr. Butler had something to do with her going missing?"

Harold's face paled. "Are we in any kind of trouble for not reporting what Elsie witnessed that night?"

"Report what?" Daisy leaned forward. "That a car drove across Curtis Butler's lawn in the dark? I'm an attorney, and I assure you both you've done nothing wrong. Besides everything you've shared will remain between the four of us."

Elsie patted her husband's arm. "Daisy's right, dear. We have nothing to worry about." She turned to David. "I suppose it's time someone finds out what happened that night. I'm not saying Mr. Butler did anything illegal, mind you. But if he has, well, even rich people eventually have to pay for their wrongdoings."

"Indeed they do." David closed his notepad. "Now do you mind if I enjoy one of those delicious cookies?"

"Be my guest." Elsie removed the napkin and pushed the plate to David.

After chatting about Elsie's garden for nearly an hour, Daisy and David returned to his truck. "I'd have never guessed we'd learn more from Curtis's housekeeper than anyone else we've talked to."

David backed out of the driveway. "As I mentioned earlier, if you want to learn the inside scoop about a wealthy family, talk to the household staff. Now we need to find out if your mom remembers anything about her mother's Friday schedule."

Poppy's heart swelled with joy as she fingered the new plaque set on the pedestal beside the hybrid rosebush. *The poppy rose, created with love to honor my beautiful wife.*

Danny strolled to her side and slipped his arm around her shoulders. "In a couple more seasons, the poppy rose will thrive in dozens of Savannah gardens."

She patted his hand. "Created by a wonderful husband and a former army guy who become a master horticulturist."

"Turns out trading guns and grenades for spades and shovels was a smart move." He nodded toward the front door. "Are you expecting David and Daisy?"

"No. Why?"

"His truck's coming up the driveway."

"Maybe they have some news." Poppy rushed out and met Daisy as she stepped out of the truck. "What a pleasant surprise." She pulled off her gardening gloves. "I hope you'll stay for supper."

Pansy dashed over and tugged on Daisy's sleeve. "Do you wanna see the pretty flower Danny made? He calls it the poppy rose."

"Oh my gosh, Mom, what a perfect gift." Daisy leaned close. "And deliciously romantic."

Sensing a flush was seconds from creeping across her cheeks, Poppy fanned her face with her straw hat. "About supper, I'm fixing your dad's favorite."

"We'd love to stay *and* see the poppy rose. But first David and I need to ask you and Aunt Pansy a few questions."

"Well then, let's go have us a meeting in our kitchen slash conference room."

"I'll fix a plate of cookies." Pansy raced ahead with Boots scampering behind her.

David laughed as they made their way to the back porch. "Soft, delicious, *and* homemade."

"Always." After climbing onto the porch and hanging her hat on a hook, Poppy settled across the kitchen table from Daisy and David. "You have questions about Mama's case, don't you?"

Daisy nodded while setting her sunglasses on the table. "We need you and Aunt Pansy to think back and remember if Rose entertained a client the same time every Friday afternoon."

What new information had they come across? Poppy pinched the bridge of her nose. Was there something special about Fridays that would trigger a memory?

"Pancakes and Inspector Gadget."

Poppy stared at her sister. Where did that comment come from?

Daisy eyed Poppy, then her aunt. "What do you remember?"

"Me and Poppy watched cartoons every Saturday morning while Mama slept late. After she woke up, she fixed us pancakes."

Poppy snapped her fingers. "Pansy's right. Mama always slept late after entertaining clients." She noted Daisy exchanging glances with David before catching her eye.

"Maybe you and I should take a walk, Mom."

Pansy tilted her head. "What secret about Mama are you gonna tell Poppy?"

Daisy's brows raised, then pinched. "Well, I—"

"I remembered 'bout Fridays." Pansy mirrored Daisy's posture. "So, how come you don't wanna tell me the secret?"

Poppy's eyes met Pansy's. She'd asked a valid question. Even if Daisy and David had discovered something devastating about Curtis, was it right to keep Pansy in the dark? "It's okay if we stay here."

"Whatever you think is best." Daisy leaned forward and crossed her arms on the table. "Earlier today David and I met with Curtis's former housekeeper."

Tension gripped the back of Poppy's neck and crept down her spine as Daisy relayed Elsie's revelations. She caught a glimpse of Pansy's bland expression. What was she thinking, and how much did she understand? Maybe she should have insisted on a walk.

The moment Daisy finished, Pansy tilted her head again and stroked her chin. "Mama's body was in that black car."

Daisy stared at her aunt.

David leaned forward. "Is that what you think?"

"Uh-huh. That's how come Papa gave Elsie that money, so she wouldn't tell anybody."

David reached across and patted Pansy's arm. "You are one smart lady."

"Could I be an investigator like you?"

"Absolutely. In fact, whenever Daisy and I learn something new, we'll run the facts by you."

"So, I can tell you what they mean?"

Pansy's banter eased the tension gripping Poppy's spine for a moment. If her sister was right, one mystery remained. Did Curtis take her mama's life, or was he covering for the actual killer? And if that was the case, who and why?

Chapter Twenty-Seven

A s dawn eased into Wednesday morning, rumbling thunder and rain pelting the window nudged Daisy awake. She yawned, then padded from the guest room to the master-bedroom window facing the side driveway and peered down at David's camper parked a mere six feet from her deck. A light shone in the window beside his dinette. Had the rain assailing his roof roused him, or had he awakened early to write another chapter? Either way, last night she'd promised to reach out to him before she fixed her first cup of coffee. After showering and donning jeans and a sweater, Daisy meandered to the kitchen and sent David a text. *"Saw your light. Are you writing?"*

"Finishing second page in new chapter. Ready for your first cup?"

"Depends." Daisy unlocked the back door. *"Are you ready to brave the storm?"*

"What storm?"

Before she could finish typing a response, David dashed in and brushed water droplets off his shoulders.

"Goodness gracious, don't you own an umbrella?"

"Didn't need one. Coffee's another story, especially if it comes with a slice of Pansy's coffee cake."

"I suggest we balance caffeine and sugar with a healthy dose of protein before we attempt to solve our number-one case."

"You mean our only case."

"At least for the moment." Daisy dropped a pod in the coffee maker, then removed a carton of eggs from the fridge. "Fried or scrambled?"

"Scrambled, and how about letting me do the honors?"

"Hmm." She tapped her finger to her cheek. "Should I trust a good-looking guy who doesn't use an umbrella to scramble my eggs?"

"The same guy who fixed sea scallops and angel-hair pasta for your family before Christmas?"

"Now that you mention it, I do recall the delicious meal he prepared. I suppose scrambled eggs aren't that much more difficult."

"Piece of cake, or should I say, coffee cake."

"Yeah, I should trust him." Daisy patted his cheek. "I'll take two."

He winked. "Coming right up."

While David hummed and whipped up breakfast, a warm sensation engulfed Daisy. While watching him work, she imagined spending every morning playfully bantering, followed by evenings sharing intimate moments. Could they continue working as a team when their relationship evolved?

"Scrambled eggs, light and fluffy." David glanced over his shoulder. "Unless you plan to eat right out of the pan, we'll need a couple of plates."

Daisy blinked. "Right." After plating the eggs and coffee cake, they settled across from each other at the dining-room table. She tasted. "Amazing."

"The eggs or the short-order cook?"

"I'd say both."

His eyes twinkled above his smile. "In that case, Counselor, would you object if Investigator slash Chef David cooks breakfast for you every morning? Rain or shine?"

"Depends. Are scrambled eggs your only early-morning specialty?"

"Hardly."

"Well then, all objections are overruled."

A half hour after finishing breakfast and cleaning the kitchen, they refilled their coffee, returned to the dining room, and sat catercorner to each other. Daisy lifted her phone off the table. "Are you ready to tackle Lambert and Butler's number-one priority?"

"Phone call number two?"

"Three. I called a second time last night. Hopefully, different hours will lead to different results." Daisy tapped Cynthia Evans' number. "It's going to voicemail. Again." She left a message, then set her phone facedown on the table. "Other than waiting for the certified letter to arrive at Curtis's door, what's our plan B if Cynthia continues to ignore my calls?"

"We could show up at the ranch and refuse to leave until Curtis grants us an audience."

"Basil and I failed both times we tried that tactic. Although that approach did work for me and Dad. I suppose because Dad threatened to expose the truth about Bobby's death if he refused to talk to us."

David drummed his fingers on the table. "Which is why we mailed that letter yesterday. Shock value."

"*If* Curtis signs for it and *if* he bothers to read it."

"Unless he's too sick to respond, curiosity will compel him to accept and read it."

"Assuming you're right, and assuming Curtis contacts us, we need to discuss our strategy."

"I'm one step ahead of you."

Daisy's eyes remained trained on David while he laid out a plan. When he finished she trilled her lips. "In other words, you want to give him enough rope to incriminate himself?"

"Cornered culprits react."

Flurries of dread built up inside Daisy as she slumped back in her chair. "Do you ever fear for your safety when you confront suspects?"

His eyes locked on hers. "You don't have to worry about your grandfather hurting us."

"Because he's old and frail."

David shook his head. "Because you're his flesh and blood."

Daisy's eyes probed. "What makes you think Curtis gives a flip about me or anyone else in my family?"

"That day back in December when Danny introduced your family to Curtis, I recognized something in your grandfather's eyes—"

"Disgust? Hatred?"

"Regret. In those few moments, however brief, I believe Curtis understood what he had missed."

"Are you suggesting that the man who rejected his sons and had a hand in my grandmother's death experienced a pang of conscience?"

"Yes, because underneath his hard-nosed, icy persona beats the heart of a father."

Daisy slumped back and recalled the moment her dad introduced Pansy as Curtis's daughter. His expression softened when she knelt in front of him and called him Papa. "I suppose facing eternity can melt even the hardest heart."

"And sometimes prompt a deathbed confession."

The front doorbell chimed. Daisy's eyes widened. "Curtis wouldn't show up at my front door, would he?"

"Not a chance."

Daisy flipped her phone faceup. "Then who would endure the rain, at nine-thirty?"

"Do you want to play a game of who's ringing my bell?" David chuckled. "Or should we answer and find out?"

"Come on, Sherlock, let's go solve the mystery." Daisy rushed to the foyer with David following close behind. She opened the door and faced a disheveled woman sporting a black eye and holding a young girl's hand. "Can I help you?"

"I think we need a lawyer."

Daisy peered around her at the umbrella lying on the porch and beyond to the empty driveway. "How'd you get here?"

"We walked."

"How far."

The woman shivered. "Couple of miles."

"Oh my goodness." Daisy stepped aside. "Please, come in. Grab a couple of towels from the linen closet, David."

"I'm on it." David dashed upstairs and returned by the time the strangers had settled at the dining-room table. He wrapped a towel around the girl's shoulders and bent to her eye level. "Are you hungry?"

She nodded.

"Then, you've come to the right place because we saved a piece of yummy coffee cake for a very special guest. Why don't you come to the kitchen with me while your mommy and Ms. Butler talk?"

The girl looked up at her mother, her eyes questioning.

"It's okay, honey. You go ahead."

David straightened and held the child's hand. "Does your mommy drink coffee?"

"Uh-huh."

"Well then, we'll fix her a nice hot cup of coffee and you a cup of delicious cocoa."

The moment David led the child away, Daisy faced the woman. "What's your name?"

"Ellie." Her eyes remained lowered. "I heard you were a lawyer from New York."

That bit of news didn't take long to spread. "Yes, but I'm not licensed to practice law in Georgia."

Ellie's chin quivered.

Daisy touched her arm. "Tell me what's wrong, and maybe I can help you."

Her shoulders curled forward. "When my husband finds out we're gone...we snuck out before he woke up."

"Did he give you the black eye?"

She nodded.

"That wasn't the first time he hit you, was it?"

She shook her head.

"The first thing we need to do is report this to the sheriff—"

"No." Ellie's face turned ashen. "He goes hunting with one of the deputies."

Daisy's heart ached for the woman. "My brother's a student at the police academy. Will you give me permission to call him?"

She hesitated.

"He'll know how to help us without involving the sheriff's department."

David peered around the corner. "How do you take your coffee, Ellie?"

"Why don't you go in the kitchen and fix your coffee any way you want while I call my brother." Daisy patted her arm. "You can trust me."

Her eyes met Daisy's. "Thank you."

The moment Ellie disappeared around the corner, Daisy grabbed her phone and pressed Basil's number.

He answered on the second ring. "What's up, noodle-noggin?"

"Are you ready for your first case as a future law-enforcement officer?"

"Did you rob a bank—"

"I'm not kidding." Daisy explained. "I'm guessing a domestic-violence issue."

"Some of the most dangerous situations. Don't let her leave. I'll be there as fast as I can."

During the following forty-five minutes, David and Daisy entertained the child while reassuring the mother. When Basil arrived, his calming approach led Ellie to allow him to take photos of her injuries, which extended beyond her eye. After a round of gentle persuasion, he also convinced her to sign a statement confirming the abuse. "You've taken the first step toward assuring you and your daughter's safety. The second is getting you to a safe place where your husband can't find you. I can take you to a secret shelter for women who deserve to live without fear."

Ellie stared at Basil, then faced Daisy.

"My brother's one of the good guys." She placed her hand on the young woman's shoulder. "You can trust him."

Ellie pulled her daughter into her arms. "When can we go?"

"Right now." Basil pocketed her statement, then kissed his sister's cheek. "Calling me was the best move you could have made."

"Thank you for responding."

Basil lifted the child into his arms and walked beside her mother as they made their way to the front door. "Are you and your mommy ready for a new adventure?"

David dropped onto the chair beside Daisy. "Did I just witness an ex-New York corporate lawyer unofficially yet expertly handle her first general-practice case?"

"Even though I didn't earn a dime, helping Ellie and her daughter was more gratifying than landing Curtis's multimillion-dollar account. I understand why attorneys take pro-bono cases." Daisy tilted her head and smiled at David. "Is that why you're drawn to difficult cold cases? Because solving them is personally satisfying?"

"In so many ways." He leaned close. "Especially now."

Daisy's breath quickened. Was David seconds away from kissing her?

He hesitated. "Your phone just pinged a text."

Terrible timing. She could ignore it, but what if Basil was trying to contact her? "Who's it from?"

David reached for her phone. "Cynthia Evans. Curtis wants to meet us at his ranch in an hour."

"Are you serious?" Daisy's pulse accelerated. "Maybe we won't need a plan B after all."

"Shock value paid off."

Chapter Twenty-Eight

David parked behind the black Tesla Daisy had seen during her three previous visits. She peered beyond the stone wall surrounding the front patio. "At least Curtis's bodyguard isn't waiting to intimidate us."

"Big difference between a surprise visit and a formal invitation." David pocketed his notepad, then rounded the front of his truck and opened the passenger door. "If luck is on our side, we're about to take a giant step toward solving this case."

"Hopefully in less than an hour." They made their way to the steps and climbed up to the patio.

The front door opened before they knocked. Cynthia stepped out and pulled the door closed behind her.

Was she denying them access? Daisy squared her shoulders. "As my grandfather requested, we're here for an appointment."

"He's not here—"

Daisy's eyes narrowed? "We're not leaving until you grant us access."

"Do you always jump to conclusions, Ms. Butler?" Cynthia's features tightened. "He's waiting for you in the stables. You can drive over."

"Thank you, Ms. Evans." David slid his arm around Daisy's shoulders as they returned to his truck. "First rule in effective investigation, maintain composure to keep the upper hand."

"The same principle applies to attorneys who win cases." Daisy cringed at her snarky tone. "Sorry, David, I didn't mean to come across as sarcastic."

"I know you didn't." His eyes radiated tenderness. "Do you need a moment?"

She forced her shoulders to relax. "I'm okay now."

"Well then, Counselor, it's time for the Lambert-Butler team to find out what our primary suspect has to say."

Elsie Harrison's revelation played in Daisy's mind as they drove around the side of the house and eased past the four-car garage separated from the house by a wide driveway. She peered over her shoulder at two windows facing the garage. From which one had Elsie witnessed a crime? Would Curtis have the courage to reveal the truth about the night Rose disappeared?

By the time they reached the stable, Daisy's palms had moistened and a dull ache attacked the base of her skull. Inside the pristine space, honey-colored paneled ceiling and walls, rustic chandeliers, and painted concrete floors created an air of elegance and wealth. At the far end of the building, Curtis leaned on his cane with one hand and stroked a horse's muzzle with the other.

Daisy counted seven horses as they passed stalls lining both sides of the building. When they reached the last stall on the left, Curtis's eyes remained trained on his horse. "The newest member of my equine family. She's from a long line of champion show horses."

David inched a step closer. "She's a beauty all right."

"My wife never understood my obsession with these magnificent animals, or that this ranch was my refuge, and these horses my prize possessions." He scoffed. "But then, like my old man, she never much understood *anything* about me." He faced Daisy, his eyes lightning fierce. "Why did you show up at my Savannah house and leave my wife your business card?"

She blinked. *Maintain composure and choose your words carefully.* "She's my grandmother. I wanted to meet her."

"Did you for once second stop to consider how an unexpected knock on her door from a New York attorney might upset her?"

Why? Because Margaret Butler had no idea she was a grandmother or because she was afraid of lawyers? "That wasn't my intention."

"I was with Daisy that day, Mr. Butler." David's voice came across as confident and measured. "She made it clear to the woman who answered the door that she was Mrs. Butler's granddaughter."

Curtis's eyes narrowed. "You have no idea the hornet's nest that little incident stirred up."

Over one business card? Something didn't add up. Daisy wiped her damp hands on her slacks. "I'll be happy to call your wife and reaffirm my intentions."

"You've done enough damage." Curtis glared at her. "For your own good, you need to leave her alone." He broke eye contact.

Daisy assessed her grandfather's profile. What did 'for your own good' mean, and when would he comment about her letter?

Curtis removed an apple from his sweater pocket and held it out for his mare. "Now that we have an understanding, you can show yourselves out."

"Since we're here—" David removed his notepad from his back pocket. "I have a few questions to run by you. First, what's your response to Daisy's letter?"

Curtis's brow pinched. "What letter?"

Daisy exchanged glances with David, then focused on her grandfather. "The one I mailed yesterday, certified for delivery today."

"I don't have the slightest idea what you're talking about."

Was he telling the truth or using a well-crafted stalling technique?

"Next question." David flipped open his notepad. "What can you tell us about Elsie Harrison?"

Curtis continued stroking his mare's muzzle. "She worked for me years ago."

"As what?"

"My housekeeper."

"What prompted you to pay off her mortgage?"

"She was a loyal employee."

Daisy remained focused on Curtis's profile. Was 'loyal' his definition of silenced? Why didn't he order them to leave or refuse to answer David's questions? Because he wanted to maintain the upper hand, or was he waiting to hear more information?

The mare whinnied and bobbed her muzzle.

"I'm curious." David clicked his pen. "Why did you choose Friday afternoons to rendezvous with Rose Fowler?"

If Daisy had blinked, she would have missed Curtis's momentary flinch. He lifted his chin and faced David, his eyes cold and hard. "Over the course of three decades, memories fade and details become scrambled. A smart investigator would do well to keep random comments made by an old woman in perspective." He removed his phone from his pants pocket and tapped the screen. "My bodyguard is on the way over."

David kept his eyes trained on Curtis while snapping his notepad shut. "Thank you for your time."

"Leave the way you came in." Curtis turned his head away and coughed.

David held Daisy's elbow as they headed back down the concrete walkway. A golfcart driven by Curtis's bodyguard pulled into the stable and sped past them as if they were invisible. When they reached the exit, Daisy glanced over her shoulder. The golfcart was gone. "We went toe-to-toe with Curtis, and he didn't crack."

"Doesn't matter. His clipped responses clarified one important point. We touched a nerve."

Daisy's brows furrowed then released. "Since he didn't repeat the story about Rose dying from an accidental fall, he likely suspects we're on to something."

"Excellent observation, Counselor."

"Maybe we should have told him about the shell casing."

"Too soon. He needs time to mull over what he heard today." David opened the passenger door. "One more fact Curtis's silence confirmed. He's covering for someone who has clout. We have to find out who."

"How? We've already interviewed everyone on your list."

"There is one person we haven't questioned."

"Who?"

"Your dad."

Daisy stared wide-eyed. "You're kidding, right?"

"I'm dead serious."

"During my entire childhood, Dad never uttered a word about his family. Not to mention the fact that we were forbidden to mention Curtis's name in his presence. So what makes you think he'll talk to us now?"

"I'm counting on his demand for justice."

Poppy stuffed her gardening gloves in her pockets and rushed from the greenhouse the moment Daisy climbed from David's truck. "The second time in two days you've stopped by for a surprise visit. Are you looking for an invitation to supper, or do you have news about Mama's case?"

Daisy brushed a gnat away from her face. "We drove straight here from Curtis's ranch."

Poppy's eyes widened. "Did he tell you the truth about Mama's death or explain what happened that night?"

"Not exactly." David relayed their conversation. "Did you tell Danny about Elsie's revelations?"

Poppy nodded. "Last night after supper."

"How did he react?"

"He walked out without saying a word and didn't come back to the house until after eleven. This morning he ate breakfast in the greenhouse."

"A good indication Dad's seething with anger." Daisy pressed her fingers to the base of her skull to help ease the escalating pain. "We're hoping he can shed some light on Curtis's relationships. Will you ask him to talk to me and David?"

"That'll take some doing." Poppy removed her straw hat and swiped her fingers across her brow. "You might as well wait in the kitchen, and don't be surprised if he refuses."

"He spent two years creating a rose for you, Mom. Believe me, you have way more influence over Dad than you realize."

"I'll do my best." Poppy returned to the greenhouse and spotted Danny sitting at his desk. Now what? Should she ease into a conversation, maybe win him over with compliments? Or come straight to the point? She breathed deeply and closed the distance to his office space.

"What'd Daisy and David want?" His attention remained focused on his computer screen.

Beating around the bush wouldn't do. "I want you to come with me, Danny."

He looked up. "What's going on?"

Poppy squared her shoulders and looked him straight in the eye. "We need you to help us solve Mama's case."

Silence enfolded the moment.

She held his gaze. "Please."

He blinked. "All right."

Poppy released a deep, gratifying sigh as Danny skirted his makeshift desk and gripped her elbow. Maybe Daisy was right. All she'd needed to do was insist.

When they walked into the kitchen, Danny pulled Poppy's chair out, then sat beside her rather than his place at the head of the table. She caught Daisy's eye and smiled. Her daughter winked. *She understood.*

Danny scooted his chair closer to the table. "What do you want to know?"

David opened his notepad. "Everything you remember about Curtis's relationships."

"What kind of relationships?"

"Friends, business associates, public officials. Anyone who comes to mind."

Danny crossed his arms and tapped his biceps. "When we were kids, Bobby and I mostly kept to ourselves. We seldom ate with the family and never attended one of our parents' parties. Except that one time. The night Bobby died." He closed his eyes and pinched the bridge of his nose.

Poppy's heart ached for him. She placed her hand on his thigh and silently prayed for God to give the man she loved the strength to continue.

Danny lowered his hand. His eyes met hers. He blinked. His brow furrowed, then released, as if a long-lost memory had broken through a barrier. "That night, before I ushered Bobby away, Curtis grabbed my arm. I remember the look of hatred in his eyes and his sinister grin." Danny faced David. "And the words he spat—'how dare you embarrass me in front of the senator. He's one of the few men whose friendship I value.'"

"Do you remember the senator's name?"

"Afraid not."

Poppy sprang from her chair. "I'll be right back." She scurried to her refuge and retrieved the Butler Family Legacy. Flurries of hope fluttered in her chest as she dashed back to the kitchen. She set the scrapbook on the table and flipped through pages until she found what she was looking for. She tapped her finger on a newspaper clipping of Curtis shaking a man's hand. "That's the senator." She pushed the scrapbook across the table

David eyed the story then read the headline aloud. "*Wealthy Business Owner Throws Support Behind Political Newcomer.* "According to the article, Curtis's endorsement was instrumental in his friend surging in the polls."

"There's another picture of Curtis clasping that man's hand the night he was elected to the state senate."

"Talk about a person higher up the food chain." David looked up. "At the very least, he's one more person of interest."

Poppy's lungs filled with deep, satisfying breaths. Little did she know the first time she'd clipped a newspaper story about Danny's family that her secret scrapbook might one day lead to justice for her mother.

Chapter Twenty-Nine

Daisy set her coffee cup on her desk and scrolled through David's laptop document. "You must have stayed up all night to pull that much material together in fewer than eighteen hours."

"I called it quits at two. The good news about politicians is the massive amounts of information available. Especially one who served in the state senate for twelve terms. Two years after he died, his son followed in his footsteps and was elected by a landslide. He's still serving. Other than typical political opponent slanders, both father and son seem squeaky clean."

"What'd you dig up about the senator's relationship with Curtis?"

"They both grew up in Savannah, but as far as I can tell their paths first crossed when they became fraternity brothers at Princeton."

"How close were they after graduation?"

"Close enough to serve as groomsmen for each other's weddings. Maybe because they were both big-time horse enthusiasts. In fact, the senator—and now his son—boarded his steeds at Curtis's stable."

"Which means they most likely spent a lot of time together."

"True. But more importantly—" David scrolled to a document page and tapped the screen. "The senator was instrumental in passing a piece of legislation that favored business and added a ton of money to Curtis's bottom line."

"Tit for tat?"

"And powerful motivation for Curtis to protect him—if he was in any way involved in Rose's death."

Daisy brushed a fleck of dust off her desk. "We'd be foolish to question anyone in the senator's family based on mere speculation. Which means our only alternative is pressuring Curtis."

"A losing battle, unless we uncover evidence of a connection between the senator and Rose."

"After all these years, fat chance of that happening." Daisy puffed her cheeks and blew a long stream of air. "Somehow we have to appeal to Curtis's sense of morality."

"Or hope for a deathbed confession."

Daisy propped her elbow on the desk and rested her cheek on her fist. "Have any of your cold-case investigations ended without a resolution?"

"Just one, at least in part. I managed to prove the only suspect couldn't possibly be guilty. Turns out that was one of my most commercially successful books. Seems even readers of real-life crime stories prefer happy endings."

"What's your prediction for the book you're writing about my grandmother?"

"Definitely a best seller."

"With a happy ending?"

"Absolutely." David paused and nodded toward the window. "It appears your new furniture has arrived."

Daisy peered at the truck easing up the driveway. "Right on schedule."

"Good time for me to go back to work and stay out of the way." David closed his laptop. "Call if you need me." He headed to the back of the house while Daisy stepped out onto the porch.

An hour after the driver raised the truck's rear door, Daisy stood on the new area rug in the master bedroom and admired her king-sized, upholstered sleigh bed. The pale blue comforter that had arrived the day before was the perfect complement to the champagne color. She draped a throw across the arm of an overstuffed settee and imagined sitting with David at the end of a long day, holding hands.

Daisy banished the image, meandered to the living room, and fingered her sofa's off-white upholstery. A silver tray and array of crystal candle holders she'd found at Maddie's store held center stage on the glass coffee table. Contemporary furniture, Agnes's antique area rug, and thrift-store finds created the perfect eclectic setting. Maybe she should paint the walls a warm shade of gray. She'd figure that out tomorrow. Tonight she and David could open a bottle of wine from Willy's Convenience Store and enjoy a cozy fire in her newly decorated living room.

She strolled to her parlor and settled in her new executive desk chair facing the bay window. Her mind drifted to Basil's update on Ellie and her daughter, now secure in a women's shelter. How many people would find their way to her doorstep if she decided to test the waters as a general-practice attorney? A handful? Dozens?

Startled by her phone's ringtone, she stared wide-eyed at the screen. "Hey, Michael, are you surviving New York's frigid weather?"

"Well enough. What about you?"

"Georgia's winters are similar to New York's springs. Not that I'm bragging." Was he calling as a friend? "What's up?"

"Are you sitting down?"

This obviously wasn't a social call. "What's going on, Michael?" A grapefruit-sized knot gripped Daisy's gut as she listened, questioned, and listened again. By the time the call ended, the tension in her neck had crept to the base of her skull and exploded in pain. She scurried to the kitchen and downed three aspirin, then made a beeline to David's camper.

"How's the new furniture?" He looked up from his laptop. His smile faded. "What's wrong?"

"We have a huge problem." She trudged in and dropped onto the dinette bench.

David slid across from her. "What kind of problem?"

"We're being sued for slander and libel."

"Who's we?"

"You and me."

"By Curtis?"

"His wife."

"Margaret Butler?" His brows arched. "How'd you find out?"

"A friend gave Michael the heads-up."

"What's the basis for the suit?"

"Michael didn't say." Daisy trilled her lips. "My own grandmother…"

"We'll need a good attorney."

"We already have one." Daisy hesitated. "Michael volunteered to represent us pro bono."

A flicker of a frown creased David's forehead. "Since his firm represents your grandfather's companies, isn't that a conflict of interest?"

"Curtis isn't named in the suit—"

"Maybe not." David drummed his fingers on the table. "But it's likely he had a hand in your grandmother's decision."

"Are you thinking Curtis told her about our investigation?"

"Unless one of our suspects contacted her, that's the most plausible explanation."

Daisy slumped back. "She wouldn't have confronted Curtis if I hadn't left my business card with her housekeeper."

"You can't blame yourself—"

"Who else should I blame?"

"No one. We'll deal with it. Is Michael a good attorney?"

"Based on his reputation, he's one of the best. He's flying down to meet with us next week. In the meantime he advised avoiding contact with either grandparent."

"Which means our investigation just came to a screeching halt. We need to tell your parents."

"Later tonight." Daisy faced the window. A squirrel perched on her deck railing nibbled an acorn. A lawsuit wouldn't exist if Pansy hadn't mailed her story about Rose's disappearance. Daisy swallowed against the tightness in her throat. And David wouldn't have found his way to her parents' doorstep. "I suppose a road encumbered by seemingly unsurmountable obstacles makes arriving at the final destination that much sweeter."

David reached across the table and interlaced his fingers with hers. "We'll overcome every roadblock and celebrate every victory as a team."

"Lambert and Butler investigative team extraordinaire." Daisy managed a smile. *Or maybe one day Lambert and Lambert.*

Hours after the sun had set and Pansy had turned in for the night, the front doorbell rang. Alarm bells resounded in Poppy's head the moment Danny led Daisy and David into the front room. She bolted off the sofa. "What's wrong? Did something happen to Lilly or Basil—"

"Everyone's fine, Mom. We have some news best delivered in person." Daisy settled on a wingback. David hiked his hip on the chair's arm.

Poppy's brows pinched as she dropped back onto the sofa.

Danny sat beside her. "News about what?"

Daisy glanced at David then crossed her leg over her knee and pumped her foot. "Michael Warner called me earlier today."

Icy fingers of dread crept up Poppy's spine as her daughter's revelation unfolded. How could a mother—a grandmother—treat her own flesh and blood with such contempt? Did an empty space exist in the woman's chest where a heart belonged?

Daisy's foot stilled. "Michael's preparing a defense."

Danny's fingers curled into fists. His nostrils flared. "My mother will do anything to protect her social status." He spat the word *mother* as if it had burned the flesh off his tongue. "I won't let that heartless woman destroy you, Daisy, or anyone else I love." He bolted to his feet and stalked out slamming, the front door behind him.

"I can't imagine the pain..." Daisy's voice faltered. "Maybe we shouldn't have told Dad."

Poppy swallowed against the ache erupting in the back of her throat. "You and David were right to come here tonight."

"Do you want us to stay and keep you company?"

"Thank you, honey, but your dad and I need time alone."

"Are you sure?"

"Positive."

David stood and held his hand out for Daisy. "We're available if you need us, Poppy."

"I'll be fine." After Daisy and David drove away, Poppy dashed to her room and yanked a jacket from the closet. Four months ago she would have crawled into bed and waited for Danny to deal with his emotions. Not tonight, and not ever again. Whether or not he would admit it, the man she loved needed her.

She rushed through the kitchen and out to the backyard. Was Danny wandering around in the dark greenhouse, or had he sought refuge someplace else? A hunch sent her ambling away from the building, past her sanctuary. Five feet behind the arbor swing, Poppy pressed her hand to her chest. Had Danny chosen their private space because he wanted her to find him? She settled beside him, then laced her fingers with his and gazed at the star-studded winter sky. Was he in the mood to talk, or would he prefer to simply sit in silence?

She waited.

Minutes passed.

An owl hooted in the distance. A shooting star streaked across the sky.

Danny's shoulders stiffened. "Rose Fowler sold her body to men because she loved her children. Margaret Butler barely tolerated her sons because she craved a place in society for her daughters. Your mother was a kind and caring woman. My mother was and still is cold and heartless."

"You have every right to feel angry and hurt, sweetheart. But somehow you have to find it in your heart to forgive your mother."

"That woman doesn't deserve forgiveness."

Poppy's heart ached for him. "Forgiveness is as important for the giver as it is for the receiver. Without compassion and mercy, anger festers and eats away at the soul."

"Where was Margaret's compassion the night Bobby disrupted her party?" He pulled his hand away. "Or after he took his own life, and she declared him dead to the family? You tell me..." His voice faltered. "Where was her compassion?"

Poppy choked back tears. What Danny needed now was her support and understanding. She slid her hand around his bicep, leaned on his shoulder, and silently prayed for God to help him find a way to move beyond his pain and anger to forgiveness.

Chapter Thirty

Poppy followed Pansy into the vacant store and marveled at the progress Andy had made. A few more weekends and he'd have the place transformed. Then what? There was far more to opening and managing a bakery than preparing a physical space. What about the adjacent stores? Would anyone walk into a bakery between two boarded-up eyesores? How would people react if news about Margaret Butler suing her granddaughter leaked?

"How much should I charge people for my cakes?" Pansy wiped a smudge off the front window. "Ten dollars? Twenty?"

"Lots of factors that go into pricing, sweetie. Think of it like Danny determining the cost of growing plants before he sets prices for his customers."

"We have to figure out how much the flour and eggs and sugar costs."

"Plus overhead."

"What's overhead?"

"Operating costs. Like electricity and water for the greenhouse and fuel for the delivery trucks."

"We'll need a computer."

"Plus someone with business experience to handle all the details."

Pansy plucked a nail off the floor. "I know how to add and subtract."

"True, but you'll be too busy baking to spend time working on financial details."

"When I move in upstairs, I'll have lots of time to bake." Pansy set the nail on the windowsill, then dashed to the back of the store and up the stairs.

Footsteps sounded overhead as Poppy resisted the urge to follow her sister. At some point she had to begin letting go and trust that God would take care of her.

Pansy returned, her face flushed with excitement. She pointed to the ceiling. "Know what's right up there?"

"What?"

"My new bedroom. When can I move my bed and new dresser up there? Maybe tomorrow?"

"We'll talk about moving later." Poppy linked arms with her. "For now we need to head over to Daisy's for lunch." After she locked the door, they walked the block and a half, crossed the street, and headed up the steep driveway.

"There's David's little house." Pansy scooted ahead, climbed onto the porch, and rang the doorbell.

Daisy responded and embraced her aunt. "My first lunch guests and right on time."

"Me and Poppy are gonna buy a computer and add up all the overhead so I know how much to sell my cakes for."

"Good for you, Aunt Pansy. You're thinking like a pro." Daisy released Pansy and hugged Poppy. "What'd you think of Andy's progress?"

"It's moving right along. Too bad the stores on both sides are so run-down."

"They'll be as good as new when Andy finishes the job."

Poppy stepped back and stared at Daisy. "You're paying him to fix all three stores?"

"I can't let Pansy's Bakery remain sandwiched between two boarded-up eyesores?"

"How can you afford to buy this house and those stores and help Pansy, and what are your plans for the other stores?"

"That's a lot of questions for one sentence, Mom." Daisy grinned. "First, securing Curtis's multimillion-dollar account paid a substantial bonus—which also explains why law-firm attorneys charge outrageous hourly rates. About plans for the other stores—with everything going on, the jury's still out. For now, on to the most important question." Daisy linked arms with her aunt. "Do you want the grand tour before or after lunch, Aunt Pansy?"

"Before. I wanna see what David's little house looks like from upstairs."

"You go on up. We'll catch up with you in a few minutes."

The moment Pansy dashed up the stairs, Daisy faced Poppy. "How's Dad dealing with the news about the lawsuit?"

"Except for the night you and David told us, he's refused to talk about it. I know it's eating him up inside."

"Michael plans to spend a few days here—"

"Where's here?"

"We have a lot of work to do—"

"He's staying at your house?"

"His time is valuable, and the closest hotel is forty minutes away. Don't worry, Mom. Michael's a friend."

"Does he know that?"

"Of course he does, and in case you're wondering, David will understand."

Poppy's brows raised. "You haven't told him?"

"Not yet."

"Then what makes you think he'll understand?"

"Because he's reasonable and practical. Anyway, what I was going to say is you need to invite Michael to supper and let him ease Dad's mind about the lawsuit. David and I will take Pansy out to dinner, so the three of you can talk in private."

"Maybe you're right."

"No maybe about it." Daisy linked arms with Poppy. "Now for your first look at your daughter's choice of décor."

"Yoohoo," Maddie's voice rang out as she headed up the driveway.

Daisy shook her head. "Either my tour is on hold, or it's about to include one more participant."

Their friend climbed the porch steps and walked inside. "Have you seen what that sleazy reporter Jones wrote?" She held up a tabloid newspaper folded to page two. "The headline is *Evidence Points to a Local Winning*

Mega Lottery. He claims most of the tickets sold at Willy's were bought by people who live around here." Maddie scratched her head. "How would he know that? Anyway, he quoted lots of anonymous sources and wrote a whole paragraph about a lawyer from a local family buying up half the town. When he asked me point blank if you'd won the lottery, Daisy, I told him your law firm paid you a big bonus. That is the truth, isn't it? Of course it is. Even though he didn't mention your name, this could kickstart you bringing your New York office here."

What was Maddie talking about? Fearing her jaw was seconds from going slack, Poppy pressed her lips tight.

Maddie handed the tabloid to Daisy. "Even though Jones wrote a shameful piece of journalism, it'll likely be a boon for the thrift store. I noticed that furniture truck in your driveway the other day. Did you buy a house full or just a few pieces?"

Daisy folded the tabloid. "Do you mind if I keep this?"

"Be my guest. There's plenty more over at Willy's."

Daisy exchanged a quick glance with Poppy before tucking the paper under her arm. "I was just about to give Mom and Aunt Pansy the grand tour. You're welcome to join us, Maddie."

"Thanks. I imagine your taste is a lot different from old Agnes's..."

Poppy tuned out Maddie's prattle as she followed her daughter and friend to the second floor. How could Daisy remain so calm and collected? What about Danny? How would he react when locals and strangers got it in their heads that Daisy had won the lottery? Would he reveal the truth to protect her? Or would he rip the check to shreds in a public spectacle? How much more would her family be forced to endure?

By the time the tour ended and Maddie returned to the thrift store, Poppy's mind raced with worse-case scenarios. She pulled Daisy aside. "Everyone around here knows you're an attorney. How are you planning to deal with this?"

"Ignore it unless asked, then laugh it off as scandalous journalism." She slid her arm around Poppy's shoulders. "I understand you're upset, and for good reason. Quite frankly, I'd like to smack Jones. However, if anyone in our family lets one smidgen of anger slip out, we'll give credence to that man's claims."

"What about your dad?"

"I'll talk to him. For now, let's enjoy each other's company and discuss my taste in home décor with Aunt Pansy."

Following lunch with her mom and aunt and a conversation with her dad, Daisy headed straight to David's camper. "You were right about Jones." She tossed the tabloid on the dinette table. "The guy's a shameless opportunist."

David shook his head while reading the article. "He's a master at exploitative journalism. No names, lots of innuendo. Unfortunately some people fail to recognize these stories for what they are. Do you understand what this means for you?"

"Yeah." Daisy plopped onto the dinette bench. "An invasion of curiosity seekers."

"Plus, good public relations, if you decide to start your own practice."

"Or enough aggravation to send me racing to another big law firm." She peered around the compact space. How *would* David react to Michael spending two nights in her guest room while he slept in his camper? "I talked to Michael again this morning."

"Anything new?"

"His time is valuable."

"That's not what I'd call a newsflash."

"The thing is—" Why was this so difficult? "Traveling back and forth takes a lot of time...so he's staying here both nights."

David hesitated, then scooted off the bench and grabbed a water bottle from the mini-fridge. "Michael's idea or yours?"

"His, but it makes sense."

"Does it?"

"Are you upset?"

"About a guy you dated who's giving up his valuable time to deal with a nuisance lawsuit, and now he's sleeping down the hall from your bedroom?"

"Michael and I are just friends."

"Does he know that?"

Second time that question had popped up. "You can trust me, David."

"That's not the point." David uncapped the water bottle. "Michael's request to stay in your home suggests he's motivated to represent us based on a lot more than goodwill."

"He's a professional."

"He's also a man, and you're a beautiful, intelligent woman—"

"Who resigned from his family's law firm after he went to bat for me."

"Which makes you that much more fascinating."

Daisy examined her short-clipped fingernails coated with clear polish. Was it possible Michael had an ulterior motive? If that was the case, how could she have missed the cues? Because she wasn't looking. That's how. "Let's assume you're right." She looked up. "I'm not saying you are, but if there's the slightest chance—"

"Slight is the wrong adjective." David downed half the water.

"What makes you so sure?"

"Instinct."

Daisy released a long sigh. "How much more complicated can this lawsuit become?"

"A rhetorical question?"

"Totally."

Back home, Poppy parked in the space David had vacated and peered at Danny loading a shrub onto the delivery truck. He seemed calm. Maybe Daisy hadn't called him. After Pansy and Boots dashed to the back porch, she climbed out and sidled over to his side. "Late delivery?"

"Tomorrow morning." Danny transferred the last plant from the cart to the truck. "Daisy called."

So she did call. "And?"

"We'll deal with it."

"You're not upset?"

He removed his cap and swiped the back of his hand across his brow. "Jones confirmed the reason I haven't cashed that check."

"Did you destroy it?"

"Not yet." He plopped his hat back on his head and pushed the cart toward the greenhouse.

Conflicting emotions unleashed a sinking sensation in Poppy's stomach. She couldn't let that so-called journalist force Danny to make a decision. "Wait." She caught up with him. "We need to talk."

"About what?"

"How you and I are going to handle the latest crisis."

Chapter Thirty-One

At four o'clock Daisy stepped back from the dining-room table and eyed the setup. Paper. Pencils. A water pitcher. Glasses. Her laptop strategically placed beside David's. "Everything we need for a proper attorney-client conference."

David draped his jacket across the back of a chair. "Everything except the defense attorney."

"He's ten minutes out." She slipped a jacket over her untucked long-sleeve shirt and peered down at her jeans and boots. How would Michael interpret her casual attire? As unprofessional? Too friendly? Should she opt for a high-powered attorney look and change into a skirt and heels? What if David was right about Michael's intentions? Better to come across as a Georgia gal rather than a New York attorney. She pulled off her jacket.

"You're as jittery as a pup cornered by a pack of hungry coyotes."

Daisy tossed her jacket on a chair. "I'm not accustomed to sitting on the client side of the table."

"Consider this as a valuable lesson in—"

"Don't you think admitting to Michael that I had failed to reveal the truth about my nonexistent relationship with my grandfather was humility enough?"

"I was going to say empathy."

"Is that what you think I need?"

"I'm just saying that experiencing sitting on the client side of the table will make you a more compassionate attorney."

Daisy crossed her arms. "So being sued or charged with a crime should be a prerequisite for passing the bar?"

"See what I mean?" David's grin reached his eyes. "Lika a typical client, just waiting to meet with your attorney is turning you into a certified basket case."

Daisy tilted her head and dropped her arms to her sides. "You really are a top-notch investigator."

"Was there ever any doubt?"

She mirrored his smile. "Maybe a smidgen."

"Are you giving me a lesson in humility?"

Daisy patted his cheek. "Empathy, honey. Empathy."

David laughed. "There's the confident, feisty gal I love." The doorbell chimed. "And just in time."

"Thank you."

He winked. "My pleasure. Now go greet our esteemed defense lawyer."

Daisy rushed to the foyer and swung the door open. Relieved to see Michael wearing a casual shirt, sport jacket, and jeans, she stepped aside. "Welcome back to my neck of the woods."

"It's good to see you again." He carried his suitcase inside, then kissed her cheek.

Daisy flinched at the scent of his signature cologne. Had David seen Michael's not-so-professional greeting? "Too bad it's under less than desirable circumstances."

David strolled over and extended his hand. "Daisy and I appreciate you taking the time to represent us."

Michael set his monographed, leather briefcase on the floor and clasped David's hand. "It's the least I could do to thank the brilliant corporate attorney who secured a multimillion dollar account for our law firm."

"Daisy's an amazing woman."

"Which is the reason we fast-tracked her to partner."

David released Michael's hand. "And why I parked my camper in her driveway."

"The fiftieth-floor office we reserved for Daisy is still vacant."

David nodded toward the parlor. "Her new office is on the first floor, *and* it has a fireplace."

Daisy's eyes shifted from David to Michael then back to David. Had she suddenly become the ball in a heated game of romantic ping pong? "If you two guys don't mind, and since your time is limited, Michael, we should cut the chitchat and get down to business."

David nodded. "She's right."

"Yes she is." Michael snatched his briefcase off the floor. "Lead the way, Daisy."

Resisting the urge to roll her eyes, Daisy marched straight to the dining room and pointed to the chair across the table. "That's your place, Michael, so David and I can maintain eye contact with you."

"Perfect client-attorney setup."

What else did he expect?

After pulling out a chair for Daisy, David sat beside her.

Michael set down his briefcase, then took his seat. "The first detail we need to unravel is the reason why Margaret Butler is suing you *both* for slander and libel. Does it have something to do with David's job as an investigative journalist?"

Daisy exchanged glances with David. How much did Michael know, and how much should they tell him?

Michael tapped his fingers on the table. "If I'm going to prepare a winning defense for you two, I need to know everything you're involved in."

David cleared his throat. "I'm investigating the thirty-year-old disappearance of Daisy's maternal grandmother."

"Actually." Daisy caught Michael's eye. "David and are I are working the case together."

"Is Margaret Curtis a suspect?"

"No." Daisy hesitated.

Michael leaned forward and crossed his arms. "What aren't you telling me?"

Daisy swallowed. She had to tell him everything. "David and I believe that Curtis was involved."

"I see." Michael opened his briefcase, removed his phone, and set it in the center of the table. "Do I have permission to record our conversation?"

David seemed to hesitate.

Daisy touched his arm. "It's standard procedure, and I trust Michael."

"All right then."

Michael tapped his phone. "Start at the beginning and cover everything you've done and what you've discovered."

For the next hour, David and Daisy shared details and responded to questions. When they finished, Michael tapped his phone. "Based on the facts, this lawsuit is intended to stop both of you from investigating Rose Fowler's case—" He eyed David. "And preventing you from publishing your book."

"Does Margaret have grounds to win her case?"

"Only if she's able to prove either of you have made or plan to make or write false and defamatory statements about her." Michael poured a glass of water. "Did either of you talk to her about your investigation?"

Daisy shook her head. "We've never talked to her about anything. Fact is, I've never met the woman."

Michael shook his head. "Your father comes from one messed-up family."

Daisy drummed her fingers. "What are you insinuating?"

"Don't take my comment personally, Daisy. I know both your parents and your aunt are amazing people."

"Then what's your point?"

"Family lawsuits are complicated and often based on emotion rather than facts."

"The same goes for most domestic crimes," added David.

Daisy filled her glass. "Now that you two guys have agreed on one point, what's our strategy."

"Tell you what." Michael tossed his phone in his briefcase. "Before we discuss the next steps, I'll treat you both to dinner."

"No need. I have prearranged supper." Daisy scooted to the kitchen and returned with a tray, plates, and napkins. "Gourmet sandwiches from Willy's Convenience Store."

"That'll work, especially with my contribution." Michael walked outside and returned moments later with a bottle of white wine. "All we need are glasses and a corkscrew."

"I'm on it." Daisy returned to the kitchen. Was the wine a gift or proof that Michael had ulterior motives? She'd definitely need to keep her guard up. She returned to the dining room and handed over the corkscrew. "Did you bring one of the fancy French wines from your parents' cellar?"

"Nope." Michael pulled the cork. "California cabernet sauvignon."

"You know, we have some excellent wineries here in Georgia."

"In that case—" Michael poured. "You can supply tomorrow night's bottle."

"About that." Daisy swirled her glass. "Mom invited you to supper."

"Another enjoyable evening engaging with your family *and* a delicious meal."

Should she tell him she wouldn't accompany him to her parents' home now or wait until tomorrow? Best to wait.

Michael lifted his glass. "Here's to putting this case to bed."

After devouring the sandwiches and polishing off the wine, Michael leaned back. "I need to prepare for an early morning conference call with another client, so let's pick back up tomorrow afternoon."

Was client prep an actual motive, or was he hoping David would leave them alone? "You obviously need some private time, and I need a good night's sleep. The guest room is up the stairs and to the right. Make yourself at home, and I'll see both you guys in the morning. How's eight for breakfast?"

"Count me out." Michael closed his briefcase. "I'll be tied up until noon."

So, he really did have an early morning task. "We'll make it brunch at 12:30."

"That'll work."

"First thing tomorrow morning, I'll buy ingredients for a killer omelet." David closed his laptop and nudged Daisy. "Walk me out."

Daisy accompanied him to the back door. "Perhaps we, or rather you, miscalculated Michael's intentions."

"For the moment he's playing it cool. Coffee at seven?"

Daisy tilted her head. "My place or yours?"

"Yours." David kissed her cheek. "Sleep well."

She breathed in the lingering scent of shampoo. "You too." Daisy closed the door behind him and returned to the dining room. Michael had turned his back toward the table. His earbud and one-sided conversation made it clear he was engaged in a business call. Relieved, Daisy tiptoed past and continued on to her room. No need to lock the door. She could trust Michael.

Chapter Thirty-Two

Late afternoon, the day after Michael arrived at Daisy's, Poppy shaded her eyes with her hand as David's truck rolled to a stop beside her.

Daisy lowered the passenger window. "How's Dad holding up?"

"He hasn't said a word, but the lawsuit is tearing him up inside. I don't know what he'll do if Margaret wins."

David peered around Daisy. "Michael's a top-notch attorney, Poppy. He won't let that happen."

"I hope you're right. What'd you talk about during today's meeting?"

"Actually." Daisy fingered her earring. "A conference call plus a client emergency kept Michael tied up until three. So, not much other than scheduling a face-to-face meeting between the parties."

"When?"

"A week from today. Ironic." Daisy scoffed. "My first contact with my grandmother and it's over a ridiculous lawsuit."

"That's her doing, not yours. How'd Michael react to the news about you and David taking Pansy out to supper tonight?"

Daisy glanced at David. Had he noticed Michael's disappointment? "He seemed to understand."

"Yoohoo, I'm ready." Pansy, wearing a new pink ball cap, dashed across the yard. She climbed into the back and buckled her seatbelt. "Where are we going?"

David turned to face her. "Someplace extra special."

Pansy's eyes widened. "In Savanah?"

"Uh-huh. Right by the river."

"Goody."

Daisy turned back toward Poppy. "We'll have her back by nine."

"Y'all have fun." After David's truck eased down the driveway and turned onto the main road, Poppy returned to her kitchen. Savory tomato and beef aromas mingled with the sweet scent of Pansy's freshly baked carrot cake. She gripped the back of her chair and peered at her family's artwork adorning the wall. Three months ago, she was comfortable with her role as homemaker. But now—the investigation, the lottery ticket, the bakery—did God want her to accomplish more than cooking, cleaning, and helping Danny in the greenhouse? And if He did, what was she qualified to do?

Danny wandered in, freshly showered, dressed in jeans and a button-down shirt.

"I fixed fried chicken, green beans, and mashed potatoes with peach cobbler for dessert."

"Not a very sophisticated menu for a New York lawyer." He settled on his chair.

"Tonight Michael needs comfort food, not fancy fixings. Besides, this is plenty sophisticated." Poppy set down the Waterford vase Michael sent to her following the one other time he had joined the family for supper. "And now it's filled with flowers from our greenhouse."

"I still don't understand why you invited him and sent Pansy away."

"So we can talk about the lawsuit, if you decide you want to." The doorbell chimed. "Do you want me to answer?"

"You might as well."

Poppy rushed to open the front door. "Welcome back to our home, Michael."

"If I'd known about the dinner invitation, I would have come better prepared." He handed Poppy a bottle of wine. "This is the best I could find at Willy's."

She diverted her eyes, keenly aware her birthmark hadn't magically disappeared. "It's perfect."

"All afternoon, I've looked forward to enjoying another delicious supper."

"It's not New York-restaurant fancy, but plenty tasty."

He smiled. "Lots of fancy big-city restaurants are over-rated."

And this big-city lawyer was a first-rate charmer. Hopefully he'd manage to snap her husband out of his sour mood. Poppy led Michael to the kitchen.

Danny stood. "Welcome back."

"It's good to see you again, sir. I trust your business is doing well."

"Can't complain."

Poppy placed three wine glasses on the table and handed Michael a corkscrew. "Will you do the honors?"

"Glad to." He pointed to the flower arrangement. "From your greenhouse?"

"The flowers, yes." Poppy placed bowls of mashed potatoes and green beans on the table. "The beautiful vase is from you."

"I'm glad you're still enjoying it." Michael uncorked the wine and poured three glasses. After Poppy set down a platter of meatloaf on the table, he pulled her chair away from the table. "Allow me."

"Thank you." She sat, then peered at Danny, still on his feet.

He gestured toward Daisy's chair. "Please."

Michael rounded the table and complied.

Danny took his seat. "I'll return thanks."

Poppy struggled to keep her mouth from falling open. He never said grace. Why now? Was he trying to impress Michael? She closed her eyes.

Following Danny's one-sentence blessing, their guest lifted his wineglass. "Here's to Danny and Poppy Butler's incredible family."

Danny simply nodded, then took a sip.

Poppy handed Michael a platter. "The fried chicken is my mama's recipe and one of Pansy and my favorite meals."

He transferred a breast to his plate and cut a piece. "Best chicken I've ever tasted."

Danny handed the bowl of mashed potatoes to Michael. "Wait until you taste this."

Halfway through supper laced with compliments about the food and not a single word about Margaret Butler's lawsuit, Michael turned toward Danny. "I'm curious. Is the fact that you haven't changed your lifestyle an indication you rejected the winning lottery ticket?"

Danny's fork halted halfway to his mouth.

Poppy's eyes darted from Michael to Danny then back to Michael. "How did you know he won?"

"Daisy mentioned it the day she resigned. No need to worry, I've never told anyone. In fact, I'd almost forgotten about it. So, what's the deal?"

"I have the check. Never cashed it." Danny's fork found his mouth.

"You're obviously a man who stands by his convictions."

Poppy's brows pinched. What else had Daisy told him? Did he know she and David were investigating Curtis for murder?

Danny swallowed a bite of chicken. "How do you plan to win the suit against our daughter and David?"

This time Michael's fork halted mid arc. "The law's on our side. However, the more I understand about your family dynamics the better."

"What do you want to know?"

Michael set down his fork. "To start, anything you can tell me about your mother."

"She's addicted to money and social status."

"What about her relationships with her family and friends?"

"Do you wanna know what she's like?" Danny slapped his fork on the table. "The entire time I was growing up, she barely tolerated my old man and definitely didn't tolerate me or my brother. Now, I suspect she's frustrated with how my sisters turned out. One's an addict. The other marries men for their money. Her friends?" He scoffed. "Wealthy people with influence and position."

Poppy cringed at Danny's bitter tone. "Based on newspaper articles, Danny's mother is involved in a lot of fundraisers."

"What do you think is really behind Mrs. Butler's lawsuit?"

Poppy shrugged. "I suppose, she's protecting her reputation."

"My wife's dead-on right. My mother would do anything to keep from losing one iota of social standing."

"Yesterday your daughter told me about her and David's investigation into Rose Fowler's disappearance." Michael paused, his eyes remained focused on Danny. "You're aware that my law firm represents Curtis Butler's business empire."

"Thanks to my daughter."

"Do you believe your father had a hand in Rose's disappearance?"

Danny's eyes grew lightning fierce. "If he didn't kill her, he for darn sure knows who did."

Poppy cringed. "I hope the investigation doesn't damage your law firm's relationship with Curtis."

"We represent the business, not the man. The company is a separate entity." Michael fingered the expensive-looking ring on his left hand. "I can't imagine growing up in a dysfunctional environment. Kudos to you, sir, for moving beyond the past and forever changing your family's legacy. The relationship you two have with each other, as well as my admiration for Daisy, are two reasons I took on this case."

Poppy stared at Michael. Did he have romantic feelings for Daisy? If so, did he know about her relationship with David? What if he didn't and found out about it? Would he drop the case? Maybe she'd misread his comment, and the real motive behind his decision was protecting his law firm. Who could blame him? Especially after they'd paid Daisy a huge bonus.

"...what's your secret, Poppy?"

She blinked. "My secret?"

"The mashed potatoes. They're delicious."

Why the sudden change of subject? Had her expression given Michael a hint about her thoughts? "Butter and garlic."

"Maybe one day you'll have a chance to teach my mother about southern cooking."

"Does she enjoy cooking?"

"She rarely goes into the kitchen. However, she is a master at dictating menus to her kitchen staff."

Poppy's eyes widened. "She has a kitchen staff in her house?"

"One of the perks of wealth." Michael refilled all three wineglasses. "Tell me about your greenhouse. What type of plants do you grow?"

"Danny created a one-of-a-kind hybrid flower. He calls it the Poppy rose."

Michael tipped his wineglass toward Danny. "The perfect tribute to your beautiful wife. Tell me about your process."

Poppy silently thanked Michael for redirecting the conversation to Danny's accomplishments. Although she suspected he didn't give a hoot about flowers, he'd managed to take her husband's mind off the case. When Michael guided their conversation to football, Poppy mentally chuckled at questioning his motives for taking Daisy and David's case. By the time they finished second helpings of peach cobbler, Danny had managed to relax.

"That was one fine meal, Poppy. You're a wonderful hostess, and I've enjoyed our conversation." Michael pushed away from the table. "Unfortunately I have an early morning flight." He stood. "And don't worry about the lawsuit, Danny. I'll take care of everything."

After bidding their guest goodbye at the front door, Poppy faced Danny. "Now that you've had a chance to talk to Michael, are you less worried about the lawsuit?"

"It won't matter how good a lawyer he is if he's never dealt with a woman as cold and calculating as Margaret Butler." He spun and headed toward the back of the house.

"Where are you going?"

"To help you clean up the kitchen."

Chapter Thirty-Three

Daisy peered out the windshield as David turned onto her driveway. Michael's car was parked in front of the house. Light shone in the guestroom window while the main floor appeared dark.

"Our attorney has either turned in for the night, or he's working late."

David parked in front of his camper and rushed to open the passenger door. He held out his hand.

Daisy accepted, basking in the warmth of his hand.

His fingers curled around hers. "The night's still young. Why don't we sit outside and light a fire."

"Great idea. Matches are in the top kitchen drawer beside the fridge."

"You relax, I'll be back in a sec."

Daisy curled up on the wooden swing suspended from the back deck rafters. A smile played on her lips as she mentally reviewed their evening with Pansy—the way David treated her aunt with tenderness and respect. The woman he'd married for a brief moment all those years ago had no idea the amazing man she'd let go.

"Found them." David knelt and stacked wood in the hearth, then struck a match and fanned the flame. "That'll take the chill off."

"That wasn't your first fire."

David sat beside Daisy. "I was the official lighter for Mom's fireplace." He wrapped his arm around her shoulders, and pulled her close.

Passion kindled inside Daisy as heat from the flames merged with the warmth from David's body. Why had he chosen tonight to cuddle by a fire? Was he in some odd way competing with Michael? The reason didn't matter. As the gentle clink of the swing's chain links mingled with the crackling flames, she envisioned spending every evening wrapped in David's arms.

"What are you thinking right now?"

Should she tell him the truth? That she longed for him to kiss her? "This is the perfect way to end the day."

"Almost perfect." David touched her chin and gently turned her face toward his. His warm breath caressed her cheek. He kissed her, deeply, passionately, awakening every nerve in her body. When their lips parted, he gazed into her eyes.

"I've wondered how long it would take you to kiss me a second time."

He stroked her cheek. "I love you from the depths of my soul, Daisy."

"I'm blessed beyond belief to have fallen in love with a man whose words alone fan the flame of desire." This time she kissed him.

They cuddled and spoke endearments until the fireplace flames flickered and died. "We have a big day tomorrow." David escorted Daisy to her back door and kissed her gently, sweetly. "I'll count the minutes until I gaze at your beautiful face in the morning light."

"Good night, my love," she whispered.

Savoring the magical evening, Daisy floated through the kitchen and dining room into the living room. Light shone from the stairwell. She smiled. Michael was kind to leave it on for her. She ran her fingers along her sofa's upholstery and glanced at her new mantel clock. Twelve-thirty. Tomorrow night, she and David would be alone. She'd prepare dinner for him. They'd eat by candlelight, then cuddle in front of the indoor fireplace.

Daisy strolled to the staircase, climbed onto the first step, and stopped dead in her tracks. Michael sat at the top, his arms propped across his knees. How long had he been sitting there? Was he waiting for her? She swallowed and continued climbing. "Another late night prepping for a client?"

"I finished an hour ago."

"Did everything go okay with my parents?"

"Your mom served a delicious southern supper."

She sat beside him. "You've finally learned what we southerners call our evening meal."

"I admire the way they've both overcome painful pasts and thrived. Your dad is still undecided about cashing that lottery check. That takes character."

As Daisy eyed Michael's profile, her attorney instincts kicked in. "What's really on your mind, Michael?"

He hesitated. "I haven't been completely honest about the reason I took this case."

"I understand your law firm wanting to protect my grandfather's account—"

"My decision had nothing to do with Curtis Butler." He faced her. "And everything to do with his granddaughter."

Avoiding eye contact, Daisy focused on the unadorned stairwell wall. "What are you trying to tell me?"

"I want you to come back to the firm."

Dread bubbled up like soda in a shaken can. "There are plenty of corporate attorneys with far more experience who'd jump at the chance to work for your firm."

"This isn't about the position—"

"Please, Michael—"

"Let me finish. The day you resigned and walked out of my office, I believed I could let you go and move on. The truth is, I never stopped having feelings for you."

Daisy swallowed against the dryness in her throat. "You know we come from two different worlds."

"A minor detail."

"A fact that's way beyond minor." Daisy faced him. "You need a sophisticated woman from a prominent family. Someone who can distinguish between a ten-dollar bottle of wine and a priceless bottle from your parents' cellar." She touched his arm. "Deep down, you know we're not right for each other."

"I'd hoped my instincts were off base. Turns out I read the signals with dead-on accuracy." Michael's eyes met hers. "You and David are lovers, aren't you?"

If she told him the truth, would he abandon their lawsuit? "David and I are *in* love."

"But not lovers." He looked away. "Is that the reason he sleeps in his camper?"

"We're taking things slow."

"Another southern custom?" Michael held up his palm. "A response isn't required."

"Good, because I didn't intend to provide one."

"David's one lucky guy."

"Thank you for understanding."

"I'm man enough to accept defeat with a modicum of dignity."

"You're a good man, Michael."

"Just not the right one for you." He lifted his arms off his knees. "In case you're wondering, I'm also an attorney with unquestionable scruples."

"Meaning you won't let my relationship with David interfere with the lawsuit?"

"You are one perceptive woman, Daisy Butler."

"Whatever your motivation." She kissed his cheek. "We're fortunate you took our case."

Michael chuckled. "The second time she kisses me, and it's a consolation prize. I suppose coming in second place has its advantages."

Daisy laughed. "I couldn't ask for a better friend, especially one with an impressive law degree from Yale. So, Mr. Bulldog fan, why don't you join David and me for breakfast before you leave?"

Michael fingered his college ring. "I don't know."

"Trust me. You don't want to miss the chance to savor Aunt Pansy's scrumptious coffeecake." She stood and stepped onto the landing. "Seven-thirty sharp."

He pushed up. "How can I refuse such an intriguing offer?"

"You can't." Daisy smiled, then ambled into her bedroom, and closed the door. She meandered to the window and peered down at the camper's dark windows. David had been right about Michael's intentions after all. At least she'd managed to disassemble the triangle without inflicting too much damage on their attorney's ego or threatening their lawsuit.

She moved away from the window. After changing into cozy pajamas, she slid beneath her down comforter and stared at the ceiling. What had Michael meant by his 'another southern custom' comment? Maybe she should invite David to move into her guestroom. She closed her eyes as the passion kindled by his kiss skated across her mind. Could she resist temptation if he slept twenty feet from her door? Did it matter?

Chapter Thirty-Four

Daisy awoke as dawn peeked over the horizon and reality crept in. The man she loved slept in a camper beneath her window, while the one she'd rejected slept down the hall. Had she made a mistake inviting both men to breakfast? Too late to question what might have been a moment of insanity. She rolled out of bed and padded to the bathroom, counting on a hot shower to ease her escalating anxiety.

At seven Daisy finished blow-drying her hair and stepped out to the hall. The whoosh of running water implied that Michael might be showering. How would he treat David after her rejection? As a professional, that's how. Daisy dashed down the stairs and headed to the kitchen, confused by the fresh aroma of coffee wafting through the living and dining rooms.

David leaned against the counter.

"You're early."

He pulled her in his arms and kissed her. "Good morning."

She stroked his cheek. "Your greeting is much better than mine."

"Is Michael joining us for breakfast?"

"At seven-thirty."

"Want me to scramble some eggs?"

"I'd rather taste another one of your delicious kisses."

"Glad to oblige. Except our attorney showed up early."

Daisy spun toward a not-so-subtle throat clearing.

Michael strolled in, casually dressed with his phone clipped to his belt, and his hair still wet. "I thought Pansy's famous coffee cake was the only item on the menu."

Sensing her cheeks were seconds from turning multiple shades of pink, Daisy removed a coffee mug from the cabinet. "What's your preference, Michael? Regular or dark roast?"

"Dark roast. Black. I could use a big dose of caffeine."

Daisy dropped in a pod. Inviting Michael to share breakfast with his rival had been a huge mistake. And why had both men showed up a half hour early? "What time's your flight?"

"As soon as I show up at the airport."

Why had she asked that question? She knew he traveled in the law firm's private jet. What about next week? Did he expect to stay in her guest room again? Should she invite him or wait for him to invite himself? She handed Michael his coffee. "I hope the guest room was suitable."

"Comfortable and convenient. However, since our next meeting is scheduled to take place in the opposing attorney's Savannah office, I'll have my assistant reserve a hotel room."

"That makes sense." Relieved Michael had made the accommodation decision, Daisy unwrapped the coffee cake, releasing mouthwatering scents of cinnamon and vanilla.

Michael sniffed. "Your mom's peach cobbler last night and Pansy's specialty this morning? How lucky can a New York lawyer get? Right, David?"

Daisy peered over her shoulder. Why the snarky tone? Had Michael's damaged male ego superseded his professionalism? "I'll send you off with an extra slice of coffee cake, in case hunger pangs attack before you land in New York. Since you're leaving soon, I suggest we enjoy breakfast while reviewing our plans for next week."

"A take-charge woman. No wonder she's a brilliant attorney." Michael set down his coffee, then held up a finger with one hand and tapped his earbud with the other. He listened, then nodded. "I'll be back in the office by noon." He tapped his earbud again. "Sorry to run before indulging, but I need to head back to the airport. Wrap up a slice of that coffee cake, Daisy, and give us guys a couple minutes alone." He clasped his hand on David's shoulder. "Come with me."

Fighting the urge to intervene, Daisy wrapped aluminum foil around the remaining coffee cake and stuffed the to-go package into a plastic grocery bag. Now what? Should she wait in the kitchen? For how long? Another minute? What would a take-charge attorney do? Definitely not wait. She strode to the foyer and handed it to Michael.

"Fancy packaging."

"Were you expecting me to bring it gift wrapped?"

He chuckled. "Take-charge and humorous."

"I packed enough for you and your jet crew."

"Good move." Michael retrieved his carry-on bag and briefcase from the bottom step. "The three of us need to meet an hour before next week's meeting. I'll text you details in a couple days. Until then, avoid communication with Margaret and Curtis."

David nodded. "Will do." He remained standing at the open door.

After their attorney descended the porch steps and climbed into his car, Daisy faced David. "What was that all about?"

"I was spot-on about Michael's feelings for you, and you were right about his character."

"Why? What did he say?"

David placed his hands on her shoulders. A smile lit his face. "He couldn't have lost to a better man."

"Those exact words?"

"Verbatim."

She tilted her head and patted David's cheek. "He's right."

"I know." He winked. "How about I scramble us up some eggs?"

"You're on, as soon as we find out who just drove up my driveway."

David pivoted toward the open door.

An old car with more than a few dings and dents parked in front of the house. A woman climbed from the driver's side, then lifted a toddler from a rear car seat and climbed up the porch steps.

David leaned close to Daisy. "Odds are she's either a scam artist or a panhandler."

"What makes you say that?"

"Experience."

The young woman dressed in jeans and a tattered sweater stopped a foot from the door. "I'm sorry to bother you, Miss, but ...well..." Her bottom lip appeared to tremble. She sniffled. "The man over at Willy's said you were a nice lady." Her child sneezed. "My baby sneezes when she's hungry."

Were David's instincts accurate? "What can we do for you, ma'am?"

"I'm hoping you'll take pity on me and my baby and...you know...loan me some money? Just until I get my job back."

David stepped forward. "You read that tabloid article, didn't you?"

"Sort of."

"We're sorry you're down on your luck, ma'am, but that article was nothing more than a figment of the writer's imagination."

The woman's brows pinched. "What do you mean?"

"Ms. Butler didn't win the lottery."

The woman craned her neck and peered around David. "I understand why you might be kind of...you know, skeptical. I would be too if some stranger showed up at my door asking for a handout." Her lip trembled again. "But I need help."

Daisy eyed the woman's manicured fingernails. Was she the real deal or a well-rehearsed scammer? Only one way to find out. "Tell you what. I'll give you a basket of food, twenty dollars, and the address for a shelter in Savannah. The people who work there can help you get back on your feet."

"That's mighty nice of you, but...well...I'd be grateful if you could find it in your heart to spare a little more money for me and my precious baby. You see, she has this heart condition, and I'm on the way to take her to the hospital. I only hope they'll take charity cases." She sniffled again. "I just love her so much."

Okay, lady, I'll play along. "I can only imagine the stress you're under."

"It's so hard thinking about my baby suffering because I can't afford proper medical care."

She's really laying it on thick. "How much more money do you think you need?"

"Well...there's the surgery...and I'll need a place to stay. Mind you, I'd pay back every cent. So I'm thinking a couple thousand? You seem like a real understanding, charitable lady, so maybe five?"

Talk about an over-the-top, bogus sales pitch. "What's your name, honey?"

"Stella."

"I'm so sorry about all your trouble, Stella. Oh my goodness. A sick baby must be heartbreaking."

"I just knew you'd understand."

"Oh, I do."

The woman's eyes lit.

Daisy imagined her salivating with anticipation. "But you see, Stella, here's the thing. I really didn't win the lottery."

Stella's smile evaporated. "Are you serious?"

"Not a plug nickel. Plus, this handsome man is a private investigator specializing in fraud, and my brother is a law-enforcement officer."

Her face paled. "I don't mean no harm." Stella hiked her child on her hip and spun toward the stairs. "I'm just trying to earn a living."

David shook his head. "That woman has a warped idea about the meaning of *earning* a living, and I guarantee her name's not Stella."

The woman strapped her child in the car seat then climbed behind the wheel and slammed the door shut.

Daisy folded her arms across her chest. "Do people actually fall for such obvious scams?"

"You'd be surprised."

"Dad's skepticism about cashing that check is valid. One rumor about winning the lottery, and freeloaders come out of the woodwork." Daisy closed and locked the door. "What if Dad decides to cash the check and directs me to give the money away? Unless he wants to donate it all to existing charities, how would I distinguish between scammers and legitimately needy people? If Stella hadn't been so obvious, I might have fallen for her scam."

David wrapped his arms around her waist. "Which is why you would need a cracker-jack investigator on your team."

Daisy tilted her head. "Do you intend to hang around a while longer?"

"Absolutely." He winked. "After all, *your* parents already consider me part of the family."

"Well then, as a member of the Butler inner circle, I believe I'll put you to work."

"Cooking breakfast?"

"A bit more labor intensive. Lilly's coming over at ten to help paint my ten-foot-high office."

"What?" He grinned. "You haven't warmed up to Agnes's fondness for lavender?"

"Neither the color nor the scent. And considering my pregnant sister has no business climbing a ladder, and I chose not to..." She stroked his bicep. "We need a strong, handsome man to join our little crew. After you scramble us some eggs."

"At your service, partner."

Chapter Thirty-Five

F atigued from fretting over Danny's despair and listening to Pansy's detailed account of last night's trip to Savannah, Poppy retreated to the front porch. Grateful for a few minutes alone, she plopped onto a rocking chair and set it in motion. Her mind drifted to the last time her family had taken a family vacation—three days on Tybee Island. Daisy was still in high school. She and Danny had never taken a trip alone. Maybe after Michael settled the lawsuit and David solved her mama's case, she'd find a way to entice him to take a vacation. Just the two of them, far away from crowds and prying eyes.

Poppy closed her eyes and imagined holding hands while she and Danny strolled in the surf, listening to the ocean's gentle roar. Breathing the salty sea air. The cool, foamy sand squishing between her toes. If Danny cashed the lottery check and kept a little bit of the money, they could afford to rent a house on a secluded beach. Maybe even hire a private chef, like Michael's mother. Even if he didn't take the money, they needed time away.

Gravel crunching beneath tires shattered Poppy's mental musings. Her eyes opened as Lilly's car rolled to a stop beside the porch. Hoping her youngest child hadn't shown up to probe her dad's decision, she stood and motioned her over. "What a nice surprise." She embraced her daughter. "Can you stay for lunch?"

Lilly shook her head. "I'm on my way to Daisy's to help her paint, but I rushed over here first to warn you about a reporter."

"We already know about him, honey—"

"Not the guy who wrote the article."

Poppy grimaced. "What guy are you talking about?"

Lilly spun and jabbed her finger toward a late-model sedan easing up the driveway. "That one. He showed up at my house the same time I was leaving and asked all kinds of questions about Daisy and the lottery ticket."

The sudden urge to dash inside, grab Danny's rifle, and order the intruder off her property quickened Poppy's pulse.

"He didn't believe me when I told him Daisy didn't win all that money."

"We need to let your dad handle this."

They raced through the house and found Danny standing at the greenhouse entrance. He placed his hand on Lilly's arm. "Did that man follow you here?"

"Seems so. He's a reporter, Dad."

"He questioned Lilly about Daisy winning the lottery," added Poppy.

The man climbed out of his car and appeared to eye the house while heading in their direction.

"You and your mom, wait here." Danny strode away from the greenhouse and stopped the intruder beside the delivery truck. "Can I help you?"

"I believe you can?" The man handed over a business card. "I write human-interest stories about people who win mega lotteries. I'm interested in learning more about your daughter's winning ticket."

Danny crossed his arms. "I believe the daughter you questioned earlier made it perfectly clear that her sister didn't win the lottery."

"Look, I understand why Ms. Butler might not want anyone to know about her good fortune—"

"You're not listening to me. No matter what you've read or what you think you know, my daughter...did...not...win...the lottery." He crossed his arms. "So, I suggest you return to your car and drive off my property before I call the sheriff and report you for unlawful trespassing."

"Whoa." The man held up both hands. "There's no need for threats. I'm simply following up on a lead."

"And I'm simply informing you that your so-called lead is worthless." Danny pointed toward the driveway. His tone remained firm and measured. "Which means it's in your best interest to accept what I've told you as the truth and leave everyone in my family alone."

The man cocked his head. "Whatever you say." He spun around and returned to his car.

Lilly rushed to her dad's side. "I'm sorry I couldn't make him believe me."

"It's not your fault the man's a nuisance."

"He made me afraid I'd say the wrong thing and let our family's secret slip out."

"Now, do you understand why I haven't cashed that check?"

"I'm beginning to."

Poppy approached. "We need to warn Daisy."

"I'm on it." Danny unclipped his phone from his belt, pressed a number, and headed back toward the greenhouse.

Lilly pressed her hand to her belly. "I don't think Dad's threats will stop that man."

Danny returned. "I gave Daisy a heads-up." He punched a number and pressed his phone to his ear.

"Who are you calling?"

Danny eyed Poppy and held up his index finger. "Yes, sir. I'm calling to inquire about installing a security gate on my property."

Poppy's arms fell limp to her sides as she stared down the driveway. One undeniable fact loomed large. Life as she'd known it was changing, and not necessarily for the better.

Daisy set her phone on the desk and peered out the bay window. "Another annoying reporter is likely to show up on my doorstep before noon. I wonder if the guy knows the check hasn't been cashed." She spun toward David. "You're an investigative reporter. What would it take to make you stop investigating a rumor?"

"Credible denials." He finished spreading a tarp over the floor. "Unfortunately, some freelancers are like old dogs sniffing for buried bones. Their hunger for a story hinders their ability to recognize truth."

"Maybe I should take Dad's lead and install a gate across my driveway? Except wouldn't two members of our family making such a move raise suspicions?"

"Now you're thinking like an investigator." David pried the lid off a can of paint.

"Michael's parents have a gate across the driveway to their multi-million-dollar Southampton mansion, and Dad has a business to protect. But somehow it seems a bit presumptuous to block people from driving up to my house. Especially if one day I decided to hang an open-for-legal-business sign."

"You could adopt a dog."

Or invite David to move into the guest room. "I've been thinking."

"Good skill for a lawyer."

"If I decide to buy a dog, I'd want to raise it from a pup. Which means it would take at least a year before it qualified as a serious watch-dog. What if some stranger knocks on my door after dark tonight or tomorrow night?"

"You have a lot of ifs floating around in your head."

"What I'm trying to say..." Daisy handed him a stir stick. "I want you to move into my guest room."

"Wow." He laid the stick across the top of the paint can. "Are you sure?"

"Do you have reservations?"

"Sleeping a couple of long strides from you would require a heap of self-control."

Could she resist inviting David into her room?

"If you're having second thoughts—"

Did she even want to resist? Daisy leaned her hip on the corner of her desk. "We're already eating our meals together. And since you seem opposed to using an umbrella, you won't drip water on my kitchen floor following a dash from your camper during an early-morning rain storm."

"Excellent points, Counselor."

"Plus, I'd feel safer with you close by."

He moved close. His smile sent a twinkle to his eyes. "Your guest room is a tad too feminine for my taste."

"We'll paint the walls a color more suitable to your masculine sensibilities."

He stroked her cheek. "Seems I need to begin exercising resistance now."

"To moving in?"

"To kissing you. We have company."

Daisy spun toward the window the moment a late-model sedan parked in her driveway. "Odds are it's that pesky reporter."

"Do you want me to handle this?"

"Please."

David strode from the office and stepped out to the porch, leaving the front door ajar.

Muffled voices drifted in. Daisy tiptoed to the foyer and gripped the front-door handle. If she submitted to her impulse to rush out and confront the stranger, would she undermine David's role as her protector? She released the handle and forced her compulsion into submission.

Minutes passed.

She tapped her foot. Maybe she should intervene.

Footsteps.

A car engine.

David strolled back inside. "The guy's a legitimate reporter, and he has connections."

"Meaning?"

"He knows the check remains uncashed. Which means he'll also know when and if that changes."

"Did you have any luck persuading him to back off?"

"Let's just say we came to an understanding—one professional to another."

Daisy laced her fingers behind David's neck. "Will a kiss suffice as a proper thank you?"

"Before or after Lilly shows up?"

"I'm thinking both."

"I love the way your mind works. However, you'd better kiss me quick because I just heard another car pull onto your driveway."

Daisy huffed. "What is it with all the untimely disruptions?"

"I imagine our visitor is your sister and not another pesky reporter. About that kiss—"

"Later." Daisy unlaced her fingers and patted his cheek. "I'll make it worth the wait." She backed away, spun around, and opened the front door.

David eased behind her, his breath brushing her ear. "I'll hold you to your promise."

Heat inched up Daisy's neck as she wrestled the impulse to close the door and pretend she wasn't home.

Lilly scurried up the porch steps with a plaid garment draped over her arm. "Another reporter cornered me, then bothered Mom and Dad. He's likely to show up at your door any minute."

"He already has." Daisy embraced her sister. "David sent him packing."

"Good for you, David." Lilly pulled away from Daisy. "Facing that man twice in one day was way more than enough." She donned the plaid shirt over her long-sleeve turtleneck and rolled back the cuffs. "One of Andy's rejects. I'm ready to start working off my debt."

"Well then." Daisy linked arms with her sister. "Let's get this painting party started."

Chapter Thirty-Six

A week after David moved into the guest room, Daisy rolled out of her bed before dawn. Exhausted from awakening half a dozen times during the night, she trudged to her bathroom, turned on the shower, and waited for steam to fog the mirror. Hoping hot water cascading over her body would wash away her anxiety, she stepped into the shower stall and closed her eyes. Newspaper photos in her mom's scrapbook rolled through her mind. Her maternal grandmother posing and smiling while hosting fundraisers and social events. She seemed like a decent enough person.

By the time Daisy turned off the water and planted her feet on the bath mat, her tense muscles had relaxed. Until she swiped her towel across the foggy mirror and stared at her image. In a few hours she would officially meet the woman she'd only seen in photos. Except the one time she and her mom had driven by her house and spotted her clipping roses beside her driveway. Daisy gripped the sink. Somehow she had to keep her emotions reined in and face her legal adversary as a dispassionate professional.

After drying her hair and dressing, Daisy meandered to the hall. Light spilled from the open guest-room door. She peeked inside. The bed was made. The jacket David had worn the first day she met him laid across a chair. Had he also found it difficult to sleep? She descended the stairs, breathed in the fresh scent of coffee, and moseyed to the kitchen.

David leaned against the counter. "Good morning."

"How long have you been awake?"

"About an hour." He prepared a cup of coffee for her. "Are you hungry?"

"What was I thinking, knocking on my grandmother's door without an invitation?" Daisy trilled her lips. "If I hadn't left my business card with her housekeeper, chances are this lawsuit would never have happened."

"Eventually, Margaret would have discovered what we're up to."

"Maybe *after* you published your book."

"It's better to nip this in the bud before publication." He popped in another pod. "And we have a top-notch attorney, despite the fact that he came in second place."

"A distant second, mind you, and he couldn't have lost to a better man." Daisy patted David's cheek, then took a sip. "Especially one who knows how to prepare a perfect cup of coffee."

"Which brings me back to my question. Are you hungry?"

"Hardly. I don't know. Maybe an egg and a piece of toast?"

"Today you definitely need more than a caffeine jolt." David removed a carton of eggs from the fridge. "One protein-rich, anxiety-easing breakfast coming up."

"If your investigative journalist gig doesn't work out, you could survive as a short-order cook. Maybe open a breakfast cafe next to Pansy's bakery."

"Just one minor problem." David chuckled while cracking eggs into a frying pan. "I only cook for beautiful women and their amazing families."

"I see. How many women have you impressed with your culinary skills?"

"Let me think." He dropped two pieces of bread in the toaster. "There's...nope not her. Maybe...hmm...not her either." He flipped an egg. "Seems there's just one. A lady lawyer who can't decide whether or not she's hungry."

"Amazing." Daisy relished the unexpected release of tension from her neck and shoulders. "You've accomplished what a hot shower failed to do."

David peered over his shoulder. "Ease a serious case of anxiety?"

"Another noteworthy skill to add to your resume." Daisy's phone pinged a text. "It's from Michael. He wants us to meet him at the airport at nine."

"Which should give us enough time to strategize before we face our formidable opponent."

"We might need a lot more time and more than one cup of coffee."

After picking Michael up at the airport and strategizing for an hour, Daisy and David followed him into a glass-enclosed conference room in a Savannah law office.

The opposing attorney extended his hand to Michael. "Walter Campbell."

"Michael Warner."

Campbell motioned to chairs across the table from his client. "Please, have a seat."

Michael pulled a chair out for Daisy, then set his briefcase on the table and lowered onto the seat to her left. David settled on her right.

Daisy peered at Margaret Butler sitting ramrod straight directly across from her. Smartly dressed in a pale pink suit, the silver-haired woman appeared years younger than her age, an indication she'd enriched at least one skilled surgeon.

Her attorney opened a file folder and removed a document. "We'll begin by reiterating the details in Mrs. Butler's lawsuit." When he finished reading the brief, he placed it back in the folder. "My client is willing to drop this suit if Mr. Lambert and Ms. Butler cease and desist all investigation of her husband and commit to never publishing a book about her family."

Michael leaned forward, his fingers laced on the table. "On what grounds is she making her request, Mr. Campbell?"

"Defamation of character."

"An investigation that reveals truth about a crime doesn't qualify as character defamation, nor does an accurate written account of that same truth."

"Mrs. Butler's claim of libel and slander are based on false accusations."

"What proof does your client have that either Mr. Lambert or Ms. Butler have made any false accusations?"

"Comments from a person they interviewed."

Daisy's brow furrowed. Who had she talked to? The DA? Curtis's personal attorney? Surely, not his former housekeeper.

"Who are you referring to?" asked Michael.

"I'm not at liberty to say."

"Has it occurred to you that your informant could be mistaken?"

"The individual is a reliable source."

As the bantering between Michael and Campbell continued, Daisy drew one obvious conclusion. Her grandmother's lawyer knew her lawsuit was baseless but was willing to milk it for all it was worth financially.

Following what seemed an eternity of the lawyers batting questions back and forth, Margaret Butler appeared to have had enough. She lifted her chin and locked eyes with Daisy. "I have a question for the woman who claims she's my granddaughter."

Daisy refused to look away. No way she'd let Margaret Butler intimidate her. "Danny Butler is my father, which biologically and irrefutably qualifies you as my paternal grandmother. So, what is your question?"

"Did your grandfather reward you with his business account?"

She'd obviously talked to Curtis. "The firm I worked for, not me personally."

"Why are you party to Mr. Lambert's ill-conceived investigation?"

Margaret's attorney touched his client's arm. "Perhaps you should leave the questioning to the attorneys."

Her eyes remained trained on Daisy. "I'm perfectly capable of handling this, Walter. What's your answer, Ms. Butler?"

You want to take me on, lady? Okay, here goes. "Mr. Lambert is investigating a legitimate crime that involves my maternal grandmother. To answer your question about my involvement, I'm functioning as my family's legal counsel."

Margaret's eyes grew lightning fierce. "You have no idea what you're getting yourself into, young lady."

"Why don't you enlighten me, Mrs. Butler?"

"Perhaps you're unaware how much of a pillar I am in the Savannah community." Margaret's chin lifted higher. "Politicians seek my endorsements. Charities rely on my contributions and support. I appear on society pages more than anyone in my social circle."

The woman definitely suffered from a serious case of unabashed arrogance. "Although your contributions are noteworthy, and I'm sure much appreciated, your relationships with public officials as well as your charitable donations are irrelevant to this case."

"Ms. Butler is correct," added David. "The fact is, neither she nor I have said anything to slander you, and since no one other than the two of us has read my manuscript, your claim of libel is unfounded."

"My family is far too important to let you continue down this destructive path."

Daisy's nostrils flared. "This path—"

Michael touched her arm making it clear she had come close to letting her grandmother needle her way under her skin.

She pressed her lips tight to prevent the words remaining on her tongue from tumbling out.

Michael poured a glass of water. "Every family is important, Mrs. Butler, including your son's. However, there is no legitimate reason for either of my clients to discontinue their investigation. And I believe your attorney will confirm that unless Mr. Lambert's manuscript contains falsehoods, he is within his rights to publish a book about their discoveries."

Margaret Butler glared at Michael. "I have no intention of dropping this lawsuit."

"That's your prerogative." Michael closed his briefcase. "Unless you have a change of heart, we'll see you in court. In the meantime I advise both parties to avoid contact with each other." He pushed his chair back and stood.

Daisy noted the opposing attorney's barely visible headshake as she and David followed Michael to the door. The three remained silent during their elevator ride to the ground floor. Outside the building and on the way to David's truck, Daisy's pent-up frustration erupted. "That was a total waste of time."

"Not necessarily." Michael opened the back door. "There appears to be more involved than Margaret Butler's social standing."

David nodded. "Definitely."

"Which is why you and Daisy need to expand your investigation and discover the real reason your grandmother is spending a fortune to stop you."

"We're on it."

After dropping Michael off at the airport, Daisy faced David. "We need to stop by Mom and Dad's on the way home."

"To give them an update on today's meeting?"

"And pick up what could become an important source of evidence."

Chapter Thirty-Seven

Daisy sat at her desk studying twenty-plus years of clippings in her mom's Butler Family Legacy scrapbook. "My grandmother didn't exaggerate her influence among Savannah's social elite." She tapped a photo. "She entertained at least one U.S. president and First Lady."

David looked up from his laptop. "Before or after he held office?"

"During."

"Impressive."

"Maybe Michael is wrong about a hidden agenda. It seems more likely that Margaret's lawsuit is driven by a desperate effort to protect her image." Daisy leaned back and brushed her fingers through her hair. "Are you thirsty?"

David's eyes remained laser focused on his laptop screen. "I could use a drink."

"Water or lemonade?"

"Is it too early for a beer?"

Daisy eyed the mantel clock—her newest thrift-store find. "Nope." She pushed off her chair. "Two beers coming up." On the way to the kitchen, she paused beside the living room and peered out the window. A deer posed at the driveway's edge, her nose pointed to the porch as if sensing she'd been spotted. Would she bolt or remain still? Daisy waited. The deer turned and slipped back into the woods. Would she and David have any success uncovering details that would force Margaret to quietly slip away and abandon her nuisance lawsuit?

She continued on to the kitchen and slid koozies on two beer bottles, then returned to her office. "Any luck?" She handed David a beer.

"You won't believe this." He set the beer on the desk and turned his laptop toward her.

She stared at a color photograph. "Is that Margaret?" She leaned closer and focused on the handsome young man—his face inches from her grandmother's, his hand touching her cheek. "Are you kidding me?"

"Read the blurb under the picture."

"*What handsome East Georgia Chief Deputy and wealthy Savannah socialite are secretly involved in a romantic rendezvous?*" Daisy's mouth fell open. "Oh my gosh, Margaret Butler and Hank Bennett were lovers? When was this photo taken and where is it from?"

"Thirty-six years ago. A defunct gossip magazine."

"Let me get this straight. While Curtis was involved with one of my grandmothers, my other grandmother more than likely had her own clandestine affair going on?"

"Lifestyles of the rich and well-connected. The question is, did Curtis have a clue about his wife's affair?"

An image flashed across Daisy's mind. "Hold on." She flipped back through the scrapbook, searching for a specific page. "There it is." Daisy tapped a picture of Margaret posing between Curtis and the chief at a fundraising affair.

David leaned close. "The date on that publication confirms the picture was taken shortlyafter the magazine photo."

"Margaret and the chief are smiling. Curtis looks like he swallowed a sour pickle."

"Based on his scowl, I'd say he knows or at least suspects his wife and so-called friend had a thing going."

"You need to forward this information to Michael."

David tapped his screen. "Done." He grabbed his phone off the desk and punched in a number.

"Who are you calling?"

"The Savannah assisted-living facility." David tapped the speaker icon.

A woman answered.

"I'd like to speak to Hank Bennett."

"Whom may I tell Mr. Bennett is calling?"

"David Lambert."

"Please hold, Mr. Lambert."

David placed his hand over the phone. "He's obviously having his calls screened."

"Did you not hear me when I told you not to contact me again?" The former deputy's harsh tone made it clear he was more than mildly perturbed.

"Some new information has surfaced, sir. Do you confirm or deny that you were romantically involved with Margaret Butler?"

"You'd best listen, Mr. Lambert, and hear me loud and clear." Bennett's voice remained ruthless, despite being barely above a whisper. "My private life, both past and present, is none of your business. If you call me again, I'll have you arrested for harassment." He ended the call.

"Talk about a confirmation." Daisy tapped her beer to David's. "Well done, partner. I'd say we've stumbled across a plausible motivation behind Margaret's lawsuit. Except their affair happened a long time ago, so why worry about it now? Unless their secret tryst continued for years."

"Your dad was right about Margaret Butler doing anything to protect her image."

"Which makes her more than a little dangerous." Movement on the driveway caught Daisy's attention. "We have company." She rushed to open the front door.

Maddie gripped the railing and climbed onto the porch, pausing at the top step to take a deep breath. "You'd think climbing stairs to my apartment every day would make trekking up your driveway a whole lot easier."

Daisy gripped her friend's arm. "Steep inclines are tough."

"I hope I'm not interrupting anything important."

"You're always welcome." Daisy escorted Maddie to her living-room sofa.

David wandered in and propped his foot on the hearth. "How's it going, Maddie?"

"Good for me. Not so much for my cousin over in Jesup. She's always had too much of a hankering for beer, if you know what I mean."

Daisy inched away wondering if her breath had revealed the two sips she'd swallowed.

"I'm not saying her drinking a couple beers every afternoon—maybe more than a couple—is bad. Except when she ends up behind the wheel and struggles to drive in a straight line."

"Was your cousin charged with a DUI?"

"Second time in three years. I told her you're a good lawyer who can help her out."

How should she handle this, especially since Maddie had made assumptions about her bringing her New York office to Georgia? "I understand her predicament, but I'm not licensed to practice law in this state."

"Not even a little bit?"

"When it comes to the law, there's no such thing as a little bit."

"Daisy's right." David unclipped his ringing phone. "If you ladies will excuse me." He tapped the screen and headed straight to the office.

Maddie's shoulders slumped. "I suppose my careless cousin deserves whatever happens to her. Except her husband's half blind, and both her sons live in other states. If she loses her license I don't know how they'll get around. I suppose they could walk a couple miles to the grocery store. The problem is her knees don't work so good."

"Tell you what, I'll at least look into her options."

"I knew I could count on you." Maddie pulled a piece of paper from her pocket. "My cousin's name and phone number. I'll let her know she's in good hands."

"I can't promise anything."

"You're a smart lawyer. I know you'll come through." Maddie rose to her feet and dashed out the front door.

David returned and handed Daisy her beer. "Your second unofficial client?"

"Why do I keep getting into these predicaments?"

"While Maddie was playing on your emotions, I answered a call from Lawrence Baker."

Daisy's brows lifted. "The former district attorney?"

"He wants to talk to us in person."

"When? Where?"

David sat beside her. "Tomorrow, same place as last time."

"Bud's Bar and Grill with the flickering B?"

"That's the place. Maybe you and I should wear leather jackets so we're not so conspicuous. That is, if you own one."

"What kind of statement do you suppose a red leather jacket will make?"

"That you're a fashionable biker gal who rides in a truck instead of on a motorcycle."

"All right then." She tapped her beer to his. "Tomorrow biker gal and pickup-truck dude will rule the day."

Chapter Thirty-Eight

With just two days before the security gate's scheduled installation, Poppy swept the walkway at the far end of the greenhouse while Danny watered a row of boxwoods. He hadn't spoken more than a few sentences since confronting that annoying reporter in their driveway. Who could blame him, with all the drama going on in their lives. At least Pansy's sunny disposition added a bit of cheer to their meals. Sometimes she envied how her sister viewed life through rose-colored glasses. She truly was God's gift to her family.

Poppy leaned on her broom handle and peered beyond the glass at a bright red cardinal perched on a potted oak tree. The bird took flight then landed on the ground. Such a beautiful creature—free to fly anywhere, anytime.

"Yoohoo. He's here." Pansy's voice radiated excitement.

Poppy spun toward her sister racing up the walkway, Boots bounding beside her. "Who's here, sweetie?"

"Papa. He's on the porch. That man with the big muscles brought him."

Poppy gasped as her eyes focused on a black car parked beside the house. The broom slipped from her fingers and landed on the ground with a thud.

Danny released the garden-hose nozzle and let it fall to the gravel.

Pansy grabbed his hand. "Come on."

"Wait." Danny yanked his hand from Pansy's grip.

"It's okay, Danny. Papa just wants to visit us." Pansy headed back up the walkway.

The intensity of Danny's glare sent a shiver cascading down Poppy's spine. Somehow she had to strike a balance between her sister's innocence and her husband's grasp of reality. She slid her hand around Danny's arm and leaned close. "The least we can do is welcome him to our home."

"My old man hasn't shown up since the night your mother disappeared. You can bet this isn't a friendly visit." Danny's barely audible voice escaped through clenched teeth.

"You and I understand that, sweetheart, but Pansy doesn't."

Her sister halted and turned toward them. "Are you coming?"

Poppy leaned close. "We have to make the best of this, for Pansy's sake."

"Let's get this over with," he murmured.

Poppy matched Danny's pace as they caught up with Pansy and made their way around the house and onto the front porch. Curtis's bodyguard stood beside the railing with his arms crossed. "He's inside."

"Thank you." Poppy's response escaped before Danny had a chance to voice the retort she suspected was seconds from rolling off his tongue.

Pansy and Boots rushed inside.

Poppy and Danny followed.

Curtis leaned on his cane, gazing into the bedroom where Rose once slept and entertained men. The room with the blood-stained floor. The room where he likely took her life.

Poppy cringed. Was he remembering the hours he had spent with her mother, or the last time he'd seen her alive?

Curtis pivoted toward them. "Did you keep your mother's brass bed?"

Surprised that his appearance seemed a bit better than it had weeks earlier, Poppy nodded. "It's in the attic."

"Rose was more than a beautiful woman. She possessed a kind and gentle soul."

Danny's jaw tensed. "Why have you come here?"

"Can't a father visit his son's family without raising suspicion?" Curtis's cane tapped the wooden floor as he strolled to the front room without making eye contact. "Rose and I always began our evenings together in this room, on that couch. I see that drawing is still where she hung it."

Pansy's face beamed. "I drew that one, Papa. You can have it if you want."

"It looks perfect right where it's been all these years."

Poppy pointed to the sofa. "Would you like to have a seat?"

"I prefer the chair." Curtis lowered onto a wingback.

Poppy ushered Pansy to the sofa and sat beside her.

Danny hiked his hip on the other wingback's arm and peered down at his father. "You didn't answer my question. Why are you here?"

Curtis placed his cane between his knees and gripped the handle with both hands. "I'm taking an experimental cancer-treatment drug developed by a Swedish doctor. Costs five grand a shot."

"Is the medicine making you better, Papa?"

"Prognosis is less grim than it was two months ago."

"What's prognosis?"

Curtis stared at Pansy as if she'd asked the most ridiculous question he'd ever heard.

Fearing Danny was moments from exploding, Poppy patted her sister's hand. "It's like a prediction, sweetie. Why don't you go fix a tray of cookies? Take one to the man on the porch before you bring us the plate."

"Okay." Pansy scurried from the room with Boots trailing behind her.

Poppy eased off the sofa and sat on the wingback beside her husband.

Danny took the cue. "Cut to the chase now, old man."

Curtis drilled his fingers on his cane handle. "Your daughter and her cohort are creating turmoil for your mother."

Danny's nostrils flared. "Margaret ceased being my mother the day she shunned Bobby in front of her so-called friends."

"I'm not here to dredge up the past. However, I am asking you politely to put a stop to the investigation."

"You lost every right to ask anything of me that same day."

Curtis's grip on his cane tightened. "Look, if I could go back and keep your brother from taking his own life, I would. But I can't. What I can do is pay whatever amount you name if you convince your family to accept my explanation about Rose's death and move on."

"Is our capitulation that important to you?"

Poppy bristled at Danny's harsh tone and bulging neck vein.

Curtis shrugged. "I wouldn't call my offer a surrender."

"Then what would you call it?"

"A settlement."

"I don't settle."

"In that case we have nothing further to discuss." Curtis lifted off the chair.

Danny jabbed his finger toward his father. "Sit back down."

Curtis cocked a brow. "I beg your pardon?"

"You're in my home now. My rules. The daughter you never claimed happens to love you, so you'll keep your butt in that chair long enough to eat one of her cookies and exchange a few pleasantries."

Poppy clasped her knees tight at the sight of Curtis's narrowed eyes and clenched jaw. Would he comply or call his bodyguard to the rescue?

Pansy waltzed in. "I gave that nice man two cookies." She held the plate out to Curtis. "How many do you want, Papa?"

Boots sat on his haunches at Curtis's feet, as if daring him to stand.

Curtis blinked, then eased back down. "I'll start with one."

"They're chocolate chip. Daisy's favorite."

Curtis tasted. "This is good."

Pansy sat on the coffee table, facing Curtis. "You can take some home if you want. Do you have a dog?"

"No. I have horses."

"In that barn behind your house?"

"Yes."

"Can I come visit them some day?"

"Maybe." Curtis fidgeted. "Yes, I think so."

"Do you wanna see my ball cap collection, Papa?"

"Not today, I have business to tend to."

Her head tilted. "'Cause you're a tycoon like Danny?"

Curtis's wide-eyed stare forced Poppy to suppress the urge to expel a nervous laugh. "Bring your favorite hats in here to show your Papa, Pansy."

"Okay." She scooted out. Boots remained at Curtis's feet.

Danny glared at his old man. "Make a fuss over Pansy's hats, then leave."

"Who do you think you are, giving orders to a man who controls a business empire."

"A husband and father who knows how to love and respect his family."

Curtis flinched.

Pansy returned with a half-dozen caps in hand and the sparkly New York cap on her head. After sharing where each came from, she placed one on Curtis's lap. "This one's for you, Papa."

Poppy pressed her hand to her chest. The cap was one of her sister's favorites. She silently prayed for the man her husband detested to find it in his heart to accept the gift with grace.

Curtis fingered the embroidered hearts adorning the bill. "This is a fine cap." He placed it on his head.

Pansy's face beamed. "I'll wrap up some cookies for you and the man with big muscles." She dashed to the kitchen.

Curtis pushed up and faced Danny. "If you reconsider my offer—"

"I won't."

"You're a stubborn man."

Pansy returned and handed over cookies wrapped in aluminum foil. "They taste extra good with milk."

"Thank you for the tip, and the cap." Curtis stood.

Boots growled.

Pansy gripped his collar. "It's okay. He's my papa."

Curtis cleared his throat, then eased past Danny without acknowledging his existence and walked out of his home.

Poppy held Danny's hand as they moved to the front door and watched Pansy and her dog follow the two men to the Tesla. "Why do you think Curtis showed up all these years after Mama disappeared?"

"He's terrified Daisy and David will discover the truth about Rose's death."

Chapter Thirty-Nine

D aisy lifted a fitted red leather jacket off the back of her office chair and slipped it on over her black turtleneck. "You look more than a little intimidating." She smiled while fingering David's bomber-jacket zipper.

He stroked her collar. "Nice jacket."

"One of my bargains from a New York consignment shop. Cost me forty bucks."

"Money well spent. Except you look more like a sophisticated lawyer than a motorcycle gal."

"Do you suppose the guys in that bar will notice?"

"Oh, yeah."

"In that case, I'll need to adopt my best biker-gal swagger."

David's eyes probed hers. "You're apprehensive about this meeting, aren't you?"

He had no idea. "As a chipmunk skittering from a hungry hawk." Daisy sashayed toward the foyer.

"You remind me more of the soaring hawk than the scampering chipmunk."

"There you go." She peered over her shoulder. "My swagger's already working."

"Definitely."

"Let's get a move on, pickup-truck dude. We don't want to be late for our clandestine meeting at Bud's Bar and Grill with the flickering B's."

David chuckled while following her out the front door. "Right with you, biker gal." He held her hand as they descended the porch steps and headed to his truck.

During the drive they reviewed what they'd learned about Rose's case while speculating why the former DA had called today's meeting. Fifty-five minutes after pulling out of Daisy's driveway, David turned off the two-lane road onto the gravel and eased past three motorcycles and two trucks. Both B's still flickered on the neon sign stretched across the windowless single-story building. Country music greeted them as they stepped inside the dark interior. Greasy food and beer scents still hung heavy in the air.

Lawrence Baker motioned them to the same booth he'd occupied during their first visit. Daisy held onto David's arm as they eased past five women and six men, some sitting at the bar others at tables. At least this time no one turned in their direction. Had their attire and her swagger pegged them as regulars, or had the men avoided staring because other ladies were in the joint? Whatever the reason, she released a grateful sigh. When they reached the booth, Daisy slid onto the seat across from the former district attorney. David settled beside her.

Baker clutched a bottle of lite beer in one hand and motioned to the waitress with the other. "We'll come across as less conspicuous if you two eat something."

"Good idea." After placing an order for two ginger ales and one order of french fries, David removed his notepad and a pen from his jacket pocket and set both on the table. "What's on your mind, Mr. Baker?"

"My friends call me Larry."

David leaned back, assuming a relaxed posture. "First names work for me. What about you, Daisy?"

Had they driven all this way for nothing more than a friendly chat? "Sure. Why not."

Larry sipped his beer, seemingly avoiding eye contact. "Following our last meeting, a few details I'd forgotten over the years reemerged." He paused, as if debating what to say next. "One fact became clear during my tenure as county DA. Some wealthy people believed their money and position gave them the license to supersede the law. My job was to prove most of them wrong."

Was he admitting he'd taken a bribe? Daisy mirrored David's relaxed position. "What do you mean by most?"

"You're an attorney, so I suspect you've come across your share of clients who have enough influence to buy their way out of any jam."

"Thus far, I've only worked on corporate accounts."

He tipped his bottle toward Daisy. "Then you know exactly what I'm talking about."

Yeah, she did.

The waitress moseyed over with their drinks and a plate piled high with greasy french fries.

Larry squirted a puddle of ketchup onto the plate, then dipped a fry. "Try one. They're delicious."

David complied. "Better than most."

Larry grabbed another fry. "In a perfect world, all fries would be healthy, and justice would outweigh power."

Daisy slipped a straw into her ginger ale and pressed her lips tight to keep from probing.

Larry wolfed down five more fries, followed by a swig of beer. "Margaret Butler is not a stupid woman. Which is why I questioned the reason she'd bother to file a lame lawsuit she had no chance of winning. Until I cobbled a few facts together." Larry wiped his fingers with a paper napkin. "What I'm about to tell you is strictly off the record."

David nodded. "Understood."

Daisy's pulse quickened. "Same here."

"First, you need to know that the Butler's marriage had been on the rocks for years before Curtis moved from the Savannah house to the ranch. Rumors about Curtis planning to divorce Margaret ran rampant. Never one to let an opportunity slip by to garner leverage, she hired a private detective to dig up dirt on her husband."

Larry pushed the plate of fries aside and planted his arms on the table. "She found out about Curtis's relationship with Rose Fowler. Despite the fact that her husband was involved with a prostitute, the last thing Margaret wanted was a nasty divorce. So, she did what any vindictive, irrational wife would do. She initiated her own affair—" Larry shook his head. "With an unlikely candidate for a socialite, except for the protection he'd provide should she ever need it."

David and Daisy exchanged knowing glances.

Larry peered from one to the other. "You already know about the chief deputy, don't you?"

"We dug up that detail yesterday." David leaned forward. "Any idea how long Margaret's affair lasted?"

"Couple of years, maybe."

"Did Curtis know what she was up to?"

"Very little gets by Curtis. He knew." Larry fingered his beer bottle. "I'm convinced his wife's behavior soothed his conscience about cheating on her."

Curtis had a conscience?

David's gaze fastened on the former D.A. "I'm curious. Why did you decide to share these details with us?"

Larry hesitated for a long moment. "The mind has a unique way of rationalizing poor decisions. Margaret's attempt to stifle a legitimate investigation presented the opportunity for me to assuage my own conscience."

Daisy's attorney instincts kicked in. "You know what happened to Rose, don't you."

He broke eye contact and downed the last of his beer. "Curtis was and still is a friend. I've done my duty. Uncovering the truth about the woman he and I both loved is now your problem, not mine." He slapped a twenty on the table and strode out.

Daisy slumped back. "He knows more than he's letting on."

"No doubt." David placed two tens on top of the twenty and scooted off the bench. "We need to make one more stop before heading home."

"A restaurant that offers at least a few healthy choices?"

He shook his head. "Your parents' house."

"I'm not sure that's a good idea."

"Your dad deserves to hear the latest news from us, not from some stranger."

"You're right. But you need to entertain Pansy while I bring them up to speed."

"Why does everyone in your family assume she isn't capable of dealing with the truth?"

"I don't know." Daisy lifted a shoulder. "Maybe because we've always tried to protect her."

"Pansy's the daughter of a prostitute and one of Rose's lovers who's also her brother-in-law's old man. Trust me, if that soap opera didn't shake her up, nothing will."

"Point well taken."

After returning to the two-lane road and driving forty-five minutes David parked beside Danny's delivery truck. "Do you want me to take the lead?"

Daisy pushed her door open. "Our latest discovery might be a bit easier coming from me."

They entered the kitchen as her mom, dad, and Aunt Pansy were finishing supper.

"What a pleasant surprise." Her mom set a freshly baked pie on the table. "You're just in time for dessert."

After settling beside Daisy and across from her mom, David faced Pansy. "Nice cap. Is it your favorite?"

She shook her head. "I gave my favorite hat to Papa."

"You did? When?"

"Yesterday, when he came here to visit."

Daisy's jaw dropped. "I can't believe Curtis showed up at your house." She faced her dad. "What did he want?"

"To stop your investigation."

David tapped his fingers on the table. "He's afraid we're coming too close to the truth."

Daisy's focus shifted to her mother, then back to her dad. "David and I met with the former D.A. again today." To protect Pansy, she chose her words carefully while relaying Lawrence Baker's revelations. A chill crept up her spine at the sight of her dad's eyes growing ice-cold. When she finished, he slammed his fist on the table.

Pansy jumped. "Uh-oh, Danny's mad about Papa."

Daisy's mom caught her bottom lip between the teeth.

Her dad uncurled his fingers. "It's time to confront Margaret face-to-face."

This wasn't going well. "Not a good idea, Dad."

"Give me one good reason."

"Because her lawsuit prohibits us from having any contact with her."

"That suit is aimed at you and David, not me and your mother."

"True, but—"

"My mind's made up." He bolted from his seat and stormed out the back door.

Daisy's eyes pleaded with her mother. "You have to talk some sense into him, Mom."

"I'm not sure I want to." She diverted her eyes. "Especially after Curtis showed up here to offer your dad a bribe."

Daisy imagined random puzzle pieces falling into place. "Margaret and Curtis are collaborating."

Pansy's head tilted. "What's collaborating?"

"Working together." Daisy scooted away from the table. "The million-dollar question is why?"

Chapter Forty

Poppy swung open her closet door and peered at her options—mostly work clothes purchased from Maddie's thrift store. Did it even matter what she wore, considering one of Margaret Butler's outfits likely cost more than her entire wardrobe?

Danny eased beside her. "Can't make up your mind?"

She spun toward him and fingered his white button-down shirt collar. "Are you sure you want me to go with you?"

"Want and need." He pulled out a green dress with a fitted waist—one of three Daisy had bought for her. "You look real pretty in this one."

At least he wasn't ashamed to take her out in public. Poppy slipped into the dress and chose a pair of her mother's gold hoop earrings, hoping they looked expensive. She grabbed a clutch purse—another thrift-store find—and rushed outside as Pansy climbed into the truck's back seat.

After dropping her at Daisy's and backing from her driveway, Danny braked at the three-way stop.

Poppy peered down the side street at the three abandoned stores. "Pansy still has the notion she's going to move into the apartment over the space Andy's fixing up for her."

"It's time to let her find her own way."

"She's never lived on her own."

"Doesn't mean she isn't capable."

"I never imagined her living anyplace other than our house."

"We'll both miss her." He drove through the intersection. "Which doesn't give us the right to deny her wishes."

"I know. It's just…I don't know…maybe we're too protective."

After passing Willy's gas station and convenience store, Danny turned the radio to a classic-rock station, making it clear he wasn't in the mood for more conversation.

During the drive to Savannah, conflicting thoughts and emotions played havoc in Poppy's head. How would Danny's mother react to coming face-to-face with her son for the first time in more than three decades? If she was home and *if* she agreed to talk to them. What about Danny? Could he control his anger in the house where his brother had taken his own life?

Fighting the urge to beg him to turn around and drive back home, Poppy forced her eyes to focus on the passing scenery and her ears to tune into the music. By the time they rolled past the wrought-iron gate blocking the driveway and parked on the street in front of Danny's childhood home, her palms were damp and her chest as tight as a stretched rubber band.

Danny reached across the console and placed his hand on Poppy's shoulder. "Thank you for coming with me. I couldn't go through with this without you by my side."

Poppy squeezed his fingers. "No matter what happens inside that house, you and I are a team."

"Always." Danny released her shoulder, then dashed to the passenger side and opened her door.

She stepped onto the sidewalk and gazed up at the third-story windows. Had Bobby slept in that room the night before he died?

Danny opened the gate guarding the sidewalk leading to the brick house.

Poppy's heart pounded against her ribs as they closed the distance to the front porch. He rang the bell.

A thin, middle-aged woman wearing a maid's uniform responded. She eyed Poppy, then Danny. "May I help you?"

"Tell Mrs. Butler her son and daughter-in-law are here for a visit."

The woman's eyes widened, then narrowed. "Is she expecting you?"

"Perhaps."

The woman hesitated. "Wait here." She closed the door.

Poppy swallowed against the dryness in her throat. "What if she refuses to see us?"

"She won't."

Minutes passed.

Poppy clutched her purse to her stomach to ease the churn. How long would Margaret leave them standing on the porch?

The door swung open.

"Come with me." The uniformed woman led them through a two-story foyer into a large room. A massive crystal chandelier illuminated the elaborate coffered ceiling. "Mrs. Butler will join you shortly."

Poppy peered around the formal space. She recognized the grand piano and ornate fireplace from pictures in her scrapbook. Somehow, standing in the room she'd viewed in photos countless times over the years seemed eerie and at the same time appropriate. After all, she was related by marriage to the woman who lived here. She ran her fingers along the brocade fabric covering the sofa facing the fireplace. Had Danny and Bobby warmed their hands in front of a fire in this room when they were boys, or had the Butler children been banned from entering the space where their mother hosted countless events?

Heels clicking on the marble foyer announced a new arrival.

Poppy mentally pictured herself as a lioness standing beside her mate—proud and confident. She drew on the image to muster enough willpower to keep her left hand pinned to her thigh and away from her stained cheek.

Margaret Butler sauntered into the room, elegantly dressed in dark slacks and a brightly colored silk tunic. "It's been a long time, Daniel." Her tone lacked even a smidgen of emotion.

"The place hasn't changed much."

"Why alter perfection?" Margaret failed to glance at Poppy or even acknowledge her presence. She aimed her open palm toward the sofa. "Please."

Danny ignored her gesture and remained standing.

Margaret shrugged. "Suit yourself." She strolled to the hearth and spun to face her son. "I'm not surprised you showed up on my doorstep without an invitation. However, if you believe you're capable of convincing me to drop the lawsuit, you're sadly mistaken."

"The case is a sham."

"It suits my purpose." She lifted a photo off the mantel. "Not one time when you were growing up did you ever appreciate the value of social status."

He scoffed. "Like my sisters?"

Margaret returned the photo to the mantel. "What do you want from me, Daniel?"

"Some answers." Danny's jaw tightened. "Beginning with the rationale behind your affair."

"I have no idea what you're talking about."

"Do you deny the fact that you and Chief Deputy Bennett were lovers?"

Margaret's eyes narrowed to a slit. "Who do you think you are—"

"Was your affair revenge for Curtis falling in love with a woman your society friends would snub?" Danny took a step closer to the woman he refused to refer to as mother. "Were you aware that your husband fathered one of Rose Fowler's daughters? Her name is Pansy. She's a gentle soul, the same as Bobby. Except her family treats her with the respect she deserves."

Poppy cringed at Margaret's intense glare.

Danny scowled. "Did you have a hand in Rose Fowler's disappearance?"

Margaret's wide-eyed expression surprised Poppy. Was it possible she wasn't aware of the connection?

"Ironic, isn't it?" Danny gave his mother a droll look. "You're attempting to sue your granddaughter who is also the granddaughter of the woman whose case she and David Lambert are attempting to solve."

"I had no idea Daisy Butler existed until she also showed up unannounced on my doorstep."

"Did you help cover up Rose Fowler's murder to protect Curtis or to save your own reputation?"

Margaret eyes narrowed for a split second before she lifted her chin. ""Do you have any idea how many distinguished people I've entertained in this room? Senators. Presidents. Individuals who matter."

"How is that relevant to my question?"

"I'm important to this community."

Danny scoffed. "You've always had an over-inflated notion about your importance."

"Spoken by a man who has no social standing."

"Why did you reject my brother in front of your so-called friends?"

Margaret's composure appeared to slip for brief moment, then returned to exaggerated confidence. "This encounter is over. If you wish to speak with me again, contact my attorney. You may show yourselves out" She squared her shoulders, pivoted, and strode toward the foyer.

Danny turned his back on his mother. "This is the room where Margaret and my old man publicly shunned Bobby—" His voice cracked. "The night they shattered his spirit."

Poppy reached for his hand and stroked his fingers. "You were brave to come here, sweetheart."

"Today is the last time I'll ever step foot in this house." He continued holding her hand as they headed to the front door and out to the sidewalk.

Poppy glanced over her shoulder at the house that harbored dark secrets and mountains of pain. Would the man she loved ever find it in his heart to forgive his parents?

After returning to the truck, Danny gripped the steering wheel. "Margaret's up to her neck in your mother's disappearance."

"Maybe you're right." Her brows drew in. "The question is how?"

He started the engine. "If David's worth his salt as an investigator, he'll find out."

Moments after Danny and Poppy climbed from the truck in Daisy's driveway, Pansy dashed out to the front porch and down the steps. "We looked at the apartment over my bakery."

Poppy climbed down from the passenger seat. "You did?"

"Uh-huh. It's almost ready to move in, 'cept there's no furniture."

"Well now." Danny slid his arm around Pansy's shoulders. "Seems you have a lot to tell us, after Poppy and I talk to Daisy and David."

"About Mama's disappearance?"

"Sort of."

"Can I listen?"

He eyed Poppy. "What do you think?"

Why deny her? Especially since Pansy had been part of the investigation from the beginning. "I suspect she can help us solve the case."

Pansy's face beamed.

Daisy and David greeted them at the door. "Based on your expressions, I'm guessing Margaret talked to you two?"

"Long enough."

Pansy bounced in. "I'm gonna help solve Mama's case." She gripped Danny's hand and pulled him toward the dining room.

Daisy leaned close to Poppy. "About the apartment Andy's creating for Aunt Pansy, I didn't mean to overstep any boundaries. It's just she's excited about living on her own, and in my opinion, ready for independence. Especially with me living less than a minute away."

Poppy released a long sigh. "Same thing your dad said."

Pansy peered over her shoulder. "Come on, you guys, we've got important stuff to talk about."

David grinned. "I do believe we've been summoned."

After gathering everyone around the table and listening to Danny relay the conversation with his mother, Pansy tilted her head. "Margaret is Papa Curtis's wife, isn't she?"

Danny nodded. "She is."

"I don't think she liked that her husband loved Mama more than he loved her."

Danny stared at his sister.

Poppy's mouth fell open.

David snapped his fingers. "You are one smart investigator, Pansy. In fact, so smart you deserve an ice cream treat from Willy's."

"Then I'll show Danny my new apartment."

Poppy exchanged glances with Danny, then eyed her sister. "You're excited about moving aren't you?"

"Uh-huh. Did you know that me and Daisy are gonna fix a little yard behind the store for Boots?"

Pansy's expression along with the excitement in her voice tugged on Poppy's heartstrings. Somehow she had to find the courage to let her fly from the nest and live her life to the fullest.

Chapter Forty-One

After returning her mom's Butler Family Legacy scrapbook, Daisy stood on her front porch beside David and waved as her dad drove down the driveway. "Aunt Pansy is over the moon about her new adventure, and I think Mom is close to accepting the inevitable. Her and Dad's trek to Savannah, on the other hand, was a colossal waste of time and energy."

"From a legal perspective, maybe. Not from an investigative point of view."

"As far as I can tell, they failed to garner any new evidence from Margaret."

"True. However, if Danny's description of her reaction was accurate, she confirmed our suspicions about her involvement in Rose's disappearance."

"I'll give you that. The unanswered question is, how was she involved?"

David clasped Daisy's hand. "Come with me."

"Where are we going?"

"To Butler and Lambert's inner sanctum to review everything we know about the case thus far." He escorted her to the desk in the parlor-turned-investigative office. "We'll start at the beginning." David flipped his notepad open.

Fifteen minutes into their discussion Daisy's phone signaled a call from Lilly. "My siblings have an irritating way of interrupting at the most inconvenient times." She pressed the speaker icon. "Hey, sis. What's up?"

"Drop everything you're doing and pull up today's Savannah Snooper's podcast—"

"Who is this person, and why do I need to listen to some random podcast?"

"She's a lady who knows everything that's going on in Savannah. Trust me, you want to hear what she talked about today. Call me after you listen."

The line went dead.

Daisy eyed David. "What do you think that's all about?"

He leaned back. "We could spend the next half hour coming up with possible answers, or here's a novel idea. Why don't we upload the app and find out what your celebrity-adoring sister finds so important?"

"Hmm, why would an investigative journalist suggest taking all the fun out of random speculating? I know." Daisy set down her phone while playfully tilting her head. "Because he's intrigued by a woman who calls herself the Savannah Snooper."

"Score one for the counselor."

"Are we keeping score?"

"Absolutely."

"Okay, then." Daisy uploaded the app. "Let's find out what fascinating bit of news has captured my sister's attention and disrupted our investigative agenda." She pressed play.

"*Good morning, friends and fellow snoopers. Welcome to juicy tidbits from Savannah's number-one snooping citizen. First question for today, what prompted the society darling with the initials M. B. to file a lawsuit against a woman with the same last name, and an out-of-town journalist? Perhaps their investigation into a thirty-five-year-old missing prostitute cold case?*"

Heat flushed through Daisy. She punched pause. "Are you believing this woman with the irritating sing-song voice, which I admit is also captivating? Does she snoop into everyone's private lives or only those of high-profile citizens?"

"You know the answer."

Daisy trilled her lips. "Unfortunately." She pressed play and stared at her phone.

"*The big question is why has M.B. filed now? Could it have something to do with C. B., the litigant's estranged husband who manages his business empire from his middle-of-nowhere ranch? Is it possible the missing prostitute is the*" *reason he moved out of the Savanah house? Will M. B.'s lawsuit go to trial, or will the parties settle out of court? What about the defendant D. B.? Is she related to one of the couple's daughters? Perhaps an out-of-wedlock secret? Such intriguing questions to ponder. For now, on to other celebrity news."*

Daisy listened for another minute, then cut off the podcaster's mono-logue. "At least the snooper didn't speculate about me being related to Margaret and Curtis's son."

"Your dad's been out of the picture for three decades, which means she likely has no idea he exists."

"Until she digs deeper."

"I doubt she does a deep dive into any story."

Daisy released a sigh. "Meaning she goes for shock value, then moves on to the next sensational bit of gossip. Hopefully, her audience is relatively small." Daisy pressed her sister's number and activated Facetime.

Lilly's face appeared on the screen. "Did you listen?"

"We did."

"How do you think the snooper found out about the case?"

"By combing through public records, that's how. What I want to know is how you stumbled on that woman's podcast, and why do you listen to it?"

"A friend at work clued me in, and I listen because most of the time she talks about rich people's parties and stuff like that."

"She's a gossip."

"I know. But she's kind of fascinating."

Daisy rolled her eyes. "Any idea how many people find her brand of gossip appealing?"

"I doubt she has all that many followers, especially since her first podcast was last year on Halloween—"

Daisy scoffed. "That's appropriate."

"Maybe you and David should sue her socks off for invasion of privacy."

Daisy tapped her fingers on the desk. "Could work. Using someone's initials is innuendo and if the community could recognize them, is treated the same as if she'd said the names. But what's the point? Don't you know that in today's world there's no such thing as privacy?"

"If Dad hears about this, he'll have one more reason not to cash that check."

"You're not suggesting we keep our parents in the dark, are you?"

"No. Well, maybe."

"Look, sis, I understand how all this drama is unnerving. Especially since we don't have a clue about what Dad will decide, but—"

"I know what you're going to say." Lilly huffed. "We need to trust him to do what's best for our family, and I do. It's just...if Andy and I had more money, he could start his own construction company, and I wouldn't have to go back to work after Jonah's born."

Her sister's downcast eyes tugged on Daisy's heartstrings. "I have an idea. Why don't we have another fun painting party to help you work off your debt?"

"Are you trying to cheer me up?"

"Yeah. Am I succeeding?"

"Barely. How about Sunday while Andy's working on the bakery project?"

"Works for me." After nailing down a time, Daisy ended the call and flopped back in her chair. "How many more bombs are waiting to drop in our laps?"

"Know what I think?" David closed his notepad. "We need to forget about the case for the rest of the day and drive somewhere for dinner."

"Are you suggesting an honest-to-goodness date?"

"With my beautiful, fascinating partner."

"This grateful lady accepts." She tapped her phone. "After she gives Mom and Dad a heads-up on the Savannah snooper."

The moment Danny parked beside the greenhouse, Pansy climbed out of the truck and raced to the backyard. Poppy peered over her shoulder at her sister embracing Boots. "Do you suppose there are rules about dogs hanging out in bakeries?"

"Probably. That won't stop Pansy." Danny headed to the greenhouse.

Desperate for a few minutes alone, Poppy clutched her Butler Family Legacy scrapbook to her chest and meandered to her private retreat. Inside the familiar space, she set her no-longer-secret collection in her trunk and removed her new project. She flipped past the family's Christmas photo and Pansy's birthday card to page three and ran her finger over the empty space. How many hours had she devoted during the past two-plus decades to creating her original scrapbook? Hundreds? Thousands?

Daisy's ringtone disrupted the silence. "Hi, honey."

"Do you have a minute?"

"For you, always." When Daisy finished sharing details about the Savannah Snooper's podcast, Poppy leaned back and eyed the vase sitting on the windowsill.

"What are you thinking?"

"I need to replace that wilted flower with a fresh stem."

"What about the podcast?"

"All these years I've lived in other people's shadows. Cooking. Cleaning. Working in the greenhouse."

"Are you okay, Mom?"

"Maybe it's time I do more than collect memorabilia and photographs of other family members." Poppy closed her new scrapbook. "Thanks for calling, honey. We'll talk more tomorrow." She ended the call, set Poppy and Danny Butler's Family Legacy back in the trunk, and walked out as the germ of an idea planted itself in her mind.

Daisy swallowed against the tightness in her throat. "I think Mom's having a mental breakdown."

"Because she didn't react the way you expected?"

"You heard her rambling. She didn't even acknowledge the reason for my call."

"The mind can only take so much." David caught Daisy's eye. "You mom is likely dealing with drama and information overload."

"By talking nonsense?"

"If you ask me, she was simply redirecting her thoughts."

Daisy glared at David. "Are you suddenly an expert on human behavior?"

"An expert? No. A keen observer? Absolutely." He cradled her hand in his. "If you're worried, call your dad and ask him to check on her."

Daisy mentally replayed her mom's comments. "It's possible my call disrupted Mom's self-reflection." A sudden wave of exhaustion washed over her. "Maybe I'm suffering from drama overload myself."

"I know the perfect cure." David stood and pulled Daisy to her feet. "A night on the town with a good-looking investigator who promises not to utter a single word about anything related to that drama."

Daisy managed a smile. "As long as there's kissing involved, I'm all in."

Chapter Forty-Two

After listening to Pansy's exuberant monologue about plans for her bakery and apartment, Poppy parked across from Willy's house, behind her son-in-law's truck.

Pansy jumped from the passenger seat, raced across the sidewalk, and dashed into the abandoned store.

Poppy climbed out and pulled her coat tight against the chill from the frigid cold front that had moved deep into Georgia overnight. She hurried inside the work in progress.

Andy strode in from the back. "Upstairs is all set up for you gals to paint."

"Goody." Pansy scurried to the back.

Andy eyed the ceiling as footsteps resounded overhead. "She's as excited as a kid on Christmas morning."

"The idea of moving into her own place is a thrilling new adventure. How long before you finish this project?"

"A month at the outside. Three more weeks for the stores on both sides."

"That should give us enough time to put plans in place."

"You and Daisy are doing a good thing helping Pansy achieve her dream."

"It will take some getting used to." Poppy ran her palm along the top of the new counter. "Snow is forecast for tonight."

"A rare weather event this far south."

"The last time it snowed down here, Pansy built a snow family in our front yard."

Pansy raced in from the back. "I already opened the paint cans. One's blue, the other's yellow. Just like I wanted."

Andy nudged Pansy's arm. "If it snows tomorrow, will you build another snow family?"

"That's for little kids. I've got more important stuff to do."

Poppy couldn't help but giggle. Would her sister resist the urge when a blanket of snow covered the front lawn?

Pansy tugged on her arm. "We need to go upstairs before the paint dries up."

"You two go on." Andy removed a drill from his tool belt. "Call if you need me."

"We won't." Pansy raced to the back.

"Seems the Butler sisters' painting party is about to begin." Poppy waved over her shoulder as she stepped into what would become a baker's kitchen. She imagined her sister standing at a worktable mixing ingredients for one of her cakes. How would people discover a bakery on a little side street miles away from a town of any size? Maybe it didn't matter as long as Pansy was happy.

"Yoo-hoo. Are you coming?"

Poppy climbed the stairs and strolled into the apartment. Drop cloths protected the floor. Open cans of paint, rollers, and pans were lined up in the middle of the room.

Pansy stood at the window facing the back of the property. "Over there's where me and Daisy are gonna build a yard for Boots." She spun around. "This is my front room, 'cept it's in the back." She pointed to a wall of built-in bookcases. "Andy built those. That's where I'm gonna put my hats and treasures." Her voice radiated with excitement.

"The perfect place." Poppy followed her sister between a small kitchen and a bathroom and through an open door.

"This is my bedroom. Daisy says I can buy a grown-up bed to put under that window."

"What's a grown-up bed?"

"A big one, same as yours and Danny's."

Conflicting thoughts collided as Poppy strolled to the window and peered at the sidewalk below. In a few weeks her sweet sister, who she'd spent a lifetime protecting, would step out on her own and become a grownup. Was she ready or even capable of living on her own?

Pansy inched beside her. "Are you sad 'cause I'm not gonna live with you and Danny?"

"I'll miss you."

"Don't worry." Pansy wrapped her arm around Poppy's waist. "You can visit me and Boots every day. 'Cept I'll be extra busy baking cakes and cookies."

Poppy choked back tears. "I'm so proud of you, sweetie. You're going to make a lot of people happy."

"When they buy my cakes?"

"And see your sweet smile." Poppy faced her sister. "What do you say we start painting in the front room."

"It's gonna be yellow, like the sun."

The perfect color for a woman who spread sunshine to everyone she met.

Five hours after rolling the first row of paint on the front room wall, Poppy turned off the main road and braked in front of the newly installed gate guarding their driveway. Pansy aimed the remote. The gate eased open.

As they drove past the open barrier, Pansy peered over her shoulder. "Does that gate always close all by itself?"

"Every time." Poppy eased up her driveway and parked beside the delivery truck. Boots bounded across the backyard to greet them. Poppy peered at the gray sky as she strolled into the greenhouse and headed toward Danny's makeshift office. "Good thing the heating system is working."

"First time I've activated it since last year."

"I've been thinking." She dropped onto a metal chair. "It won't be long before Pansy moves out...and...maybe it's time I learn more about the business side of managing the greenhouse."

Danny looked up. He stared at her, his expression stoic.

She swallowed. Did he doubt her ability or question her motive? "That is...if you think I'm smart enough to learn."

"You're the mother of a successful corporate lawyer. Of course, you're smart enough."

"Then you'll teach me?"

"Beginning tomorrow, and in case you're wondering, I think it's a good idea."

Poppy's chest puffed. Danny's approval watered the little seed planted in her mind. With his help, perhaps it would emerge from the germ of an idea to a full-blown plan.

Chapter Forty-Three

Daisy's eyes eased open and adjusted to the light streaming into her bedroom. She crawled from beneath her comforter, ambled to the front window, and peered at the winter wonderland blanketing her front driveway and the woods beyond. Eager to follow the family tradition of enjoying hot cocoa when it snowed, she donned her robe and dashed downstairs.

"Good morning, sleepyhead." David's cheery voice emanated from the office.

She tightened her robe's belt, then smoothed her hair and eased to the French doors. Flames flickered in the fireplace. David's laptop sat open on the desk. "Are you enjoying the view or working?"

He smiled. "Perfect day for both."

"I'll join you as soon as I shower and dress."

"And after I fix us a killer omelet."

"You're turning that old saying about food being the way to a *man's* heart totally upside down."

"You know the best chefs are men."

Daisy giggled. "Not in the Butler family."

"I'm starting a new tradition."

"Lucky me. I'll meet you in the kitchen in ten." A warm sensation engulfed Daisy as she climbed the stairs and headed straight to the shower.

After savoring the best omelet Daisy had ever tasted, she and David carried mugs of hot cocoa with dollops of whipped cream out to the front porch. She set her mug on the wrought-iron table and snapped photos of the sun glistening on the blanket of snow to capture the southern snowfall—here today, gone tomorrow. "The first real winter day in our new home." She caught the words seconds after they'd escaped. Had she meant to say *our* home? She glanced sideways at David. Had he noticed?

"The first of many."

He'd definitely noticed. "Enough pictures for now." The frigid air sent a shiver cascading through Daisy as she pocketed her phone, grabbed her mug, and hurried back inside. She strolled into the office and planted her feet in front of the fire to ward off the chill. "What's the Lambert and Butler investigative team's agenda for today?"

"Puzzle solving."

"Do you believe we have enough information to create an accurate picture?"

"At the very least, we'll identify missing pieces."

"That makes sense." Daisy settled on her desk chair. "Where do you want to start?"

"At the beginning." David opened his notepad.

She sipped her cocoa as he flipped to the first entry. His changing facial expressions and the way his fingers traced the words he'd penned both intrigued and troubled her. He found collecting information and knitting the clues into a logical pattern thrilling and satisfying. And he was a master at his profession. A sigh threatened to escape. She had fallen in love with a man destined to spend months away from home. Unless they continued to work as a team—

"What's your opinion?"

Daisy blinked. "What?"

"Is my partner daydreaming rather than focusing?"

His smile warmed her heart. "A momentary mental wandering. I'm back now."

For the next two hours, Daisy managed to remain focused on the case. By the time they finished reviewing David's notes, mountains of details whirled in her head. "I'm more confused now than before we began. Unless we can find someone else to talk to, I don't know how we'll ever identify Rose's killer." She paused. "What about Curtis's senator friend?"

"I ruled him out."

Daisy slumped back in her chair. "In that case, we've run out of memories to tap into."

A faraway look clouded David's eyes. His brows drew together. "Maybe not." He flipped through his notepad and stopped on a page toward the end. "Elsie claimed she'd noticed something unusual about the car that drove onto Curtis's driveway the night Rose disappeared."

"Which she couldn't remember."

"Perhaps her memory needs a little more jogging." David grabbed his phone, pressed a number, and activated the speaker. It rang three times. She answered.

"Hi, Elsie. It's David Lambert."

"It's nice to hear from you, David. How's Daisy? Did you get much snow in your neck of the woods? I covered all my plants, so I hope they're okay. Did you solve the missing-prostitute case?"

"Daisy and I are still working on it. Which is why I'm calling."

"How can I help?"

"You told us the car you saw in Curtis's driveway was black with dark windows."

"Black as the night."

"You also mentioned that you noticed something unusual but couldn't remember what. I need you to close your eyes and picture that car in your mind."

"Okay. My eyes are closed."

"Good. Was there something about the headlights? Or maybe the logo identifying the make?"

"Let me think."

David's eyes remained locked on the phone, as if he willed a detail to jog Elsie's memory.

They waited.

"Hold on. It's coming back now. There was some kind of round ornament on the hood." She described it. "I remember thinking that car must belong to a rich person. Does that help?"

"Indeed, it does. After we solve this case, Daisy and I will treat you and your husband to dinner."

The second David ended the call, he tapped on his key board. "My research buddy sent this to me yesterday." He turned the screen toward Daisy.

A burst of air escaped her lungs as she mentally processed the detail David's contact had uncovered. "We need to bring Michael into the loop." She pressed his private number.

He answered. "I'm due in court in ten minutes."

"I'll make this quick." Daisy relayed what David had discovered. "What's our next move?"

"A meeting with both parties. I'll text you the details." Michael ended the call.

The tension in Daisy's neck crept down her spine. "Talk about an explosive missing piece."

David reached across the desk and grasped Daisy's hand. "You need to give your parents a heads-up."

"You're right." Daisy pressed her mom's number.

She answered. "Are you and David enjoying the snow?"

"Not as much as Aunt Pansy. How many snowmen has she created?"

"Not a single one. Would you believe she spent the past two hours making snow ice cream? She wants to add it to her bakery menu."

"Good for her." Daisy drew in a deep breath and forced her anxiety into submission. "I need to tell you something David and I discovered." She shared the details.

Silence enfolded the moment.

Daisy's heart ached for her mom. "Do you want me to tell Dad?"

"It's best Danny hears the news from me."

"Call me after you tell him."

"I will."

The moment her mother ended the call, Daisy slumped back in her chair. How much more would her parents have to endure before the nightmare ended?

Chapter Forty-Four

By Monday morning every trace of snow had melted, and the weather had returned to a seasonal normal in South Georgia. Sitting in David's truck outside the airport terminal, Daisy fought the cold fingers of dread churning inside.

He reached across the console and held her hand. "Your skin is as cold as ice."

The warmth from his flesh did little to ease the chill. "What if we've drawn the wrong conclusions?"

"Based on the evidence, I'm confident we've landed on the truth. If by some chance we're off base, our attorney will find out soon enough."

"After the damage has been done."

Michael exited the terminal, headed straight to the truck, and climbed into the back seat. "It's a heat wave down here compared to New York. Twenty-seven degrees when I arrived at La Guardia."

Daisy peered over her shoulder. "If you think it's warm now, wait until we ignite a firestorm."

"Which we'll douse with the truth."

"Or fan into a roaring flame," Daisy mumbled under her breath as she faced the windshield. During the short drive into town, she concentrated on breathing deeply to ease her escalating anxiety. Which worked until David pulled into the parking lot, and she spotted her parents and aunt standing outside the building's front entrance.

Michael tapped her shoulder. "Did you know they planned to show up?"

"No, although I'm not surprised."

"Let me handle this." Michael led the way after they climbed from the truck. "Despite the circumstances, it's nice to see you folks again." He placed his hand on Danny's shoulder. "You wanting to offer moral support to your daughter is admirable. However, I can't let you participate in our meeting."

"We didn't expect to." Her dad's taut features offered more than a hint of the anger brewing inside.

Daisy's mom clung to his arm. "It's easier for us to wait here than at home."

"Believe me, I understand." Michael smiled as he held the lobby door open. "It's also best if the opposing party doesn't know you're here."

"We'll wait over there." Daisy's family turned toward the seating area while she, David, and Michael headed straight to an open elevator.

Daisy's pulse accelerated as they stepped out at the second floor.

Walter Campbell stood at the glass-enclosed conference room door. "Welcome back, Mr. Warner." His smug grin indicated he had no idea what lay ahead.

"Thank you for arranging this meeting on such short notice." After setting his briefcase on the table, Michael pulled out a chair for Daisy.

Sandwiched between David and their attorney, Daisy's eyes followed Margaret's attorney as he settled between his client and Curtis Butler.

Michael opened his briefcase. "Does Mr. Butler's attorney plan to join us?"

Curtis lifted his chin, his expression smacking of arrogance. "He's on call."

"Suit yourself." Michael removed a document from his briefcase.

Campbell opened the folder sitting on the table in front of him. "I assume your clients requested this meeting to consent to Mrs. Butler's request."

Michael appeared to focus on the document. "Quite the contrary." He paused for a long moment.

Daisy recognized his tactic. Let the comment simmer to create tension and stir doubt.

"Actually—" Michael looked up. "My clients and I are here to present the facts in our case."

Campbell leaned forward. "What case?"

"Rose Fowler's disappearance." Michael's tone remained neutral. "Are you aware that your client's husband was involved in a long-term relationship with Rose Fowler?"

"Mrs. Butler made me aware of that fact."

"Did she also tell you that Curtis Butler and Rose Fowler are Pansy Butler's biological parents?"

Campbell's brow twitch hinted that today was the first time he'd heard that bit of news. "Do you have proof?"

"Irrefutable."

Campbell stole a quick glance at Margaret, then eyed Michael. "How is that relevant to my client's law suit?"

"A private detective hired by your client provided proof of her husband's illicit affair."

"Again, how is that relevant?"

"I'm getting there." Michael paused while running his finger down his document.

Campbell fidgeted.

"My clients have become aware that Curtis Butler had a standing date at Rose Fowler's home every Friday afternoon." Michael looked up. "The last time Ms. Fowler's daughters saw their mother alive was a Friday afternoon thirty-five-years ago."

Curtis glared at Michael. "What's your point?"

"A deputy sheriff found a piece of evidence in Rose's bedroom a few days after she disappeared." Michael removed the bag containing the shell casing from his pocket and let it spill out on the table. The casing rolled to a stop in front of Margaret.

Her flinch was barely perceptible.

"We're also aware that Mr. and Mrs. Butler keep guns at the ranch and in the their Savannah house."

Campbell squared his shoulders. "As do half the citizens in Savannah."

Michael's focus shifted to Margaret. "Did you and your husband reject your son Bobby because he embarrassed you?"

Margaret's eyes narrowed to a slit. "How dare you ask me that question."

"Were you aware that the child your husband fathered with a prostitute is a gentle soul like Bobby?"

Daisy cringed at her grandmother's intense glare. Had Curtis told her about Pansy?

Michael broke eye contact and shifted his focus back to his document. "Mrs. Butler was involved in a romantic relationship with former Chief Deputy Hank Bennett at the time of Rose Fowler's disappearance. Bennett quashed the investigation."

Campbell cleared his throat. "What are you insinuating, Mr. Warner?"

"I'm simply stating facts, sir." Michael faced Curtis. "Are you as particular as your wife about the kind of car you drive?"

"I have a driver."

"Good point. However, Mrs. Curtis prefers to drive herself. Correct?"

"As far as I know."

Daisy exchanged a knowing glance with David. The firestorm was moments from erupting.

Michael's focus shifted to Margaret. "You never purchase any make other than Mercedes Benz, do you, Mrs. Butler?"

Campbell touched his client's arm. "You don't have to answer."

"Stay out of this, Walter." Margaret kept her eyes trained on Michael. "I only drive the best."

"Understandable for a woman with your social position."

Margaret lifted her chin and sniffed, as if an offensive odor had suddenly wafted into the room.

"New details recently surfaced about the night Rose disappeared." Michael's expression and tone remained measured.

Curtis's nostrils flared. "Your law firm represents my business empire, Mr. Warner."

"But not you personally."

"You have no right—"

"To do what? State the fact that a Benz drove across the lawn to the woods bordering your ranch the night Rose Fowler disappeared?"

Margaret flinched.

Curtis's jaw clenched.

Michael leaned forward, keeping his eyes focused on Curtis. "Did your wife kill your lover to protect her reputation or out of revenge?"

Margaret's eyes shot daggers at her accuser. "Who do you think you are—"

"It's all right, Margaret." Campbell touched her arm. "Mr. Warner has done nothing more than present a laundry list of circumstantial evidence."

"Circumstantial evidence is enough to have your client arrested for murder, Mr. Campbell."

"Enough!" Curtis slammed his fist on the table. "If you want revenge or blood, then arrest me for killing Rose."

Daisy's heart pounded. She could no longer remain silent. "You're guilty of a cover-up, not murder."

"I'll be dead and buried before this case ever goes to trial."

Campbell cleared his throat. "Everyone needs to take a breather. Mr. Warner, escort your clients to the lobby and wait for my assistant to call you back in."

Curtis's eyes narrowed. "What are you doing, Walter?"

"Putting an end to this case once and for all."

Chapter Forty-Five

Daisy dropped onto a leather sofa in the second-floor lobby. "What do you think they're up to, Michael?"

"A diversion or delaying tactic." He remained standing. "Smart move on their part."

Daisy crossed her leg and pumped her foot. "I can't believe Curtis is willing to trash his reputation and put his business at risk to protect Margaret."

David sat beside her. "A guilty conscience can force a rational person to make irrational decisions."

"His need for redemption will likely allow my grandmother's killer to go unpunished."

Michael hiked his hip on a chair's armrest. "It's a waste of time to draw conclusions until Campbell shows his cards."

"You're right." David propped his foot on his knee and fingered his sock.

Michael removed his phone from his belt clip and pressed the screen.

Daisy picked at a fingernail. How long would their opponents make them wait? Her foot pumped faster. If Campbell's ploy was meant to drive their anxiety through the roof, it was definitely working.

Five more minutes passed.

A woman approached. "Please come with me." She led them back to the conference room. "Mr. Campbell will join you momentarily."

Daisy, David, and their attorney returned to their seats. Michael set his briefcase on the table and leaned back assuming a relaxed, confident position.

The tension emanating from the other side of the table was palpable. Daisy stole glances at her dad's parents. Neither made eye contact with her or anyone else in the room. Did they have any idea what was going on, or were they as much in the dark as she was?

Two more minutes passed.

The door swung open. Campbell stood aside. A thin, middle-aged woman with short dark hair strode in and sat at the end of the table.

The color drained from Margaret's face.

Curtis jabbed a finger toward his wife's attorney. "How dare you drag her into this."

"No one dragged her; she came voluntarily." Campbell sat at the opposite end of the table from the new arrival. "Mr. Warner, Mr. Lambert, Ms. Butler, meet Victoria Butler, Margaret and Curtis's daughter."

Daisy gaped at her aunt. The woman's gaunt appearance hinted that she was Danny's alcohol-and-drug addicted sister. Was she here to provide an alibi for her mother or confirm her father's confession?

Curtis glared at his daughter. "What do you think you're doing?"

"What I should have done a long time ago."

He lifted off his chair. "Don't—"

"You still don't understand, do you?"

Curtis hesitated, then lowered to his chair. "You're not thinking clearly."

"Believe me, I'm thinking more clearly than I have in years." Victoria faced Daisy. "I'm sorry about Rose. I was there that night. She didn't deserve to die."

Daisy's pulse quickened. Danny's sister knew which parent pulled the trigger.

Victoria continued to eye Daisy. "How much has your father told you about life in the Butler household before Bobby died?"

"Enough."

"Then you know ours was one messed-up family."

Margaret splayed her left hand across her chest. "My daughter's memory is compromised."

"Why?" Victoria smirked. "Because I've spent most of my life wallowing in self-destructive behavior? The cold hard fact is no amount of alcohol or drugs could erase what happened, or wash away my shame."

Margaret faced her attorney, her eyes pleading. "Do something, Walter."

"Either sit quietly and listen, or leave the room." Campbell waited.

Margaret pressed her lips tight.

"Good." He turned from his client to her daughter. "Please continue, Ms. Butler."

A distant, dull stare clouded Victoria's eyes. "When I was a little girl, I longed for my daddy's love and approval. I wanted him to tell me stories and tuck me in at night. In our house that task belonged to nannies. Over time, I abandoned every hope of having a loving relationship with him. Until the country club my mother revered planned a father-daughter dance—scheduled for the Friday before my fifteenth birthday. After Mother told me he'd accepted my invitation, we went shopping. I bought a pretty blue dress and high heels."

Victoria paused. Her eyes downcast. "I couldn't understand why my daddy didn't show up to take me to that dance. Until I learned that every Friday he visited a prostitute. In my confused mind, I blamed Rose Fowler for my daddy's failure as a father."

Curtis's chin dropped to his chest.

Margaret's features grew slack.

"I believed if I told Rose to leave my daddy alone, he'd come back home. I begged Mother to drive me to her house. She refused. That's when I stole her keys and threatened to drive there by myself. She gave in. When we arrived at the house, we found my father's car parked in the driveway. I wanted to back out and go home. Mother told me we hadn't come that far to slink away as if we were cowards. She climbed out and closed the door without making a sound. I hesitated, not sure what to do. In a moment of clarity, I made a fateful decision, then followed her to the porch. The front door was unlocked. We crept inside. I heard my daddy—" Her voice faltered. "Telling a prostitute she was the only woman he had ever loved. Mother swung the bedroom door open."

Victoria faced Daisy. "Rose wore a pretty blue dress, the same shade as the one I'd bought for the father-daughter dance. My daddy held her in his arms. Mother called her a terrible name. His reaction and the look in his eyes told me everything I needed to know. He loved Rose more than he could ever love his wife or his children."

Daisy stole a knowing glance at David. Had he been right all along? Was Curtis guilty of covering up rather than committing the murder?

"Mother had no idea what I'd taken out of the glovebox." Victoria's eyes reddened. "I pulled the weapon from my pocket and pointed it at my father. Mother pushed me the instant the gun fired. The bullet missed its target and slammed into Rose's chest. She fell into my daddy's arms."

Daisy gasped.

David grasped her hand.

Curtis jabbed his finger toward David. "If you hadn't meddled in my family's business, Rose's disappearance would have remained a long-forgotten mystery, and our daughter wouldn't face a possible life sentence."

"Don't you understand?" Tears tracked down Victoria's cheeks. "Spending the rest of my life behind bars will be a welcome relief from the mental prison I've been locked in for the past thirty-five years." She sniffled and turned toward Daisy. "I owe your parents a long overdue apology. When can I meet with them?"

"In five minutes." Daisy dabbed at her own tears. "They're downstairs."

"I want to break the news to them. Alone and in private."

Poppy's heart beat wildly in her chest as she settled on a leather sofa between her husband and Pansy. Why had Danny's sister requested a private meeting? To apologize for her parents' crimes? Or to beg them not to press charges?

Danny propped his forearms across his knees and stared at the floor.

Pansy wound a strand of hair around her finger while peering around the room.

The door opened. A thin woman who looked vaguely familiar walked in. "Hello, Danny."

He straightened but remained seated. "Victoria."

She sat on the coffee table in front of the sofa and eyed Pansy then Poppy. "Thank you for agreeing to meet with me."

Poppy forced her hands to remain in her lap, away from her birthmarked cheek. "You're family."

Pansy tilted her head. "You, me, and Danny have the same papa but not the same mama."

"Which makes us half-sisters." Victoria's eyes shifted to her brother. "I'm sorry about what happened to Bobby."

"If you're here to apologize for our parents' heartless souls, forget it."

"I understand why you're still bitter—"

"How could you?"

"Because I know what it's like to live with tormenting regret." Victoria clasped her hands in her lap. "There's something you need to know about the night Rose Fowler disappeared." As Victoria shared her story, a pained expression emerged and clouded Danny's eyes.

The pain in the back of Poppy's throat dissolved into heart-wrenching grief. Dark secrets had burdened the Butler family far too long. Would the truth about her mother's death heal Danny's wounds or drive them deeper below the surface?

Seconds after Victoria confessed to killing Rose Fowler, stunned silence permeated the space. Poppy's limbs remained frozen. A tragic accident driven by a daughter's yearning for her father's love had killed her mother and nearly destroyed the young girl who pulled the trigger.

Victoria's chin quivered. "I'm ready to accept the punishment I deserve." Tears pooled and escaped. "I only hope one day you'll find it in your hearts to forgive me."

Pansy scooted off the sofa, sat beside her half-sister, and slid her arm around her shoulders. "Everything's okay. Mama lives with Jesus now."

Poppy peered at her husband's downcast eyes. She swallowed, then faced Victoria. "The guilt you've carried in your heart all these years has taken a terrible toll. It's time you find some peace." She reached across the space and touched her sister-in-law's knee. "I forgive you."

Her chin quivered "Thank you." Her voice was barely above a whisper.

Pansy kissed Victoria's cheek. "That's from Mama. She forgives you too."

"You're a beautiful soul, Pansy. So was my sweet brother—" Victoria's voice cracked.

Danny bolted to his feet and stormed from the room.

Poppy bit her lip to stop the rush of tears "Your confession came as quite a shock. Danny needs more time."

"Who can blame him for detesting me? The way our family treated him and Bobby."

"He doesn't hate you." The moment the words tumbled out, Poppy prayed they held at least a smidgen of truth.

"Thank you." Victoria buried her face in her hands and sobbed.

The tears Poppy had held at bay tracked down her cheeks. Tonight in private, she'd draw on her strength to help the man she loved come to terms with his past and find forgiveness in his heart.

Chapter Forty-Six

Five mornings after Victoria's confession, Daisy and David settled side by side at her parents' kitchen table. Her mom served coffee, then took her seat. Pansy sat in her usual spot, drawing a picture in her sketchpad. Daisy's mouth turned to cotton the moment her dad ambled in from the back porch and lowered onto his chair. How would he react to the latest development? With anger? Disappointment? She took a sip of coffee to counter her parched throat.

Her dad caught her eye. "I assume you have an update."

Daisy set down her coffee and laced her fingers. *Here goes.* "This morning I spoke to Michael about Victoria's case. It seems Curtis wields a lot of influence with the current district attorney."

Her dad's brows raised. "They're cutting a deal, aren't they?"

"Two years in a minimum-security prison with the possibility of parole in sixteen months." Daisy's focus shifted from her dad to her mom. "You have every right to contest the decision and plead for a longer term."

Her mom fingered her wedding band. "While I've been blessed to have a wonderful husband, a loving family, and a good life, Victoria spent the past thirty-five years in a tormenting prison of addiction and mental anguish. Sixteen months behind bars is more than enough additional punishment."

Did her dad share her mom's sentiments, or was he still consumed with bitterness? She faced him. "Do you agree with Mom?"

"There's no doubt Margaret and Curtis Butler created a legacy of misery and suffering." He fell silent, his brow furrowed, his hand clenched.

Confused by her mother's relaxed posture and serene expression, Daisy pressed her hand to her stomach to ease the fluttering sensation.

Moment's passed.

"Then that night happened." Her dad's fingers slowly uncurled. "In a moment of clarity, Margaret and Curtis Butler understood how miserably they had failed as parents and chose to risk everything to protect their daughter. Tragically, their decision to conceal the crime forced Victoria to spend more than half her life locked behind invisible bars." His brow relaxed. "A few months in a physical cell are more than adequate punishment. With regard to my parents, I'll never understand or even learn to love them. However, my grace-filled wife persuaded me to forgive them for the pain they've inflicted on our family."

Pansy looked up from her sketchpad. "Is Papa part of our family now?"

Daisy's eyes shifted from her aunt to her father's passive expression. How would he respond?

The hint of a smile softened his features. "He has your favorite hat, right?"

"Uh-huh." Pansy's brow pinched. "Is Papa's wife still gonna sue Daisy and David?"

Daisy marveled at her aunt's grasp of reality. "Good question, Aunt Pansy. Since Rose's disappearance is solved, Margaret dropped her case against me."

"But not me." David crossed his arms on the table. "Unless I allow her to review my book before publication to ensure I depict her as a pillar of the community." He faced the man of the house. "Your family has endured enough, so I agreed."

"My mother's a piece of work."

Daisy's jaw dropped. Her dad's reference to Margaret as his mother was nothing short of miracle.

Pansy's head tilted. "What's a community pillar?"

David uncrossed his arms. "Someone important, like a leader."

Pansy plucked a blue pencil from her pencil box. "Me and Poppy are gonna be pillars in our bakery."

Daisy eyed her mom. "Meaning?"

"Chef Pansy will handle the baking, while I take care of business details."

"Good for you, Mom." A warm sensation cascaded through Daisy. "Poppy and Pansy Butler, the family's newest business tycoons."

Pansy giggled. "Same as you and Papa Curtis, right, Danny?"

"Even better." He cleared his throat. "Now that the bakery's future is in good hands and the Rose Fowler mystery is solved, it's time to share a long-overdue decision." He clutched his coffee mug and stared at the dark liquid.

Daisy's pulse accelerated. After remaining suspended in a time warp for nearly three months, was she moments away from learning what her future held? Why hadn't her parents invited Lilly, Andy, and Basil to join them?

"A couple days ago I read that it's best to choose a good name over riches, and favor is better than gold or silver."

Daisy did a double take. Had she heard correctly? Had the man who vowed never to set foot inside a church just paraphrased scripture?

Her dad glanced at her mom, then faced Daisy. "Your mother and I made the decision together."

Daisy forced her anxiety into submission. No matter the challenges, she'd support whatever they'd decided.

"We're cashing the check. Your first order of business as our family's attorney is to purchase Agnes Watkins' land."

"All of it?"

"Every acre. Anonymously."

"How long do you want to keep your good fortune secret?"

"Indefinitely. Can you make that happen?"

Daisy puffed her cheeks and blew out air. They hadn't made her job easy. "I'll find a way." Her mind spun back to the cash-or-don't-cash check list she'd helped create. Which item on the pro column had tipped the scale? "Why is purchasing land my first task?"

"'Cause Danny's gonna build a town and we're gonna name it Roseville."

Daisy gawked at her aunt, then her dad. "Is she serious?"

"Roseville won't be an ordinary town."

Daisy's brows pinched. "What do you mean by not ordinary?"

"We'll create a community where people who need second chances are given a hand up instead of a handout." He cleared his throat. "A spin on Pansy's 'build it and they will come' concept."

Daisy leaned back and folded her arms across her chest. "How on earth do you and Mom propose turning Pansy's idea into any kind reality without revealing your identity?"

"We don't have a clue. Which is why we're counting on you and David to develop and implement a plan."

"Have you bothered to ask David if he's interested in collaborating?"

"Not yet."

"Don't you think you should before committing him?"

David drummed his fingers on the table. "In case you've both had a momentary lapse of memory, I'm sitting right here."

"All right, then." Daisy's elbowed him. "What's your opinion of my family's bizarre plan?"

"Some of the biggest successes began as seemingly impossible concepts." His eyes met Daisy's. "I'm confident the Butler-Lambert team is capable of delivering a huge victory to the Butler family legacy."

No matter how outrageous, at least her family's wild idea would keep David from leaving. She resisted the urge to kiss him and turned toward her dad. "One more question. When will you and Mom share your decision with Basil and Lilly?"

"After we come to terms with an unresolved detail." He fell silent.

Daisy probed her mom's expression and understood. Her parents were at an impasse on how much money, if any, to give to each of their children.

An hour after leaving her parents' home, Daisy stood beside David in her living room and peered out the window at a hawk perched on the porch railing. "We've committed to a monumental task."

"I prefer to call our joint venture a new beginning for the Butler family." David wrapped his arm around her waist. "We'll need a legitimate cover to protect your family's privacy."

"Are you thinking a new shingle in town?"

"Butler and Lambert, legal and investigative services, handling all sorts of mundane cases, and one top-secret operation."

Daisy's eyes met his. "Unless you have second thoughts about abandoning your mission to solve cold cases."

"First, I have a question. Will you miss working with corporate types to represent down-home country folks?"

"I'll manage."

David stroked her cheek. "And I'll love working with the most charming, beautiful attorney in the entire south. Of course, I might find it difficult to resist kissing her every time she smiles."

"Oh my." Daisy emphasized her best southern-belle accent while fanning her face. "How you make my heart flutter."

David winked. "My dear, you should be kissed, and by someone who knows how."

Daisy giggled. "Did my partner just misquote Rhett Butler?"

"Even better. I combined two of his famous lines into one brilliant retort."

"You're obviously a *Gone with the Wind* fan."

"I've seen the movie a time or two. It was one of my mother's favorites."

"I wish I'd had the chance to know her."

"Mom would have adored you almost as much as I do."

"I...um...think the hawk just flew away."

David grinned. "Expert lawyer move—redirect."

"You noticed."

"I'm a top-notch investigator." His smile crinkled the skin around his eyes. "Plus, your cheeks now match your ears."

Daisy tilted her head. "Well, fiddle-dee-dee, Captain Lambert, how you do carry on."

David burst out laughing. "Is that your best Scarlett O'Hara imitation?"

"Yeah. How'd I do?"

"If I was Rhett, I'd sweep you into my arms and carry you up that grand staircase."

Daisy snapped her fingers. "And if I'd written the story, that's exactly how the movie would have ended."

David gathered her into his arms. "What do you say we forget Scarlet and Rhett and continue creating our own magical love story?"

She breathed in the lingering scent of soap and shampoo. "I believe the time has come to begin writing the next chapter."

"The first of many." He kissed her with a passion she understood would sustain them through every peak and valley they were destined to travel in the months ahead.

Thank you for reading Truth and Forgiveness, the second book in the Butler Family Legacy series. Are you eager to learn what happens next? New Beginnings, the third book in the series:

https://www.amazon.com/dp/B0BSYH857H

Afterword

A Note From the Author

One of the most rewarding aspects of my writing journey is interacting with readers and book club members. If you're not already one of my newsletter friends, I would love to connect with you and send you a free copy of *The Vet and Valentine's Day*, an award-winning short story. Simply go to:

https://www.subscribepage.com/pat-nichols-newsletter
Follow me on Bookbub and you'll receive notices of my new releases:

https://www.bookbub.com/authors/pat-nichols?follow=true
Would you like to learn more about my books and my writing journey?
https://patnicholsauthor.blog

You can also find me on Goodreads, Face Book, Twitter, Instagram

Acknowledgments

The road to publication is never traveled alone. A heartfelt thanks to all who join me on this journey.

Sherri Stewart, my editor and mentor, for her expertise and commitment to excellence.

My beta readers Pat Davis, Beverly Feldkamp, Kitty Metzger, Kathy Warner, and Carlene Dunn for their critique and suggestions during the final stage of my writing process.

My launch team members for their reviews and to all those readers who aren't on the team but take the time to write reviews.

My author friends at American Christian Fiction Writers Georgia Chapter for creating a warm and welcoming environment and for providing valuable insight and education. My Word Weavers International, Greater Atlanta Chapter partners, for their critiques and positive reinforcement.

A special thanks to my amazing family for believing in my journey and encouraging me to continue pursuing my dream.

Above all, as a Christ follower I thank God for His grace and the gift of eternal life.